"We obviou
for a spouse a

"Please don't say anything to my family, Jake. Promise me," Leah said.

"Okay…but on one condition." His gunmetal-gray eyes snagged hers.

"What's that?"

"That you'll help me pick out a wife." He held up his own package of letters with a crooked grin.

"Why do you need *my* help?"

"You're a great judge of character, and you know me better than anyone else. Do we have ourselves an agreement or not?"

"Agreed." Leah smiled up at Jake and the dimples on each side of her pink lips winked. How he would love to— Jake stopped his mind from taking him down that well-worn path to nowhere. Soon Leah would be another man's wife.

"Well, let's get this over with," Leah said, her smile looking forced now.

"Have to put it that way?"

"No, no. I just meant…"

Jake placed his fingertips on Leah's soft lips. "It's okay—I know what you meant."

Books by Debra Ullrick

Love Inspired Historical

The Unexpected Bride
The Unlikely Wife
Groom Wanted

DEBRA ULLRICK

is an award-winning Christian romance author. In addition to multiple full-length novels, her stories have been featured in several novella collections, one of which made the *New York Times* bestseller list. Debra is happily married to her husband of thirty-eight years and has one daughter. For more than twenty-five years, they lived and worked on cattle ranches in the Colorado Mountains. She now lives in the Colorado flatlands. Debra loves animals, classic cars, mud-bog racing and monster trucks. When she's not writing, she's reading, drawing Western art, feeding wild birds and watching Jane Austen movies, COPS, or Castle.

Debra loves hearing from her readers. You can contact her through her website at www.DebraUllrick.com.

DEBRA ULLRICK

Groom Wanted

Love Inspired

Recycling programs for this product may not exist in your area.

ISBN-13: 978-0-373-82929-3

GROOM WANTED

This edition published by arrangement with Love Inspired Books.

www.LoveInspiredBooks.com

Printed in U.S.A.

A man's heart deviseth his way,
but the Lord directeth his steps.
—*Proverbs* 16:9

To my daughter, Sharmane Wikberg.

Remember, kiddo, when you brought home those Christian romance books from the library eons ago, and how you had to beg me to read them? Look what happened when I finally did. Who would have ever thought it, huh? Thank you, Sharmy. And thanks for being such a loving daughter. God sure blessed me when He gave me you. I love you, girl.

((MEGA HUGS))

Chapter One

Paradise Haven
Idaho Territory, 1886

Nine men had replied to her "Groom Wanted" ad.

Leah Bowen couldn't believe she'd received so many that quickly. Her heart skipped as she fingered the envelopes that might very well hold her future and her only avenue of escape from the nightmares that plagued her.

"You, too, huh?"

"Twinkling stars above!" Leah gasped and whirled toward the sound of Jake Lure's deep voice. Her nose came within an inch of jamming into the napped wool shirt covering her friend's massive chest. Pleasant scents of springtime and sunshine floated from him.

Near the front door of Paradise Haven's post office Jake stood, looking over her shoulder at the posts in her hand. Most people were intimidated by his massive size, but she wasn't. Underneath that outdoorsy, muscular exterior was a gentle giant.

"What—what do you mean, 'you, too'?" Leah glanced at the top envelope with the very noticeable masculine script and tucked them into her reticule. She tossed the end of her purple knit scarf over her shoulder and gathered the edges of the collar of her wool coat closer together.

Jake held up a packet of letters. "Got these in the mail today."

"Oh? What are they?" she asked with all the innocence she could muster.

"Same thing as that stack you just put in your purse."

"What? You mean letters?"

"Those envelopes you have aren't just any ole letters." One of Jake's eyebrows rose. "They're answers to *your* advertisement."

Advertisement? She swallowed hard. Did he know she'd placed an ad for a husband? "What are you talking about?" Leah hated playacting, but she had no choice. She refused to offer Jake any information concerning her personal ad. Just because he had mentioned how he wanted to place an advertisement for a wife during one of the many times she and Abby had visited him over the past eleven months didn't mean she had to confide in him that she, too, had wanted to do that very same thing. So how did he know? Or was he only speculating?

Jake cupped her elbow.

Her gaze flew to the spot where his large calloused hand rested, then back onto his face. "What are you doing?"

"Taking you someplace where we can talk without being overheard." Even through a whisper, his voice sounded deep.

Their footsteps echoed on the plank-covered boardwalk as he led her away from prying eyes to a more secluded place to protect her reputation, no doubt, for which she was extremely grateful though she still tried to look annoyed. Truth was she didn't want people getting the wrong idea about the two of them. They were friends and nothing more.

They'd become good friends after he'd slipped on some shale at the top of a hill on his place almost a year ago. He'd tumbled down and hit his head, leaving him with a bleeding gash on his forehead and rendering him unconscious. If Leah's brother Michael and his wife, Selina, hadn't found Jake that day, he may have died. Selina's kindness in doctoring him and making sure he had food and his needs were met changed Jake. He realized how wrong he had been for judging her for her lack of social graces and regretted his heckling. After that, he changed, and he had become the person to everyone else that he had always been to her.

Through it all, Leah had always believed that Jake was a nice man, a good man, even when he was heckling people. Years before, she'd learned that most people who teased others were either jealous or insecure or did it to protect themselves. Leah wasn't sure just why Jake had. But her friend Dottie Aimsley had once told her that she'd heard the reason Jake acted like that was because when he was growing up he himself had been ridiculed because he had a fear of crowds. Although Leah didn't know all the particulars of his phobia, hearing that had secured her compassion toward him, and the two had quickly become the best of friends.

And he was a handsome friend at that.

A man who could charm any woman. Except her, that was. Leah had her sights set on a different type of man. A man exactly like her late father—before he had become a rancher. The mere thought of him brought the pain surging into her chest. She couldn't let it reside there, though. She had to evict it as she had so many times before or it would escalate until it became so bad she could barely breathe.

She sighed and blew out a long breath. It really was a shame Jake wasn't a city man. City men didn't encounter anywhere near the hazards farmers and ranchers did. She knew that for a fact because, even though it had been fifteen years since her family had moved from New York to the Idaho Territory, she still kept in contact with her friends back East and all of their fathers were still alive.

Marrying a farmer or a rancher who risked his life every day working with unpredictable animals and dangerous farm tools and equipment wasn't for her.

And Jake was one of them. Her father had been one of them, too. Getting away from city life and owning a ranch had been her father's dream. It was that dream that had gotten him killed.

Her heart felt the pain of his loss as if it had just happened yesterday instead of years ago. Her hand balled into a fist and pressed against the center of her chest as she tried to make the memories stop. But they came with even greater force. In desperation, her mind grasped backward through time to the father who had doted on her.

Had loved her.

Had made her feel special.

Secure.

Protected.

And fearless, even.

Oh, sure, after his death her older brothers—Haydon, Jesse and Michael—had tried to take his place. Tried to make her feel secure. But no one could take the place of a father. Especially in a little girl's heart. No one.

And no one could stop the nightmares that visited her on a regular basis since his death.

She'd learn to suppress the nightmares because she had to be strong for her little sister, Abby, and her mother, whose grief at that time had ripped at Leah's soul. Oh, if only she hadn't heard her father gasping for air as his lungs filled with blood or had seen his broken body crushed underneath that huge tree. But she had.

Leah slammed her eyelids shut to blot out the gruesome memory that chased her like a haunting ghost. In one shaky breath she willed her father's healthy face to come into focus, but only a shadowed image filled her mind. Time had faded his features until she could no longer see them clearly. And that scared her.

It was all Paradise Haven's fault. She despised and blamed the Idaho Territory for the loss of the one person she had loved most in the world. Moving back to New York would help the nightmares stop. Of that she was convinced because there were no phantoms there. Only fond memories.

Memories of better, happier times.

Memories of her father walking and talking and holding her until whatever was bothering her at that time disappeared. Father had made everything okay. Only he couldn't make this okay. Nothing would bring him back to life. This place had killed him.

New York was where she longed to be.

Getting there couldn't happen fast enough for her. Why she had waited this long she didn't know. But the sooner she moved, the better off she would be. And maybe, just maybe when she finally got there, those dreaded nightmares would end.

"Leah?"

She blinked and yanked her attention upward and onto Jake. "What?"

"You okay?" His dark blond brows met in the middle.

"I'm fine." Or she soon would be when she moved away from here.

The look on his face said he didn't believe her. "You gonna answer my question?"

"I just did. I said I was fine."

"No. Not that question. Still waiting for an answer to—" he pointed to the stack of posts in her reticule "—if those letters are what I think they are."

"I don't know. What do you think they are?"

He gave a quick glance around. No one milled about anywhere close to them. "Answers to your advertisement."

She studied his eyes, gazing at her from under his brown cowboy hat. His irises were a light silver-gray with a dark gray circle surrounding them, reminding her of a tabby cat she once had. A knowing look filled them. There was no denying it any longer.

"How did you know?"

"Put two-and-two together."

"What do you mean?" Panic and fear settled into her spirit, knowing that if anyone in her family discovered what she was doing and why, they would put a stop to it right away. It didn't matter that Haydon and Michael had gotten wonderful wives that way. There was no way they would let their sister traipse off to New York by herself to meet a complete stranger, even if she was twenty-four years old.

Jake's gaze slipped to the boards at their feet. "Truth is, Leah, I saw your advertisement when I looked through the papers for the one I'd placed. We obviously posted ads for a spouse at the same time."

Oh, no. He did know. Fear dug its claws into her chest.

"You don't look too good. You okay?"

She nodded, then changing her mind, she slowly shook her head. "No." She gazed up at him, imploring her eyes to show how much this affected her. "Please don't tell my family."

"You mean they don't know?"

"No. I didn't tell them. Please don't say anything to them, Jake. Promise me you won't." Desperation pricked her skin.

He ran his fingers down the place that once had a thick, dark blond mustache but now only held stubble and kept repeating the action. "On one condition." His gunmetal-gray eyes snagged onto hers.

"What's that?" Worry nipped at the heels of her mind as she waited for his response.

"That you'll help me pick out a wife." He held his own package of letters up, and his lips tilted into that normally lazy, crooked grin of his. The one that really was quite endearing.

"Are you serious?"

"Yep. Sure am."

"Why do you need me to help you do that?"

"'Cause. I don't trust myself. When it comes to women, I haven't had the best of luck."

Heat rushed to her cheeks. Turning down Jake's marriage-of-convenience proposal a couple months back had nothing to do with his luck with women but with her wanting to flee this place. "What makes you think I'll do any better?"

"You're a great judge of character, and you know me better than anyone else. Not only that— Women seem to have a sense about these things. Men don't. So. Do we have ourselves an agreement or not?" He held his hand out for her to shake.

She stared at it, debating what to do, until she realized she didn't have any other choice. Having peace in her life depended on her moving. With a short nod, she clasped his hand, and gave it a quick shake before releasing it. "Agreed."

* * *

Jake shook Leah's hand and plastered a smile on his face. He wasn't kidding when he said he needed help picking out a wife. His past record had proven that. At eighteen he'd asked Gabby Marcel to marry him, but she'd said no, saying she wanted to marry Jeffrey Smith. He didn't even know she liked the man. Jake thought Gabby was in love with him, but she'd just used him to get close to his friend. Backfired on her big time. Jeffrey wanted nothing to do with her and neither had Jake after that.

Then a few months back Leah had turned him down, too, saying she had her reasons and that it had nothing to do with him, but her.

Too bad she hadn't accepted his proposal. He didn't blame her for rejecting him, though. Nothing had been mentioned about love. Only about how it would be nice since they were friends and all. A friendship he treasured and didn't want to lose. Jake's hope at the time had been that if they did marry one day his heart would love Leah the way a man loves a woman, but right now he only felt friendship toward her. So, it was probably best she'd turned him down.

Besides, she was way out of his league, anyway. Going from a large home to a small three-room house would be hard for anyone used to living in the luxury she was accustomed to. Plus, staying where she was, Leah never had to want for anything. If she married him, she would. Oh, he could support her by keeping food on the table and clothes on her back, but there wouldn't be much left for anything extra. And the woman deserved every good thing life had to offer. None of that mattered now, anyway. Leah had made it clear that nothing would stop her from moving back to New York. Why she wanted to go there, he had no idea.

Personally, he hated the city and would go crazy if he ever went to one again.

Literally.

His childhood had seen to that. In 1864 fire blazed throughout Atlantic City. The crowd had gone berserk trying to flee to safety and in the process he had gotten separated from his mother. The crowd trampled him, leaving him for dead at six years old. Ever since then, he had a fear of crowds. He could be around a small group of people, but he couldn't handle being closed in a building or surrounded by people—he felt trapped. For twenty-two of his twenty-eight years he'd tried to overcome his fear. Had even made a trip back to Atlantic City. Big mistake that was. While walking down the crowded streets, suddenly everyone seemed as if they were right on top of him again, just like when he was six.

He'd felt trapped.

Closed in, even.

His heart had pounded hard and fast, his breathing came in short gasps, his arms felt heavy, his palms coated with moisture, and his head swam until his vision clouded.

The need to flee had pressed in on him.

Only when he had escaped to an open field had his heart stopped racing and his breathing returned to normal.

Even now, whenever he found himself crowded in, even by the smallest mob of people, fear stampeded over him. His only recourse was to get alone until his heart and breathing returned to normal and the fear lifted. When people asked him what was wrong, he'd make up an excuse because a long time ago, he'd learned not to tell anyone or ask for help. The few times he had he'd been made fun of and he hated how small that made him feel. For a man his size, it was hard to make him feel small, but ridicule did. The worst part of this whole thing was his phobia punctured the dream of him ever moving to New York to be with Leah.

"You do know, Jake, that I will have to bring Abby with me again. Propriety and all that, you know." Leah's voice snatched his mind back from the dark caves of the past. "That means she'll know what you're doing, too."

"Already figured as much. Wouldn't have it any other way. Wouldn't do anything to ruin your reputation, even if that means having Abby know what I'm up to." He gave a quick nod. "So be it. Besides, I enjoy your sister. Who wouldn't? She's a pistol."

"She sure is. A very discreet pistol, though, I assure you." Leah smiled and the dimples on each side of her pink lips winked.

"Well, let's get this over with."

"Have to put it that way?"

Leah waved her hand, "No, no. I didn't mean it like that. I just meant..."

He placed his fingertips on her soft lips. "It's okay, Leah. You don't have to explain. I know what you meant. Was just teasing you." When he realized where his fingers were, he quickly removed them.

"When do you want to start?" She fiddled with the strings of her reticule.

"Now, if that works for you."

Leah's gaze brushed his. She tilted her head in that cute way of hers, then stared at him as if she were considering his offer.

"Hmm." She settled her fingertip against her lips. "I am finished in town, and Mother isn't expecting me until later. So now will work just fine. I'll run and go get Abby, then follow you to your place."

"No."

"What do you mean, 'no'?" Leah tilted her head even farther and a blond lock slipped across her eye.

He reached to brush it away, then snatched his hand back to his side. Doing that seemed intimate somehow. A line friends didn't cross. "Think about it, Leah. How would that look, us riding off together?"

Leah tapped her forehead. "How could I have been so dim-witted? Of course, you're right. Thank you, Jake."

He glanced out to the dirt street that ran right through town. "Tell you what. I'll head on out now. You and Abby leave ten or fifteen minutes after me?"

"What time is it now?"

He pulled his pocket watch out of his vest pocket and flipped it open. "One forty-five."

"I'm supposed to meet Abby at her friend Phoebe's house around two. So that will work perfectly." There were those dimples again.

"Great. See you at my place in about half an hour then?"

This smile went all the way up to her eyes. Eyes the color of a spring day dotted with clouds.

"We'll be there."

Unable to think of anything else to say, Jake clasped the brim of his hat, gave a quick nod and headed toward the blacksmith shop to pick up his horse.

"Phoebe!" Leah gaped at Abby's friend, who was a little more than a year older than Abby's seventeen. "Your wedding dress is absolutely gorgeous. You look so beautiful in it. Like Cinderella at the ball."

Phoebe's lips curled upward and her face turned as red as her hair. Her big green eyes were shielded when her eyelids lowered. How the sweet girl ever managed to snag Markus Donahue, the banker's son, when she was so shy was beyond Leah, but she was glad Phoebe had. If anyone deserved a nice man like Markus, it was Phoebe.

"Tomorrow's the big day. Are you excited?" Leah curled a stray strand of hair around her ear.

Phoebe dipped her head down and nodded. Two seconds later her head popped upward and alarm marched across her face. "You two are still coming, aren't you?"

Leah walked over to Phoebe and grabbed her hands. "Of course we'll be there. Nothing would stop us from coming."

"But you know how unpredictable the weather is here in May. What if it rains or snows and you can't get into town because the roads are too muddy?"

Horrified was the only way Leah could describe Phoebe's face.

"Then we'll ride the horses into town. They'll be able to make it even if the buggy can't."

Phoebe's head jerked with short, nervous nods. "Oh. Okay."

Leah clasped Phoebe's hands again. "We'll be there, Phoebe. I promise. Now." She released her hands. "Come on, Abbynormal." Leah used the nickname she often called her sister. The one that best suited Abby's personality. Abby was anything but normal, but Leah loved her sister for it and envied her at the same time. How wonderful it would be to be so carefree. "We need to get going."

Abby stopped talking with Phoebe and faced her. "Why?"

"Because…" She gave Abby that look. The one that let her know she was going to Jake's again. Something the two of them had done ever since his accident many months back when he'd fallen and hit his head. Back then, the idea of him alone and needing help had eaten at Leah until she couldn't bear it. She was so glad Abby had agreed to go with her to help him until he had healed. During that time Leah and Jake had become great friends.

Make that the three of them. Abby enjoyed going to Jake's farm as much as Leah did and thought it was great fun playing the role of her older sister's chaperone. Leah was glad she found it fun, but it was necessary more than anything. If she didn't drag her sister along, Leah could never have gone to a single man's house alone. It would be improper and, most importantly, her reputation would be ruined.

Being seen with Jake too much in public would give people the wrong idea about the two of them. Like a wildfire out of control, all of Paradise Haven would spread rumors that they were courting. She'd seen it happen to several other couples who eventually wed or ended the whole thing in a ruinous scandal—neither of which she wanted with Jake. Besides, it wasn't like that between her and Jake. To be sure, they enjoyed each other's company, but neither of them had feelings that went beyond friendship.

Leah loved having a male friend as special and caring as Jake. She looked forward to their visits. Despite the fact they wanted different things out of life, he was the one person she felt she could talk to about anything.

Well, almost anything.

He didn't know the real reasons why she had turned down his proposal and why she wanted to move. No one knew about the nightmares except for her former friend Marie. Former for two reasons—one, Marie had moved away, and two, Leah hadn't associated with her since the day she'd confided in Marie about the nightmares and how she blamed this place for killing her father. Marie had laughed and said she was just being silly and that she needed to get over it. Oh sure, as if it were that easy.

"Ohhh." Abby nodded, then turned to her friend. "I'd better scoot along now, Phoebe. Sister dear has places to go and things to see. But fear not, I shall see you on the morrow. You have my word." Abby, the dramatic one in the family, grabbed her cloak, swung it around her shoulders with the grace of a queen and, with her arm outstretched holding her cloak, glided toward the door.

"Thank you so much for helping me make my dress and for putting the finishing touches on it." Phoebe scurried after Abby and hugged her.

Abby pulled back and waved off her friend. "You are quite welcome, my dear." Abby's British accent imitation needed help. She sounded nothing like the Manvilles, their British neighbors back in New York City, or even like Rainee, their sister-in-law, who mixed British with Southern quite nicely. "And now, I must make haste and take my leave." Abby swung the door open and, with a flourish, headed outside.

Leah shrugged toward Phoebe's direction. "What can I say? You can't help but love her." With that, she followed Abby out the door and onto the wagon. They turned and waved goodbye to Phoebe before she disappeared into her house.

"So, we're heading to Jake's again." Abby waggled her eyebrows.

"We sure are."

"Well, then, sister dear, what are we waiting for?" Abby faced forward. "Make haste. Make haste, my dear."

Leah shook her head. She should have never let Abby read the well-worn copy of *Pride and Prejudice* that Rainee had given Leah years ago. Ever since then, Abby imitated the British often. She hoped Abby never found the copy of *Sense and Sensibility* that she kept hidden in the bottom lining of her trunk. She shuddered just thinking about how Abby would act after reading that one.

Leah wondered if Abby would follow in her footsteps.

The real Mr. Darcy in *Pride and Prejudice,* not the one Elizabeth Bennet thought he was before she had gotten to know him better, reminded Leah of her father. Mr. Darcy had rescued Elizabeth's family when Lydia's infidelity would have shamed them. He was a man with integrity, a big heart, a protector, just like her father. From the moment that realization had struck Leah, her love and respect for Mr. Darcy had her praying that someday she would find her very own Mr. Darcy—a man who represented everything her father had stood for.

"C'mon, Leah. What are you waiting for?"

"Pushy."

"Me, pushy? You were the one who was in such an all-fired big hurry to go." Abby nudged Leah's shoulder.

"True. True. I hate it when you're right." Leah tittered and with a quick slap of the lines on her horse's rump the buggy pitched forward. "Oh, you won't believe this, Abbs, but Jake knows about my advertisement."

Abby whipped her head so fast in Leah's direction that one of her curls whacked her sister across the face. "How'd he find out?" Abby's eyes gleamed as she searched Leah's. Her sister loved a good story and loved to tell them, too, but she wouldn't tell this one. She'd been sworn to secrecy.

"He started getting newspapers from all over, including back East where I placed mine. When he searched the papers to see his ad, he saw mine and put two-and-two together."

"Oh. What are you going to do if he tells Michael?"

"He won't."

"How do you know he won't? Jake and Michael are good friends. If Michael finds out, you know he'll tell the rest of the family. And Haydon and Mother will put a stop to your plans."

"They won't find out because Jake and I made an agreement and shook hands on the bargain."

"Oh, yeah? What kind of agreement?"

"Well—" she shifted toward Abby "—he won't tell anyone if I help him find a wife. You know, help him decide which of the letters he should respond to."

"Ohhh. This could be fun." Her sister's eyebrows danced.

Fun? Leah hadn't thought about it being fun. But it just might very well be. She gave a quick flick of the leather lines to get her horse to pick up her pace. "Don't tell anyone, Abbs. This whole thing will be our little secret, okay? Promise?"

"I haven't said anything to anyone before, have I?" Her sister looked slighted.

"No, you haven't. And I know you wouldn't, either. But with this concerning Jake, too, I just thought I would remind you, that's all. Okay?"

"Okay."

They rode in silence for a time. The only sounds were the horse's hooves clunking on the hard road and a flock of geese honking above them.

"It's too bad you have your heart set on moving to New York. Otherwise, Jake would make a great husband for you," Abby said out of nowhere.

Leah glanced over at her sister. "Jake is a friend and nothing more. But if I wasn't so dead set in pursuing my dreams, who knows, I might have considered Jake." Turning down his proposal hadn't been easy because she enjoyed his company immensely. Good thing she wasn't in love with Jake. Saying no would have been extremely hard, but necessary.

"You would?" Abby clasped her hands together and her eyes sparkled.

"I said if, Abbs, if."

"But Jake is sooo handsome," Abby said dreamily with her clasped hands pressed against her heart.

"If you think he's sooo handsome, then why don't you marry him?"

Abby yanked her hands away from her chest and her wide eyes stared at Leah. "Me? He's way too old for me. But if he wasn't, I sure would try for him."

"Why?" Leah found she really wanted to know.

"What do you mean, 'why'? Just look at him. He's dreamy and so handsome."

Handsome, yes. But dreamy? She never thought about Jake as being dreamy. "Jake is handsome. I'll give him that. But looks aren't everything, and he is not my type."

"I know, I know." Abby rolled her eyes. "Your type of man is one who wears waistcoats, ties and fancy suits and lives in a big city."

Only because that was how her father used to dress. Another pleasant memory she held on to.

Abby laid her hand on Leah's. Gone was the humor from her face. Serious now replaced it. "What if you find someone, Lee-Lee, and once you get out there, it isn't anything like what you dreamed it would be? Then what?"

Good question. Just what would she do? What if she got out there and the nightmares didn't stop? No. She couldn't think that way. She had to hold on to that hope. She just had to. "That won't happen, Abbs, because before I go anywhere, if a man intrigues me, I'll request a picture of him and ask a lot of questions. If I like his answers, then I'll go out and meet him in person first."

"You know Mother won't let you go alone."

"She won't know."

"You mean you're not going to tell her?" That same horrified look she saw on Phoebe earlier now shrouded her sister's face.

"No. And neither are you."

"I don't like this, Leah. Not one little bit."

Neither did she. But her heart was set on moving out East and nothing would stop her. Not her mother, her brothers or Jake. Jake? What did he have to do with any of this?

Chapter Two

Jake rode into the yard of his farm faster than ever before, unsaddled his horse and turned Dun loose in the corral. He ran to his house and stepped inside. One glance told him it was as bad as he had feared. Boots and jackets were sprawled on the bench and floor, dishes covered the table and newspapers surrounded his living room chair.

Every time Leah had come to his house, their visits had been planned and he always had a chance to spruce up the place first. This time that wasn't the case because he hadn't expected to see her today, much less invite her over. "Better hustle, Jake." He snatched up his jackets and hung them on the hooks, then lined his work boots neatly underneath the bench.

Dishes rattled and clanged as he gathered the breakfast mess, tossed the dishes into the sink and covered them with a towel. After washing the table down, he flocked the pile of newspapers together and laid them in a neat pile on the coffee table he'd made.

Next he plucked his clean undergarments, shirts, pants and socks down from the clothesline he'd rigged near the cookstove, tossed them onto his unmade bed and closed the bedroom door behind him.

Banjo's barking reached his ears. He peered out his living room window and saw Leah's carriage coming down the lane.

He darted toward the wash basin and checked his reflection in the shaving mirror. His thick blond hair, part of his Norwegian heritage, stuck out everywhere. He snatched up his comb and smoothed the strands down, then headed out the door and met Leah and Abby right as they pulled in front of his house.

"Hush, Banjo." His mottled-colored Australian shepherd tilted her head both directions, then darted onto the porch. Banjo laid down on the top step, placed her head between her legs, leaving her front paws dangling over the step, and let out a slow, pitiful whine.

Jake looked back at the ladies sitting in the buckboard phaeton with the parasol top, another reminder of the differences in their financial statuses in life. This phaeton was only one of the expensive carriages the Bowen family owned.

"Hi, Jake!" Abby waved.

"Howdy-do, ladies." He nodded, then offered Leah a hand.

"Thank you." She smiled up at him when she reached the ground.

He returned her smile, then helped Abby down.

"Thanks, Jake." Abby looked around the yard. "Where's Meanie?"

"In the barn. Had to put her in a stall."

Leah tilted her head. "How come?"

"Kept running off. Down to Mabel's barn. Eating all her grain. Caused all kinds of ruckus. Ornery old goat anyway."

"Jake!" Leah gasped and her eyes widened. "That isn't

nice. Once you get to know Mabel, you'll discover she's really a very sweet lady with a soft heart."

Abby giggled and darted up the steps, flopping down next to Banjo.

Jake couldn't help but laugh. "Wasn't talking about Mabel. Was talking about my pet goat, Meanie."

Leah's cheeks turned a nice shade of dark pink, the same color as the dress she had on, and her perfectly formed lips formed an *O*.

"Shall we get started?" He motioned toward his house. They walked side by side up the wide steps, past Abby and onto the porch. Jake opened the door and moved out of the way.

"You coming, Abby?"

Abby turned sideways. "Do you mind if I stay out here? It's too nice to go inside. Besides, Banjo's better company. Isn't that right, girl?" Abby rubbed his dog behind her ears.

"Hey." Leah planted her hands on her slim waist.

Abby glanced back and winked. "Just kidding, Lee-Lee. But I would like to stay out here on the porch, if you don't mind. Even though the air's a little nippy, the sun sure feels good."

Leah looked up at him as if to question if it was okay or not.

Jake shrugged, seeing no reason why she couldn't. "I don't mind if you don't."

"I don't mind. That's fine, Abbs."

"Would you like something to drink, Abby?"

"No. I had a cup of hot cocoa at Phoebe's house right before we left, so I'm fine. But you two go ahead if you'd like," she said, keeping her back to them as she continued to pet Banjo.

"You change your mind, just holler," Jake said before he and Leah stepped inside his house.

"Where do you want to sit?" Leah asked him.

"The table. That way we can spread the letters out and be in plain view of Abby."

"Sounds good to me."

Jake took Leah's wrap and hung it on a peg near the door before Leah headed toward his kitchen table.

The slab table with pine legs and the kitchen chairs made out of lodgepole pine with slab seats looked shabby next to Leah's fancy kitchen furniture. Never once had she turned her nose down at them, though. She even made a comment one time about what a great job he'd done making them, how nice his handiwork was and how beautiful she thought they were. It meant a lot coming from her.

"Want something to drink?"

"No, thanks."

A quick nod, then he hurried around Leah and held out one of the chairs and waited for her to be seated before he sat in the chair on her right. He removed the stack of envelopes from his inside vest pocket and laid them on the table in front of him.

Leah scooted her chair closer to his, and her skirt brushed against his legs when she did. Lilacs and crisp spring air swirled around her. "Well, which one would you like to read first?"

He glanced down at the pile and thumbed through them until he came across one from Tennessee. "This one."

"Any particular reason why you chose that one first?" Curiosity fluttered through her eyes.

"Yep."

"Care to share?" She looked hopeful.

He debated whether or not to tell her. She might think he was strange if he did. Clasping his hands in front of him on top of the table, he drew in a deep breath and said,

"Know this sounds odd, but ever since Michael brought Selina here, I've been hoping to find someone like her."

She shook her head and grinned. "You sound like Michael."

"Come again?" he asked, not understanding her meaning.

"Well." She dropped her hands onto her lap. "Ever since Rainee arrived, Michael wanted someone just like *her*."

"He did?" That was news to him. Shocking news at that.

"Yes."

"Don't get it. Selina's nothing like Rainee."

"I know. Everything in her letters indicated she was like her, but her friend had written the letters for her and lied so Selina would find a good husband. It was a deceptive thing for her to do, but I'm so glad she did. Selina is a remarkable person. And I'm so thrilled to have her for a sister."

Everything Leah just mentioned made him rethink what he was about to do. What if he, too, got a woman who lied to him and wasn't what she said she was? Or even worse, what if he found someone who interested him and she turned him down because *he* wasn't what *she* expected? After all, he'd been turned down twice before. Could he handle another rejection?

Leah studied Jake's face. It went from fear to confusion to sadness.

"Maybe I shouldn't do this. Maybe I should just give up this whole crazy idea." Jake plowed his hands through his bulky blond hair and sat back from the letters, staring at them.

"Why?" Leah couldn't imagine what had caused him to change his mind so suddenly.

"Well, what if the woman who writes me is nothing like she portrays herself to be?"

Oh, that's why. Leah let out a relieved sigh. "Jake, because Michael was needed on the ranch, he married Selina without going out to meet her. You don't have to do that."

"I can't afford to leave, either." Again his fingers forked through his hair. Only this time they went all the way down the back of his head until they reached his thick, muscular neck where they lingered.

"You don't have to. You can have her come here."

His hand dropped to the table. He frowned. "Why didn't Michael do that?"

"Because Selina's father wouldn't let her leave until she was married. Michael had prayed about it and had peace so he married her sight unseen."

Jake scooted back his chair, scraping it against the rough wood floor, and rose. Leah's eyes trailed up his tall, broad frame, wondering what he was doing.

He went to the sink, which she noticed was stacked with what she presumed to be dirty dishes, though a large towel covered them. Nervousness permeated his every movement. "I know I already asked you this once, but would you like something to drink now?"

"Yes. Thank you. A glass of water would be great." Her mouth felt dry as trail dust. She watched as he held the glass under the spout and raised and lowered the water pump handle in the sink. His broad shoulders and arm muscles bulged as he filled the glass. Only a few drips of water landed onto the dish towel. She hoped to find someone as tall as Jake. He had to be at least six-foot-four or -five. And at five-foot-eight-and-a-half, she was either the same height as most of the men she knew or taller. The thought of being taller than the man she married bothered her.

Jake turned and walked back toward her. What a fine

male specimen he was. He would make some woman a good husband. Of that she was certain.

He set a glass of water in front of her and one in front of himself before lowering his bulky frame onto the chair. Worry creased his forehead. This time she thought she knew why.

Wanting to put his mind at ease, she laid her hand on top of his arm, and his hard muscle jumped under her fingertips. She removed her hand and rested it on the table in front of her. "Listen, Jake. Before you get too involved with someone, you could always make it clear you want to meet them in person and spend time getting to know them before either of you make any real commitment. And..." She sat back in her chair. "I don't know what your financial situation is, but you could inform her that you would send her a round-trip ticket in case things don't work out."

His shoulders relaxed and the creases in his forehead disappeared. "That's a good idea. Think someone would do that?"

"Of course they would. It's done all the time. I know I'm going to. There is no way I'm going to marry someone without meeting him and without spending time with him and his family first."

"You scared, Leah?"

Was she? "A little. But the sooner I get away from here, the happier I'll be."

"You sure about that? Won't you miss your family?"

"Yes and yes. To be perfectly honest, the idea of staying here bothers me more than the idea of missing my family or the fear of the unknown does. I actually find that part rather thrilling."

"What do you find thrilling?"

"The fear of the unknown."

He narrowed his eyes and searched hers. "Why do you dislike it here so much?"

She shrugged, wishing she could confide in him about the nightmares and just why she hated this place as much as she did. But she didn't want him to think she was being silly like Marie had, so she used her standard reply. "I miss New York City and the lifestyle I used to have back then. Plus, I want some excitement in my life. As crazy as this may sound, I crave adventure." That part was true. She could use some adventure in her life.

"The Idaho Territory doesn't provide you with enough adventure?" A hint of humor warbled his voice.

"No. It's so boring here. Nothing exciting ever happens."

"You don't call the war with Nez Perce Indians exciting?" His blue eyes sparkled with mischief.

"There was nothing exciting about that war. Frightening was more like it." She shifted in her seat. "But I don't want to talk about that. Let's take a look at those letters. Would you like to read them first, or do you want me to?"

"If you don't mind, I'd rather you read them." Jake opened the envelope from Tennessee and gave the letter to Leah.

Leah could hardly decipher the sloppy penmanship. "Hello, my name is Betsy. I'm a single mother of four young children."

"Whoa." Jake's hand flew up. "Forget that one. Not ready to be a father yet. Especially to a herd of kids." He frowned. "How old is she, anyway? Does she say?"

Leah scanned the letter. "She's thirty-nine."

His eyes widened. "Thirty-nine? That's eleven years older than me. No, thank you." He tugged the letter from her hands and ripped it into several pieces before setting the shredded pile far from him.

Leah took the liberty of going through his stack of posts. She couldn't believe how many women were looking for husbands. "How about this one? The postmark is from Mississippi."

He shrugged, then nodded.

"Dear Mr. Lure. Me name is Samantha O'Sullivan. I be twenty-seven years old, six feet tall and one hundred and twenty pounds. Me hair is fiery red and me eyes are brown. Me pa said I must be gettin' married soon afore I become an ole maid. I dinna want to wed, but me pa said if I dinna and dinna write to you that he would toss me backside outta the house."

Leah looked over at Jake and put on her most serious face. "I think she sounds just like what you're looking for. You should write her back right away."

"You—you do?" The shock on his face pulled a guffaw out of Leah.

"No, no. Don't look so worried. I'm just teasing you, Jake."

Relief flooded over his face and his taut lips relaxed. "Whew. Had me worried there for a moment."

Leah sat up straight and in her best Irish imitation she said, "Blimey, Mister Jake. Ye must pick me. Aye, ye must, even tho' I dinna wanna marry. And even tho' me be gone in da head for even tellin' ye such a thang in da first place, won't ye please consider sendin' fer me anyway and spare me from becomin' an ole maid?"

She laughed and so did Jake, but his laughter had a nervous flutter to it.

Seconds later, Jake shredded that letter, too. "Next."

Leah continued reading the responses he'd received. Each one was worst than the first, but Jake didn't shred any more of them— He just stacked them in a pile. She opened the last one and a photograph slipped out. Leah picked it up and her mouth fell open.

"What you got there?" Jake asked.

Leah slid her attention from the photo and onto him. "She sent you a picture."

"Who did?"

Leah handed the picture to him and looked at the signature at the bottom of the letter. "Evie Scott. She's very lovely, isn't she?"

"Yep, she's pretty." He said it with very little enthusiasm.

Was the man blind or something? The woman was striking, and yet Jake seemed unfazed by her beauty.

He laid the photo on the kitchen table. "Don't care what a person looks like. I care about the type of person they are in here." He pointed to his heart. "What's her letter say?"

Leah drew in a breath and read the letter. "Dear Mr. Lure. My name is Evie Scott. As you see, I have enclosed a photograph of myself. I am twenty-two years old, five-feet-seven inches tall. Ever since the War Between the States, men have been scarce out here in Alabama. It is my desire to marry and to raise a family. I am willing to travel out West and marry straightaway, or if you so desire, we can spend time getting to know one another first before a commitment is made by either one of us. Of course, I will expect proper accommodations for a lady of my standing and—"

"Whoa. Stop right there," Jake interrupted.

Leah looked at Jake. "What's the matter?"

"Heard enough. She's not someone I'd consider marrying."

Leah tilted her head and frowned. "Why? She sounds lovely."

"Obviously, she's a woman of rank. I want a wife I can feel equal to. Not someone who comes from money."

She came from money, so why had he asked her to marry him? Wait a minute. Did he think she had turned him down because he didn't have money? That bothered her. A lot. She didn't care about that. But she didn't want to ask and embarrass him, either. So she'd let it go. For now, anyway. "Okay." Leah placed the photo in the letter and put it back into the envelope. "What now?"

"Nothing." He shrugged. "I'm in no hurry to get married. I'll wait to see if anyone else answers my ad."

"Oh, okay." She nodded.

Neither spoke.

"Leah." Abby chose that moment to appear at the door. Leah looked over at her sister. "We'd better get on home or Mother's going to wonder where we are. She may even send out a posse or the cavalry looking for us," Abby said with her usual dramatic flair.

"What time is it?"

Jake pulled out his pocket watch and told her the time.

"Sweet twinkling stars above. Abby's right." Leah scooted her chair out. "I've got to go. Mother will be worried."

Abby darted down the steps. Banjo followed her, leaping and hopping at her heels.

"Meant to ask you, where'd that expression come from, anyway?" Jake asked, following her out. "You're the only one I ever heard say it."

"Say what?"

"'Sweet twinkling stars above.'"

"Oh, that." Her face lit up. At the edge of the porch she gazed up at the sky. "When my father was alive, many warm summer nights we'd grab blankets and go lay outside. Father used to tuck me under the crook of his arm and we'd stare up at the stars. Father used to say that back in New York you couldn't see them as clearly as you could here. He even made up a song about sweet twinkling stars above and used to sing it to us."

"How's it go?"

Leah turned her attention onto him, then to where Abby was, near the phaeton playing with Banjo.

"Sweet twinkling stars above; there to remind us of our Heavenly Father's love. Each one placed by the Savior with care; as a sweet reminder that He will always be there. Oh, sweet twinkling stars above. When my children gaze upon you remind them, too, of my love. Each twinkle is a kiss from me; a hug, a prayer, a sweet memory. Oh, sweet twinkling stars above." Leah stopped singing in the softest, sweetest voice he'd ever heard. One filled with reverence and joy. And yet, her face now only showed sadness. "Okay. Now you know. And I need to get going," she blurted as if her tongue were on fire, and down the steps she bolted.

Jake caught up to her and they walked side by side until she reached her carriage. She stopped and faced him. All of a sudden, something barreled into her backside and sent her flying forward. Her face smacked into a firm wall. Her arms flung out, clutching onto something solid. Something warm. Something very muscular.

Jake stared at the top of Leah's head plastered against his chest. Her hands clung to his upper arms as he caught and held her there. He froze in place and the air around him suddenly disappeared. Having her this close to him, her hands touching him and her head so near his heart, caused his pulse to buck and kick like an untamed horse. That had never happened to him before. Course, she'd never touched him that closely before, either. Still. What was going on?

"Um, Jake, could you help me up, please?"

Jake blinked. "Oh. Yeah. Sorry." As soon as she was steady on her feet, he released her.

"What just hit me, anyway?" Leah ran her hands over her skirt.

"Meanie's what hit you," Abby said from behind Leah.

Abby had Jake's pet goat by the collar, yanking it away from her sister.

"Meanie! How'd you get out?" Jake grabbed the goat's collar and tugged her close to his leg. The animal stretched her head toward Leah and started gnawing on her skirt.

Jake yanked the cloth from the nanny's mouth and tapped her on the tip of the nose. "Stop that, you ornery old goat." Meanie latched onto Jake's fingers and shook her head fast and hard.

Banjo barked and bit Meanie in the backside. The goat chomped down harder on Jake's fingers. Jake struggled to pull them away while simultaneously holding the goat and knowing he looked like a blooming idiot. "Down, Banjo!"

The dog immediately dropped onto his belly.

Jake tugged, trying to free his now-throbbing fingers. One more yank and they were free. Shaking his hand, he glanced over at Leah. "Gonna hang that brother of yours. Should have never let Michael talk me into taking this goat off his hands."

Leah covered her mouth with her hand and her eyes crinkled into a smile.

"Go ahead and laugh. We both know you want to."

Her laughter pealed across the farmyard. It only took a second before he and Abby joined her.

With a hard jerk on his arm, Meanie broke free and

took off in the direction of Mabel's house. Banjo ran after her, nipping her heels and dodging the goat's quick kicks.

"Oh, no! Not again." Jake darted after them, hollering over his shoulder, "See you ladies tomorrow. Got a dog to stop and a goat to catch."

Their laughter followed him.

It took a quarter mile, but he finally caught up with Meanie and the dog, corralled them both and headed back to the house. He fully expected Leah and Abby to be gone, but they weren't. Keeping a tight hold on Meanie, he walked up to Leah's rig, panting from the exertion. "Something wrong?" he asked between gasps of breath. He struggled to keep the nanny from breaking free again.

"You said you would see us tomorrow, but I can't come by tomorrow."

"Won't be here even if you did."

"Huh?" Leah tilted her head in that charming way of hers.

"Guess Michael didn't tell you, then."

"Tell me what?"

"Starting tomorrow, I'll be working for him." He jerked on the goat's collar to keep her under control.

Leah's eyes widened. "Y-you are?" She glanced around his spread and then turned her attention back onto him. "But who's going to take care of your place?"

"Only gonna work part-time, until Smokey gets back from taking care of his folks' affairs and Michael feels comfortable leaving Selina home with the twins. Can you believe it? Michael. A father? To twins?"

"It's hard to picture Michael a father. But I'm so happy for my brother and Selina. It's hilarious watching him with those babies. Every little whimper and he rushes to their cradles. Selina has to almost wrestle him to the ground to keep him from picking them up all the time. He's paranoid to leave them and Selina alone.

"Mother, Abby and I promised him we'd help, but with Lottie Lynn and Joseph Michael only a few days old, he doesn't want to leave them or Selina. And if he does, it's only for a minute or two. I can understand that." She looked at Jake and her smile lit up her whole face. "I'm glad you'll be at the ranch, though. It'll be fun having you around."

Jake's insides grinned at her announcement. Maybe being a hired hand on the Bowen ranch just might be a fun thing after all.

Chapter Three

Leah removed her coat and scarf, hung them up on a wooden coat tree near the front door of her house and looked around. Dinner was on the stove waiting to be heated, everything was sparkling clean and the laundry was finished. With Abby still outside and her mother only who knew where, the house was so quiet that the only sound she heard was the grandfather clock ticking. Knowing she was alone and that she wouldn't have to wait until later to read her letters, her spirit skipped with excitement. She darted toward the stairs.

"Where are you off to in such a hurry?" Mother's voice stopped her.

Masking her disappointment for the delay in reading her posts, she put her reticule on the step and turned toward her mother. "Hi, Mother. Sorry, I didn't see you."

"Of course you didn't. I was in my room until I heard the front door. Did you have a nice time in town today?"

"I had a wonderful time." Soon Mother would know just how wonderful of a day Leah really did have. Right now, however, she had to keep that information tucked inside those hidden, secret compartments in her mind. When the time was right, she would tell Mother of her plans.

Arm in arm they went to the living room and sat down. Mother crossed her legs in Leah's direction. "Were you and Abby able to help Phoebe get everything finished for her wedding?"

"Yes, we did. Oh, Mother, Phoebe's gown is so pretty, and she looked so beautiful in it. Markus will absolutely love it."

"I'm sure he will. I wish you could find a nice man like Markus. Anyone caught your eye yet?" Eagerness and hope brightened her mother's beautiful face.

"No. Sorry, Mother. Not yet." *But hopefully someone will very soon.* She thought of the letters sitting on the stairs, waiting for her and calling out to her to come read them.

Mother patted her hand. "You will. God has someone special for you. I'm sure of it. When the time is right, He'll bring the right man into your life. Unless He already has and you don't know it yet."

She tilted her head and frowned. That same strand of hair that always seemed to escape its pins fell across her cheek. She reached up and curled it around her ear. "What do you mean? Do you have someone in mind?"

Mother leaned forward. "Let's just say I've been praying." She reached for Leah's hands and held them in her own, hands that were starting to show a few age spots and wrinkles. "Sweetheart, sometimes God places something right before our eyes but we don't see it because we're too busy looking somewhere else or for something else. Something that may or may not be God's will for us."

Did her mother know about her plans? No, she couldn't because only Abby, Jake and Selina knew, and none of them would have said anything to her. Of that she was certain. The need to know what her mother meant hovered inside her until she could no longer stand it. "What do you mean, Mother?"

"I'm just saying that there are a lot of young men here who would make a wonderful husband."

That was true. But the problem was they lived here, not in New York.

"What about Jake? You two seem to get along really well. You even entered the sack race at last year's harvest party with him. He's a nice man who loves the Lord. He'd make a wonderful husband."

Her eyes snapped to her mother's. "Mother, Jake is a nice man, but he's not the one for me."

"How do you know that?"

"I just know. Well, Mother—" Leah rose "—I'm sorry to end this conversation, but I have some things I need to do."

The look on her mother's face said Leah wasn't fooling her, but she nodded and smiled. "I need to get busy, too. Just think about what I said, okay?"

"I will." They hugged, then Leah headed up to her room. She removed the letters from her reticule and locked them in her nightstand before heading back downstairs and out the door where she planned on having a long talk with the Lord. After the conversation with her mother, she needed one.

Two hours later, after the dinner dishes were finished and the kitchen cleaned, Leah excused herself and went up to her room, shutting the door behind her. With one right turn of the passkey she locked the door, then tossed the key in her armoire drawer and quickly readied herself for bed. Against the headboard she propped up her pillows and settled herself on top of her lavender quilt. With a quick turn of the brass skeleton key, she unlocked her nightstand drawer, removed the letters, a pencil, and her Mr. Darcy diary and opened it up to the next blank page.

Dear Mr. Darcy, she penciled in as she had been doing ever since Rainee had given her the journal. Somehow Leah had felt silly just writing to her journal, but this way she felt like she was writing to a real, live person somewhere—someone who understood what she was going through. Someone who didn't make fun of her. She thought about calling it her Dear Daddy diary, but that hurt too much, so she named it the next best thing after her father, Mr. Darcy.

Today, I was pleasantly surprised to see that I had received many letters to my advertisement. I can't wait to read them, and I want you here when I do. My greatest hope is that I will find you in one of them.

For years I've dreamed of finding someone as wonderful as my father. You're the closest thing to that. But you already know that, don't you? I've shared it with you enough times.

I so desperately need to move. To escape the nightmares. I can't take them much longer. They're getting even worse and are coming more often. I just have got to find the peace I had before tragedy took Daddy away from me.

She grimaced.

Before the Idaho Territory took him from me.

Fresh anger roiled inside her.

I hate this place, Mr. Darcy! My father would still be alive if we hadn't ever moved here. I miss him terribly.

She brushed away a tear, let out a long sigh and forced her shaking hand to continue.

I want to go back to New York. That's why I placed an ad in the New York Times. *I'm going to stop writing now so I can read my letters, but I'll be back to let you know how they are. See you in awhile.*
Love,
Leah

She set her diary off to the side and picked up the first letter postmarked from New York. Her heart raced as she tore open the envelope. Was this it? Was this the man who would make everything good again? She couldn't wait to see.

Dear Madam,
I am answering your advertisement because I am in need of a wife. It is my father's wish that I marry a woman who is willing to bear me many sons so as to continue the Hamlen name and lineage.

Leah felt heat rush into her cheeks. The man was rather forward with his mention of bearing children. Such an intimate detail for him to openly share. Most inappropriate. But then again, if that was his design in marrying, then she could understand why he would bring it up. Still, the very idea that he did made her uncomfortable.

With uneasiness squirming through her, she continued to read.

The women here refuse to submit to my authority, and I will not have that. I will say straightaway that I am a strict believer in the Bible and where it

says that the man is the head over the woman and she is to submit to her husband. If you do not have a problem with being submissive to me and calling me Lord, then please contact me. If not, do not bother responding.
Signed,
Mr. Gregory Joseph Hamlen III

Leah laughed. No wonder the man was still single. What woman in her right mind would ever marry such a man as he?

She imitated Jake and tore the letter and envelope into pieces. After she did, she wished she hadn't and instead kept it to read to Jake. "If he thought some of his letters were bad, well, this one topped any of his," she whispered into the empty room.

Leah scanned through the pile of letters. One with precise penmanship snagged her attention. She looked at the return envelope and her heart skipped a beat. *Sweet twinkling stars above!* She clutched the envelope to her chest and looked upward. "Lord, is this a sign from You?"

Pulling her attention back onto the letter, she read the name on the return label again.

Fitzwilliam D. Barrington.

Fitzwilliam was Mr. Darcy's first name. She wondered what the *D* stood for. Darcy? No. Surely not. That would be too weird, even for her. Brushing all those thoughts and the strand of hair that had fallen against her cheek aside, she flipped the envelope over and carefully ran her finger over the red waxed seal with the fancy script *B* insignia.

Dear Miss Bowen,
As I have just moved to the United States of America from England, I have not had the pleasure to make

many acquaintances as of yet. The women I have met do not share your good opinion to travel and to explore the world. I must confess, your exuberant advertisement has quite intrigued me, and I must meet you. If it is agreeable with you, perhaps I could come on Tuesday next or within a fortnight to meet you. We could spend time getting acquainted to see if there could be a future for us together. If this is agreeable, then please send a post to me straightaway.

I hope to hear from you soon.

Sincerely,
Fitzwilliam D. Barrington

Relief drizzled over her. Mr. Barrington was willing to come here. She wouldn't have to risk breaking her mother's heart by traipsing off to New York by herself. She tossed everything from her lap onto the floor and rushed over to her writing desk.

Retrieving her best stationery, she dipped her pen in the ink well and penned her reply, making sure to use the swooping letters that looked so beautiful. Everything about this reply had to be perfect. After all, Fitzwilliam would make his decision about her and their future from it. Tomorrow she would take it to the post office. Bubbles of excitement popped through her. In her heart of hearts she felt she had at last found her very own Mr. Darcy who would come and whisk her away.

Jake saddled his horse and made his way to the Bowens' house. No one would be expecting him for at least another hour, but he couldn't sleep so he'd decided to head to their place early in hopes of seeing Leah. The morning nip brushed across him on a light breeze. He pulled the lapels of his wool coat tighter together, hoping the morning sun would soon penetrate the chilly air.

As he rounded the bend of pine trees nestled against the mountain leading to the Bowen ranch, his anticipation of seeing Leah caused his heart to beat erratically as he rode into their ranch yard. Leah had a way of making him feel special. He loved spending time with her.

He glanced toward the barn. There she was, sitting on a bench outside the barn door, petting Kitty, the family's pet pig. Jake reined his horse in that direction. Leah raised her head and leaped up. Grabbing the ends of her light pink wrap together, she scurried toward him, her lavender dress swinging like a bell around her feet as she did. Her warm welcome made his heart smile.

"I was hoping I would catch you this morning. You won't believe what I have to tell you." She was practically bouncing on her feet.

"Morning to you, too." He grinned.

There were those dimples again. Her eyes sparkled and her face shone brighter than the morning sun glistening off the dewdrops. Something had put that glow on her face. How he wished it was him, but he knew better.

"What won't I believe?" He dismounted and stood in front of her. Kitty nudged her nose into the palm of his hand.

"Kitty, leave Jake alone."

"She's all right."

"She's a pest." Leah leaned over and tapped the pig on the nose. "Aren't you, girl?"

Kitty sniffed the air with her round snout. Jake patted her shoulder and gave a quick scratch behind her ears. Content with the attention, Kitty waddled slowly in the direction of the field blooming with purple camas flowers, no doubt to have her fill of camas bulbs. "That pig's quite a character."

"She sure is." Leah laughed, then turned her attention from the retreating pig back onto him. "Come and sit down. I can't wait to tell you my good news." She grabbed his hand and pulled him along.

There was a lilt to her walk. The air around her rolled with joy. She let his hand go and he followed her to the same hewed-out bench she'd been sitting on when he'd arrived. After he tied his horse to a nearby hitching post, he sat down with her, careful to keep the appropriate amount of distance between them.

"Okay, bright eyes. What's your good news?"

Her smile bracketed by those dimples was contagious, and he found his own lips curling upward.

"I think I found my husband."

He wasn't expecting that, and it took him a minute to gather his wits about him. "Oh, yeah?" He knew he should be happy for her. That it would happen someday. But the thought of losing his best friend made his gut twist into a painful knot.

"Yes. He moved from England to New York City and he wants to come here to meet me. I'm sending my consent today. I'm so happy. He sounds like just the type of man I've been looking for." She went on and on oblivious to the pain her declaration was causing him. Pain he couldn't articulate.

"Morning, Jake." Michael's voice drifted toward him from yards away. "I wasn't expecting you here so early."

Jake snapped himself together and stood. "Morning, Michael."

Leah hopped up beside him. "What are you doing here?" she asked. "I thought you didn't want to leave Selina alone."

"I don't. But she's finally asleep now."

"What do you mean, 'finally'?" Leah tilted her head.

"The babies kept her up most of the night."

Jake anchored his arms across his chest. Concern for a woman he'd come to greatly respect pressed through him. "How's Selina doing?"

"Other than being exhausted, she's doing well. Having twins is a lot of hard work. But Joseph and Lottie Lynn are sure worth it." His eyes sparkled, then a wide yawn stretched his lips. It was then that Jake noticed the bags under Michael's eyes.

"So, what are you doing here?" Leah inquired again.

"I wanted to show Jake what to do."

"Can't Haydon or Jess do that?"

"They could, but..."

"You know both Haydon and Jess are going to hang you for not trusting them to show Jake what to do," Leah interrupted her brother.

Michael frowned. "It's not that I don't trust them. I wanted to be here to welcome Jake. To show him around and..."

They continued to talk about Jake as if he weren't standing right there between them.

"Fine, fine. If you insist on being the one to show him what to do, I'll run over and sit with Selina and the twins until you get back. I know that will help put your mind at ease and help you to relax a bit."

"It sure will. Thank you, Leah. But don't wake her or the babies. And don't knock. Just open the door quietly and let yourself in."

"Yes, yes, Michael." Leah dragged out the words and rolled her eyes at her brother. "You worry too much. You really need to learn to lighten up."

"Just wait until you have children. Then it will be my turn to tell *you* to lighten up."

She shook her head and glanced over at Jake. "See you later, Jake."

He gave a quick nod and watched her as she headed toward Michael's house.

"You like her, don't you?"

Jake yanked his attention to Michael. "Sure I like her. She's been a great friend to me."

"She's more than a friend. I can see it in your eyes."

Jake shook his head and waved Michael off. "The only thing you see in my eyes is respect."

"If you say so, buddy." The smirk on Michael's face bugged Jake. Couldn't a guy have a female friend without everyone making a big deal about it?

Best change the subject before Michael put together any more pieces that didn't fit. "So, what do you want me to do?"

"Changing the subject, huh?"

"Michael." Jake sent Michael a warning glare. "I'm here to help, not discuss my *friendship* with Leah. You want my help or not? Besides, thought you didn't like leaving Selina alone."

Worry crowded into Michael's face immediately followed by determination. He glanced at his pocket watch. "Oh, man. I've got to hurry. I've been gone ten minutes already."

"Ten minutes? That long, huh? We'd better hurry, then."

"Okay, wise guy. Just wait until you become a father. Then you'll understand. Come on." He motioned for them to go inside the barn.

Jake hoped someday he would know exactly how Michael felt. Once again, he wished Leah hadn't turned his marriage offer down. He knew she'd make a good wife and mother, and he admired her and respected her more than any other woman he knew.

Thoughts of Leah answering some strange man's ad and inviting him there trailed through Jake's mind. Would he be able to handle seeing his best friend hanging out with another man?

A man who could possibly become Leah's husband and take her away from him?

God, give me the grace to let my friend go and to make it through this time. Make it a large dose. 'Cause I'm sure gonna need every ounce You can spare.

Chapter Four

Steps creaked under Leah's feet. She cringed, hoping the noise wouldn't wake Selina. Michael would give her a good scolding if she did. Of that she was certain. Quietly she opened the door and stepped inside. Her eyes popped open. She'd never seen Selina's house this messy before. Never.

Dishes were scattered all over the table and piled in the sink. If Selina saw them, she would be so upset, and Leah couldn't have that. After she peeked into Selina's bedroom to make sure everything was all right, she closed the door. Leah grabbed an apron from off the hook, rolled up her sleeves and, as quietly as she could, she washed the dishes and tidied up the house.

Squeaking hinges caught her attention. She turned to find Michael stepping inside the house.

"Is she still asleep? Are the twins okay?"

She barely heard his questions his voice was so low.

"Yes. They're fine." She, too, kept her voice down.

"Good." He nodded. "Leah, would you mind doing me a favor?" He looked away and then back at her. "Oh. Thanks for doing the dishes and picking up the place. I really appreciate it. I hadn't gotten to that yet."

"You're welcome, Michael. That's what sisters are for." She smiled. "Now, what did you want?"

"We have a cow that's down and needs doctoring. Everyone else is busy and Jake will need my help. Would you mind staying here with Selina a bit longer? I don't want to leave her alone." He ran his hand over his face. "Man, I wish I didn't have to help. I hate leaving Selina. But Jake can't do it alone and no one else is around."

Leah laid her hand on his arm. "I can stay with her. She and the twins will be just fine."

Worry crowded his face. It was happening a lot these days.

"Michael." She turned and gave him a push toward the door. "Go. They'll be fine. Selina's a strong woman."

"She is, isn't she?" Pride puffed out his chest.

"Yes. Now go. I'll wait until you get back."

"If you need anything—"

"Michael, she'll be fine." This time, Leah pushed him out the door.

"I'll be back in about an hour."

"I'll be here."

She watched Michael leave, then shut the door.

With Selina and the babies still sound asleep, Leah searched her brother's cellar and pantry and made a pot of stew and some biscuits.

Nearly an hour later, Leah heard a baby cry. She headed over to the bedroom, slowly opened the door and peered inside. Lottie Lynn's little arms were moving in short, choppy movements. A wail came from Joseph's bed and his arms and legs imitated his sister's. Leah scurried inside, not knowing which one to reach for first.

"They sure have mighty good lungs," Selina said with a voice filled with sleep.

She started to rise, but Leah shot up her hand. "You stay there. I'll bring them to you."

"I ain't helpless. I can get them."

"I know you're not. But Michael would have my hide if he knew I let you get out of that bed."

Selina rolled her sleepy eyes. "Such fussin' that man does over me. I can do it."

"Please, Selina. You stay there. Let me do this for you," Leah said over the wails of the twins. She picked up Lottie Lynn, who stopped crying instantly. Leah hugged the baby girl to her chest. Someday she hoped to have a houseful of her own children. Her thoughts went to the letter still in her pocket, the one destined to be mailed today. Maybe that someday wasn't too far off.

She changed the baby's diaper and handed her to Selina who was now sitting propped against the pillows, looking more tired than Leah had ever seen her. No wonder Michael seemed so worried. She made a mental note to tell her mother that despite Michael's protest, they needed to come and help Selina…and Michael.

"Thank ya kindly, Leah."

"You're welcome."

Joey's loud wail pierced the air. Leah scuttled over to his crib and, securing his head, lifted him out. Muddy diaper odor stung Leah's nose with its potency. Ewwww. She wrinkled her nose and blinked her eyes.

"Sweet twinkling stars above. You need changing, little man," she cooed to him as she walked over to the changing table Michael had made. She laid him on the wooden slab with the feather-filled flannel quilt on top and changed her nephew's diaper. His crying stopped. She picked him up, kissed his cheek and turned toward Selina. A light blanket covered Lottie Lynn's head while she nursed.

"Do you want me to leave and you can holler when you're finished?"

"No. It don't bother me none. Unless you're uncomfortable."

She shook her head, sat down in the rocking chair next to the bed and rocked Joey.

Leah knew it was time to make the announcement. She let out a long breath to settle the butterflies flitting about in her stomach. "Well, I finally did it."

Busy with the baby, Selina hardly looked up. "Did what?"

"I placed an advertisement for a husband. And I've already received several answers."

Selina's eyes went wide as they jerked up, and her brows puckered. "Does your family know?"

"No."

"They ain't gonna like it. You goin' off to who knows where."

Leah found that weird coming from Selina, who had traveled across the country to be with Michael.

"I know what you're a-thinkin'. I did it. And I personally see nothin' wrong with it. But your family is mighty protective of you."

"I know they are. But..." She handed Joey to Selina and took the newly fed Lottie Lynn from her mother. With a cloth draped over her shoulder Leah patted her niece on the back until a loud burp echoed in the room. Selina and Leah giggled.

Selina settled Joey and then turned her attention back to Leah. "But what?"

"But, I don't think they'll have a problem with it once I tell him that Fitzwilliam will be coming here, and I won't be traveling alone."

"Fitzwilliam? Ain't that an interestin' name. Never heard it before."

"I love his name. And—" she shifted Lottie Lynn and cradled her closer "—I really believe God is in this."

"Why's that?"

"Well, ever since reading *Pride and Prejudice* I've prayed for a man like Mr. Darcy. In the book, Mr. Darcy's first name is Fitzwilliam."

"Oh. I see." She waved her head back and forth, confusion flooding her face. "No, I don't see. What's that gotta do with anythin'?"

"It's simple, really. I've been praying for a man like Mr. Darcy. Then I get a letter from a man with Mr. Darcy's first name. And he lives in New York City." Oops. She shouldn't have said that. Leah didn't want Selina asking her why that was important, so she rushed on before she could. "You see, these are all signs."

"Signs?"

"Yes. From God."

"Leah, it ain't none-a my business—"

"What isn't any of your business, sweetheart?" Michael interrupted Selina as he stepped into the room.

Leah's gaze flew to Selina. With her eyes only, she begged Selina not to tell him.

Her brother strode into the room and kissed Selina, then took Lottie Lynn from Leah. "So, how are my favorite people in the whole world doing?" Michael sat on the bed next to Selina.

"Oh, I didn't know you thought of me as one of your favorite people. I'm honored, and I'm doing great," Leah teased her brother.

"Very funny. Ha-ha. I wasn't asking you."

"Really? Could have fooled me," she teased him again.

Michael turned to his family.

Whew. Thank You, Lord. Michael's forgotten all about his question. Leah stood. "It looks like you don't need me anymore, so I'll be on my way. There's stew on the stove and biscuits in the warmer."

Michael glanced over at her. "Thank you, Leah. I appreciate your help." He turned back to Selina.

"Thank ya kindly, Leah." Selina peered around him. Then, as if she weren't even there, her brother and his wife started talking. They were so adorable to watch. Leah silently prayed for a marriage like theirs, like the marriages of all her siblings and her parents. Out of the house she bounded with a spring in her step. Time to ready her horse and head into town to mail the letter that might very well give her the future she desired.

Jake finished mucking the stalls. Rivulets of sweat streamed from underneath his cowboy hat. From his back pocket, he pulled out a handkerchief that had definitely seen better days.

"You need a new one of those." Leah stepped in front of him, and what a beautiful sight she was.

He looked at the holes in his kerchief. "Sure do."

"I'll make you some."

"You don't need to do that."

"I know I don't need to, silly. I want to."

It was hard for Jake to accept charity—always had been. He hated feeling less than in front of anyone. Feeling that way in front of Leah was even worse. "Only if I pay for them."

Leah planted her hands on her slender hips. "No. You will not pay me for them."

"Won't take them then." He crossed his arms over his chest and stood his ground.

Her eyes trailed the length of him. For some odd reason,

he hoped she liked what she saw. “You think that stance is going to stop me? Well, it won’t. Besides, you have a birthday coming up and you can’t refuse a birthday gift from a friend. It would be rude.”

She got him there. He picked up the shovel again and changed the subject. “How are Selina and the twins doing?”

“Great. They’re so cute. You should see them.”

“I’ll give Selina a few more days to recuperate before I do. Besides, don’t think Michael’s gonna let anyone near her for a few days.”

They laughed.

“He sure is protective of them, isn’t he?” Leah said through a giggle.

“I would be, too.”

“I bet you would. You’ll make a fine father someday.” As she realized what she’d said, her face turned a deep shade of red. She spun and headed toward the tack room.

Jake followed her. “What you doing?”

“I’m going to get Lambie ready so I can head into town to mail my letter.” She kept her back to him and reached for a halter.

His heart felt as if it had been thrown from a bucking bronc, but he reached for the tack just the same. “Here. Let me do that.”

She turned to him and her smile was filled with gratitude. “I can get her. But thanks anyway.”

Jake gently tugged the halter from her grasp. “How about you let me help—or no handkerchiefs?” He grinned down at her.

She tilted her head and gazed up at him with those big blue eyes. “Okay. You win. But—” she held out her hand “—only if you promise me you will accept my gift.”

Jake glanced down at her hand. “Deal.” He accepted

her handshake. Her hand felt small in his larger one. Soft, too, except for the few calluses he felt.

"Um, Jake." Leah glanced down at her hand. "You can let go now."

His attention drifted to her face and then to where their hands were still joined. "Oh, right." He dropped her hand as if it were on fire and felt heat rush up his neck and into his face. He couldn't believe it. He was blushing. Blushing. Like a woman.

Embarrassed, he spun on the heel of his boot and strode to her horse's stall. "How you doing, girl?" he asked, slipping the lead rope around Lambie's neck and then the halter on her head. Jake led the mare from her stall over to where Leah stood by the phaeton.

While they worked together to hitch up her horse Jake asked, "Lambie's a weird name for a horse, ain't it?"

"Yes. Abby named her."

"Did she name Kitty, too?" He referred to the pet pig with the huge personality.

"Yes. When she was younger she wanted to name all the animals. My brothers didn't have the heart to refuse her. They're sorry for it now." She laughed.

"Why's that?"

"Well, we have a horse named Lambie and one named Raven. Kitty the pig." She ticked each one off her fingers as she mentioned them. "Miss Piggy, the cat." She paused. "Oh and there was Taxt, one of our bulls."

"She named a bull Taxt?"

Leah laughed again. "Everyone asks that. And the answer is yes, she did."

"Poor bull."

Leah's giggle at his comment pulled a chuckle out of him. Ever since they'd become friends, he'd found himself laughing more and more. It felt good. Real good in fact.

"There. All finished."

"Thank you, Jake, for helping me."

"Welcome. Anytime."

She grabbed the lines under the horse's chin and tugged on them. Jake hurried ahead and opened the double doors.

Outside the sun had knocked the midmorning chill out of the air.

Leah looked up at the sky and all around. "It's sure a lovely day today."

Jake shifted his focus from her sleek, graceful neck and placed it upward, glad his hat shielded the bright sun from reaching his eyes. "Sure is."

"Well..." Her eyes collided with his. "I'd better go now. Mother wants me to pick up a few things for her, and I need to mail my letter." Her face brightened at that, and his outlook dimmed.

Pushing his own stupid feelings aside, he offered her a hand into the buggy, even though he really didn't want to aid her reason for going. "Mind picking up my mail while you're there?"

"No. I'd be happy to." She sat down and faced him.

"Leah." He gathered the lines but didn't hand them to her. "You sure you wanna do this?"

"Do what? Go to town? I have to. Mother needs—"

"No," he interrupted her, unable to keep the frustration from his voice. "Answer that man's ad."

"Of course I'm sure. Otherwise I wouldn't be doing it."

"How can you be so certain?"

Her eyes brushed over his face as if she were contemplating her answer. She looked away and then her attention settled on him. "For years I prayed for a man like my father and Mr. Darcy."

"Mr. Darcy? Who's that?"

Her eyelids lowered to her lap.

Jake watched as she nervously tugged on her fingertips. In a bold move, he reached for her hands and held on to them. "Leah, look at me."

Slowly, she raised her head toward him. "We're friends. You can tell me who Mr. Darcy is." Jake wondered if Mr. Darcy was the man who had just bought the livery stable. He couldn't remember the man's name, only that it started with a *D*.

"Promise you won't laugh?"

"Promise." He hiked his foot up, set it on the phaeton step and rested his forearm on his leg, waiting for her answer.

"Mr. Darcy is the hero in *Pride and Prejudice*."

"What's that?"

"A novel."

Jake forced his eyes not to bounce wide open. A novel? She wanted a man like some imaginable character out of a book? Whoa! He hadn't seen that one coming. Right now, laughing was the furthest thing from his mind.

"I know it sounds silly. But the man reminds me so much of my father."

"So this Mr. Darcy is a rancher?"

She shook her head and her bouncy curls wiggled with the motion. He longed to wrap his finger around one of them, just to see if they were as soft as they looked. "No. He's not a rancher. He reminds me of my father—before we moved here, that is." She clamped her lips together tightly.

Jake thought he saw a shimmer in her eyes but wasn't sure because she looked away. He placed his foot back onto the ground, not sure what to say or do.

Seconds ticked by. With a slow turn of her head, she dropped her attention onto him. "I'd better go, Jake. I have lots of errands to run."

That was it. No explanation. He scanned her face. Though she tried to smile, he could see in her eyes that she was upset. He hated to see her leave like this, but he didn't know what to say or do to make it better because he didn't even know what was wrong.

She reached for the lines. Reluctantly, Jake laid them in her hand when what he really wanted to do was snatch them back and ask her what was wrong. But he didn't. She said she needed to go, and he needed to respect that. He stepped back, out of her way. "Be careful."

"I will. Thank you."

"For what?"

"For helping me with my horse and for not laughing at me."

"Nothing to laugh at." His grin was meant to reassure her.

She nodded and flicked the lines. Jake watched the buggy pull out of the yard. Curious about what type of person this Mr. Darcy fellow was, he decided that he needed to purchase a copy of that book. What was it called? Oh, yes. *Pride and Prejudice.* The title alone made him nervous. He'd never been much of a reader in school, but this was important. He could only imagine what was stuck in between the pages and who this Mr. Darcy fellow was. The sooner he found out, the better.

Chapter Five

Leah couldn't believe she'd almost slipped. Telling Jake about wanting a man like her dad was bad enough, but she'd almost started to tell him why. Good thing she'd caught herself.

Two hours later, after running all of her errands, she headed for home. Seven letters had come for her and sixteen for Jake. She looked at the large bundle of Jake's posts, and without warning or understanding, jealousy snipped at her. Why, she didn't know. She wanted her friend to be happy. And if one of the women in those letters would make that happen, she'd be happy, too.

A light breeze swept by her and over the field of blooming camas. The purple flowers waved as the gentle wind drifted over them. Spring was her favorite time of the year. It meant winter was coming to an end and new life, new growth and new births were being ushered in.

From afar, she noticed Jake out in the field tending to the cattle and grinned. He had a way of making her smile. Another click of the lines, and she coaxed Lambie into a fast trot.

Jake spotted her, swung into his saddle and headed

toward her. Her heart picked up as he neared. That happened a lot lately.

"Howdy-do." Jake pulled his horse up alongside her buggy and rode next to her.

"Howdy-do yourself." She pulled her horse to a stop and raised her hand to block out the sun as she gazed up at him.

Jake moved his horse until he blocked the sun from shining in her eyes. "Did you have a pleasant trip?" He thumbed the brim of his hat upward, and she got a clear look at his tabby-gray eyes.

"I sure did." It was even more pleasurable now that her best friend was here. "How'd your day go? Did my brothers work you too hard?"

"Naw. I'm used to hard work. Think they went easy on me today, though." There was that lazy grin she enjoyed.

"Why's that?"

"'Cause. Didn't do much." He leaned over and rested his arm on his saddle horn and gazed down at her. His horse shifted and stomped its leg, trying to get rid of a pesky horsefly. Jake didn't even flinch but remained relaxed.

Leah envied how relaxed he always was, whereas she was always restless and fidgety inside and out. Oh, to have his peace. Someday. Someday soon, she encouraged herself. "What all did you do?"

"Milked the cows. Doctored a few heifers. Cleaned the barn. Checked to make sure the pigs were all okay. That was it. I'm done for the day already."

"Already?"

"Yep."

"Sweet twinkling stars above. They really did go easy on you." She grinned and nearly laughed outright.

He chuckled. "Yep. Told you they did." Jake sat up straight. "Before I forget, did I have any mail?"

"Oh. Um. Yes. You did. Quite a bit, actually." She moved

her reticule, grabbed the tied bundle of his mail and handed it to him.

"You weren't kidding." He took the generous bundle from her and turned it around.

"Sixteen, to be exact."

His attention drifted to her. "Sixteen, huh?" A knowing smirk accompanied his question.

Heat rushed to Leah's face. She wished she could blame it on the warm sun, but the sun had been there for hours, and her red face hadn't. She dipped her head and only let her eyes look up at him. "Yes. Sixteen."

There was that chuckle again. "How many you get?"

"Seven." She raised her chin, hoping her face was no longer red.

"You busy now? I mean, after you take your supplies home."

"No. Why?"

"Well, was wondering if you'd help me go through these." He raised the package of letters.

"Sure. You want to go through them now?"

"You mean right here?"

"Yes."

"What about your supplies?"

"They'll be fine. Besides, I got done earlier than I thought. Mother won't be expecting me home for another hour or so. We could…" She looked around and pointed to the trees. "We could go sit on that rock over there in the shade?"

Jake followed her line of view. "Works for me."

He dismounted, gathered both reins under his gelding's neck, and wrapped them around the saddle horn and let go.

"Won't he leave?" Leah asked, referring to his dun-colored horse.

"Nope. Dun's trained not to go far when his reins are tied to the saddle. We do this all the time."

"Our horses are trained to stand still when the reins are down, but I've never seen anyone do it like that before."

"Yeah, well, I'm different."

"That's for sure." A smile lit up her face.

It must have been lost on Jake because he whipped his head in her direction and his tone sounded defensive. "What's that supposed to mean?"

"Oh. I see how that must have sounded, but I meant that as a compliment. Truly. That's one of the things I like about you, Jake. You do things differently than most folks."

"Like what?" His forehead wrinkled as he tied off the lines on her carriage.

"Well, for one, you keep that silly goat and put up with her silly antics when no one else would."

"Yep. I do. 'Cause I know if I gave that little escape artist to someone else they would probably destroy her. That's why I keep her."

"Exactly. They would have put her down. And so you put up with all the trouble she causes rather than risk someone else destroying her." Leah watched as he shrugged off her compliment. "You're a softy when it comes to animals, Jake. That's one of the things I admire about you. And another thing you do differently is… You asked another woman to help you pick out a wife. I don't know anyone who's ever done that. Do you?" She danced her eyebrows up at him and sent him a smirch of a smile.

"Got me there." His lazy grin appeared. "Speaking of. We'd best get to it so we can get ready for Phoebe's wedding." Jake slipped the tied bundle of letters from her hand.

Under the clear blue sky the knee-high bunchgrass rustled as they walked through it side by side until they reached a large flat-topped boulder and sat down.

"Okay. What do we have here this time?" Leah pointed to the letters Jake held.

He untied the string and handed her the first one. Leah opened it and scrunched her face.

Jake leaned toward her. His breath brushed the hair near her ear, sending chills rushing up and down her back. Not understanding why that would happen, she turned her head, and her face was inches from his. Her gaze soared to his gray eyes. Eyes that searched hers, questioning hers, as her eyes did his.

A moment passed in which neither moved.

Then Jake pulled back, cleared his throat and looked straight ahead. Leah, realizing she hadn't been breathing, drew in a long, quiet breath, wondering why her insides were suddenly fluttering.

Jake willed his heartbeat to return to normal. The urge to kiss his friend just now was so strong that he'd almost given in to it. Nothing good would have come from it, of that he was certain. And he would do nothing to risk his friendship with her.

No one understood him like she did.

No one accepted him just as he was like she did.

And no one filled his thoughts more than she did.

And therein lay the danger.

She was leaving soon.

It was time for him to find a wife. He looked back at her. "Well. Let's get to it."

Leah tilted her head. "Get to what?" Confusion infused her face.

Did she know he had been about to kiss her? If so, is that what she thought he meant? "The letters. Get to the letters."

"Oh. Yes. Oh, um. Right. The letters." Her attention

dropped to the post in her hand. "I think we have to forget this one."

"Why's that?"

"Because." She placed it under his view. "I can't even read it."

He squinted, trying to make out the sloppy cursive. He could make out only a few words. Saloon. Toothless. And ten babies. "Whoa!" He balled the letter up faster than he could say the word *no.*

"What?" Leah glanced at the wad in his hands.

"You don't wanna know."

"Well, now you've got me curious. Tell me?"

Reluctantly, he un-balled the letter and smoothed the wrinkles as best as he could. Heat drifted up the back of his neck as he pointed to each of the three words.

Leah's eyes opened farther and farther with each one he pointed to. "Sweet twinkling stars above." Her hands flew to her flushed cheeks, and her wide eyes darted to his. "Oh my." She shook her head. "Oh my, my, my, my, my."

"'Oh my' is right." He took the letter from her and wadded it up again before he shoved it into his pocket to burn later. Apprehension and fear fisted inside him as he stared at the remaining pile. "Not sure I wanna do this anymore. Bad idea."

"What's a bad idea?" Leah's color had returned to normal and she seemed to have recovered from the shock.

He wished he had. His gut was still being punched around. "Don't think I want you to read anymore."

"Why?"

His own eyebrows pointed upward. "Why? You ask me why after reading that letter?"

Leah's lips quivered and her nostrils danced.

He watched, amused at her trying to hold back her

laughter. His own lips now curled and twitched. Soon a belly laugh rolled out of him.

Leah's hand rested on his arm and her sweet laughter joined his.

He didn't know how long they laughed, but it was long enough that Leah had tears rolling from her eyes.

He would offer her his handkerchief, but it was too worn and would be too embarrassing. No need, anyway. She reached inside the pocket of her skirt and pulled a lace hankie out and dabbed at her eyes.

When they both had composed themselves, Leah asked, "What do you want to do with these?"

"Burn 'em!" he blurted.

They burst out laughing again.

"Seriously," Leah said through a twitter. "What do you want to do with them?"

"Told you already. Burn 'em."

She tilted her head. "Surely they can't all be like her."

He hiked a brow.

"Okay, Jake. Tell you what. I'll turn my back to you and read them so you can't see my face. If they're bad, then I'll slip them back into the envelope. If they aren't, I'll read them to you. Sound fair?"

After that last letter, he didn't care what was in any of them. He no longer had any faith in this process. He'd rather remain single the rest of his life than marry a toothless woman who had worked in a saloon and wanted ten babies.

"Well, what do you think?"

"Think I'll just forget the whole thing."

Once again her hand rested on his arm and lingered there.

His attention trailed there and to the heat that now raced up his arm.

"Oh, sorry." She yanked it back and rested her hand on her skirt. "You sure you want to do that, Jake? There might be some lovely ladies in here." She patted the stack.

Debate did a roundup through his brain. He really wanted to get married, but some of the letters he'd received were downright scary. Okay, a few of them were. Still. Did he dare take a chance on one of them?

"Jake." Leah's soft voice reached his ears and he looked at her. "I know you're scared. So am I. But if you don't step out in faith, how will you ever know? Besides, like I said before, you can always have her come here before you make a decision. I mean, it isn't like you have to marry her or anything before meeting her." She shrugged. "What have you got to lose?"

Her words pinned his heart to the hard ground. It was once again obvious that she would never consider him. If she would, she wouldn't have suggested he send for someone else. *Is that what's been holding me back? Hoping Leah would change her mind and marry me?* Truth smacked him upside the head. That was it. Knowing that, he decided he might as well give it a try. "You're right. Don't have anything to lose. Okay. Open the next one." If only she knew how hard those words were for him to say. When what he really wanted to say was, *Are you sure you won't reconsider my proposal and stay here? At least I know what you're like. These other women are downright scary.*

Leah pulled out the next one. One after another she read, and the second to the last one caught his attention.

Dear Mr. Lure,
My name is Raquel Tobias. I am a Christian woman looking for a Christian man to share my life with. I'm twenty-three years old, five foot seven, 130 pounds,

with auburn hair and blue eyes. I'm currently residing in Chicago, taking care of my beloved Aunt Sally who encouraged me to not follow in her footsteps wishing she'd married. Therefore, I decided to take a chance by answering your advertisement.

Aunt Sally insists on paying my way there and back in case things do not work between us. It is her way of saying thanks for being a companion to her all this time. Aunt Tillie, her sister, is recently widowed and will be coming to live with her, so my aunt will not be alone if I leave.

So, if you would like to meet me, please reply to this post.

Thank you and God bless you.

Raquel Tobias

Leah shifted her focus from the letter onto him. "What do you think?"

"Well," he stood, pondering Miss Tobias's words. Seconds passed. "Like you said, I need to step out in faith, so I'll answer her." And what a leap of faith it would be. Bigger than any he'd ever taken before.

"Do you want help writing her back?" For some odd reason, the prospect of Jake actually responding to a woman who could potentially become his wife made Leah uneasy. Was the feeling a warning from God that this woman wasn't right for him? She didn't know. She couldn't rightly discern why she felt the way she did. All she knew was something didn't feel right.

"You okay?" Jake asked, shifting his vision down on her.

Leah gazed up at him. Once again, Jake, being the perfect gentleman, blocked the bright sun from shining in her eyes. She shook out the confusing thoughts. He was going to think she'd lost her mind. "Yes. Of course. I'm fine." Only she didn't feel fine. No. In fact, she felt sick. Even so, she forced a smile onto her face. Later on, when she was alone, she'd try to figure out just what was bothering her about this whole situation. After all, from the looks of things, everything seemed to be working out exactly as she had hoped. She realized then she was just being silly about all of it.

"Thanks for the offer, Leah, but I can manage." Jake crossed his arms over his chest and shrugged.

That threw her completely off track, and she turned wide, confused eyes at him. "Manage what?"

"The letter." He nodded at it still in her hand.

"Oh. Yes. That. Silly me." She gathered the letters, handed all of them to Jake and then stood. "How could I have forgotten so soon?"

"'Cause you're a woman."

"Hey." She slapped him on the arm. "What's that supposed to mean?"

"Just teasing you, Leah." He winked at her.

Winked. She couldn't believe her friend just winked at her. Even more befuddling…she couldn't believe how her heart leaped in response to his wink. What was going on with her? Whatever it was, she wasn't sure she liked it. "Yes, well, um. I'd better get home now. I have much to do before Phoebe's wedding. So, I'll see you later, Jake." She brushed past him, scurried to her buggy and climbed aboard.

"What's your hurry?"

"Me? I'm not in a hurry," she answered without meeting his eyes.

Jake hiked a brow and stared at her. "Okay, Leah. Something's wrong. What is it?"

Her hands shook and her insides weren't any better, but she forced herself to not show any of it. "Nothing's wrong. I just have a lot on my mind, that's all. And I really do have much to do before the wedding."

His eyes searched hers, though she wasn't really looking at him. She couldn't. If she did, he would see everything.

He shook his head. "Not buying it, Leah. But neither will I push you into talking about what's bothering you." Hurt and disappointment marched across Jake's face. "You got a right to keep your own counsel, I guess."

Anger with herself for handling it all so badly trounced over her. Gathering her courage, she looked down at him. "Jake, I'm honestly not sure what's bothering me, or I would tell you." She looked him right in the eye, wanting to ask but not sure she should. "Do you ever feel like something's wrong but you don't know what it is?"

"Yep. Lots of times."

"You do? What do you do about it?" It was odd being so blunt about what she was feeling. So often, her own feelings had to be tucked away in deference to duty. She took a short breath and pushed those thoughts away.

"I pray and ask God to show me what it is and what to do about it." Conviction gripped his words. He looked so settled, so solid.

"Pray," she whispered. How simple, yet why hadn't she thought of that? "That's what I'll do. Thank you, Jake."

With his free hand, he handed her the lines. "Leah, you know you can talk to me anytime about anything. That I'm here for you, right?"

"Yes." She knew without a doubt he was. "And I thank you for that. You know that I'm here for you, too, don't you?"

"Yep." Jake nodded and smiled a half grin.

After a few moments of gazing silence, he stepped back, out of the way of her buggy. "Better let you go so you can get whatever it is you need to do done. See ya this evening."

That's right. She would see Jake this evening. Joy sang through her leaping heart. She gave him her sweetest smile. "Yes. I'll see you later. I'm looking forward to it." She meant that more than even she understood and that scared her. She was starting to realize that she needed to be careful because the more time she spent with Jake, the harder it would be for her to say goodbye to him. But say goodbye she must. Her peace of mind and her very sanity depended on it.

Chapter Six

Dressed in her blue-violet dress, Leah stood at the full-length looking glass in her bedroom and studied her image. The sheer, ruffled lace around her neck, sleeves and skirt looked out of place in the Idaho Territory. Yet tonight it wouldn't be. Phoebe was marrying the banker's son, so everyone would be dressing in their best attire.

Leah gave one more glance at herself. Then she turned the key on her jewelry box, removed the tortoiseshell hair-pins, placed them into her coiffure hairstyle and stared at them. Father had given them to her for her tenth birthday.

She closed her eyes as memories of that day crashed in on her. Father had been so proud of the combs he himself had picked out. "A special gift for my special girl," he'd said before tucking them into her hair. He'd stood back and admired her. "You look beautiful, Leah. I'm so proud of you, princess." He'd hugged her, and she felt the warmth and security of that moment even to this day.

Melancholy shoved through her as she remembered also that there would never be any more hugs from her father. He was gone and nothing could bring him back. This wretched place had stolen him from her.

Short, huffy breaths whooshed between her clenched

teeth. She yanked the combs from her hair and put them back into her jewelry box where she couldn't see them anymore. The reminder of who gave them to her hurt too much.

Without warning, the image of her father gasping for air invaded her thoughts. She slapped her hand over her mouth to stifle the scream the unwelcome intruder regurgitated. Gurgling sounds of her father trying to draw breath flooded her ears. She pressed her hands over them to snuff the ghastly noise from her anguished soul. But neither the image nor the sound stopped.

The urge to scream once again siphoned up her esophagus. She wanted to let it out. To yell at the ugly things attacking her to leave her alone, but she couldn't— Her family would hear her.

She pinched her eyes shut and swallowed hard as if that would somehow make everything better. When that didn't work, she leaned over, placed her hands on her knees and drew in several long breaths, exhaling slowly each time until finally the grisly images and sounds faded, and the jitters ceased. Having won that battle, she straightened and pressed her shoulders back. Ghosts of the past would not ruin her evening. Chin up, she headed downstairs.

"Oh, Lee-Lee. You look beautiful." Abby glanced over her.

"You look pretty gorgeous yourself, Abbs." The yellow cotton frock layered with white lace on the bodice, skirt and neck brought out the yellow highlights in her sister's hair. Abby had done an incredible job on that dress. What an excellent seamstress she turned out to be. Leah was so proud of her baby sister.

"Well, look at my girls." They both turned toward the sound of their mother's voice. "You both look so lovely. Oh." She pressed her finger on her lip. "That won't do.

You girls had better go up and change. You'll outshine the bride, and we can't have that now, can we?"

"Oh, Mother." Leah waved her off and beamed under her praise. "You're so sweet. But I'm certain we, as in the three of us, won't 'outshine' the bride. Trust me. Wait until you see her."

"Yes, Mother." Abby cupped her fisted hand under her chin, batted her eyes and sighed dramatically. "It's the most beautiful gown ever, and Phoebe looks absolutely fabulous in it."

"What a silly goose you are, Abbynormal." Leah shook her head at her sister. "You are so dramatic."

"Yeah. But you love me."

"I sure do." She pulled Abby into a hug.

"Okay, ladies. We'd better go or we'll be late." Mother gathered her wrap and picked up the gloves that matched her simple yet elegant blue silk dress. "I hope you girls don't mind, but with Jess and Hannah and Haydon and Rainee having full wagonloads already, I accepted Mr. Barker's offer to come and pick us up."

Leah's excitement plummeted to her button-up shoes.

"We don't mind. Do we, Leah?" Abby beamed.

Leah wished she shared her sister's enthusiasm over her mother's growing friendship with Mr. Barker, but she didn't, and she minded—a lot. The idea of Mother sitting next to someone who wasn't her father bothered Leah enormously. Mother was lonely, that Leah knew, and she hated feeling so selfish. She tried not to think only of herself, but the idea drove through her heart like a railroad spike being plunged into the hard ground.

"Leah." Mother laid a gloved hand on her arm. "You don't mind, do you? If you do, I will have one of the hands get the surrey ready."

Despite how she felt, Leah did what she always did—

suppressed her true feelings to spare hurting someone else's. She couldn't bear to hurt her mother like that, even if it was killing her from the inside out. "No. Of course not, Mother. No need to get the surrey. It was kind of Mr. Barker to offer to take us."

The sound of wagon wheels crunching on the gravel and a horse whinnying drew their attention outside.

Wraps and gloves gathered and put on, they headed out the door.

God, please help me to overcome this discontentment and to be happy for Mother. Please.

The ride to the church seemed endless, and Leah sent up many more prayers the whole way there. At the church, Mr. Barker pulled his landau alongside the others. He hopped out and helped her and Abby down, then her mother. Mother looped her arm through his and they strolled toward the church door together. As if they were a couple.

Bile rose up Leah's throat. Everyone was watching. Everyone could see. And they appeared to not even care about that.

Leah wanted to yank her mother's arm from Mr. Barker's, but it was not her place to do so. Her mother had every right to do what she wanted and to be with whomever she wanted. Father had been gone a long time now, and this war raging inside of her was her problem, not her mother's. Still. It hurt. She closed her eyes and fought to keep the tears and frustrations down. The pain, however, was too much to bear.

"It's hard for you to see your mother on the arm of another man, isn't it?" Jake's voice, while low, reached her ears with ease as he stepped up beside her.

She stared up at him, blinking and searching for the

answer to her silent question: *How did you know?* She'd told no one.

Without another word, Jake cupped her elbow and led her out of the earshot of others. This time she didn't care what anyone thought. Right now she needed a friend more than ever. And not just any friend. She needed Jake. He had a way of comforting her. Of making her feel better when no one else could or did.

It wasn't until they'd made it around the corner of the building that she looked up into his face. "Whatever do you mean?"

"I saw the hurt on your face just now when you watched your mother walk away with Mr. Barker, Leah. And I have to say, I know exactly how you feel."

"You—you do?" She searched his eyes for the truth.

"Yep."

"How can you possibly know?"

"I know because when my mama decided to get remarried, I had a terrible time with it. Hated seeing her with someone other than Papa. But the truth is, it didn't take long to get over it."

"Why's that?" Leah needed to hear his answer. She needed the selfish feelings she harbored about this over, too. Those same feelings that now had her head lowering in guilt and shame.

"Because I saw how happy Mama was, that's why. And I realized how selfish I'd been by not considering how lonely she was without Papa around." He tilted her chin upward with his forefinger. "It gets easier. Honest. And Mr. Barker's a good man."

Tears blurred her vision and coated her heart. "But he's not Father."

"No. He isn't. And no one can take your father's place. But your father's gone, Leah. You're mother isn't. Life goes on whether we like it or not. You have a big heart. Open it up and let Mr. Barker in. If you can't do it for you, then do it for your mother. She needs you to." He released her chin.

After a brief moment, Leah shifted her attention over to the small flock of people heading into the church. "I know you're right," she said not looking at him. "I need to. For Mother's sake, if nothing else. It's just so hard sometimes. And it hurts so badly. My father was a wonderful man." Her throat constricted. "And he and Mother were so happy." She closed her eyes, fighting back the flood of unshed tears.

Jake gently turned her face toward him and held it just long enough, until her eyes opened and their gazes locked. The compassion in those soft gray eyes of his revealed just how much he really did understand what she was going through. Knowing he understood what it was like to lose a father one dearly loved, she wanted to pour out her heart to him, to tell him about the nightmares she had and how hard it had been for her all these years since her father's death.

The opportunity passed with the ringing of the church bell at that precise moment.

Another time, perhaps. She took a deep breath and let determination fill the place sorrow had been.

"We'd better get inside," Jake said as if he'd read her thoughts. He led her to a small group of people near the door. Once there, he stepped back, waiting until everyone preceded him, including her. To keep the tongues from wagging, she couldn't sit with Jake, so Leah joined her mother and even managed to smile at Mr. Barker, who returned it with a large one of his own.

Mother beamed. Her lips curled with approval, and her eyes twinkled with joy.

Yes, Leah decided. She could do this, and she would.

For her mother's sake she would try her hardest to. However, in the very next second, doubt assailed her with the question: If she accepted her mother's relationship with Mr. Barker, was she somehow denigrating the memory of her father?

Jake sat on the small bench nearest the door. Being close to a quick means of escape was the only way he could handle being shut in with such a close group of people.

The pastor began the ceremony. He talked about marriage and how sacred it was and how it shouldn't be entered into lightly.

Jake's focus slid to Leah, sitting directly in front of him. He wished it was he and Leah standing there exchanging their vows. Immediately he scattered that wishful yet ridiculous thought away with a shake of his head.

The words "Do you promise to love her?" echoed off the rafters.

Love. Markus's love for Phoebe was written all over him and the conviction of it was in his strong response, "I will."

Again Jake glanced at Leah. He knew he couldn't make that same promise before God. Sure, he cared deeply for Leah. But love? He didn't think so. He wasn't even sure how a person knew when they were in love.

Jake forced himself to remember it wouldn't be Leah standing up there when the time came, anyway. He wondered about the nameless, faceless person that would stand next to him. What would she be like? And could he ever love her the way Markus loved Phoebe?

A latecomer slipped in through the door, breaking through his thoughts. An old man looked down at Jake and with a quick jerk of his thumb motioned for Jake to move over.

Jake froze.

The world tilted and then began to close in around him. The man now stood between him and his only way of escape. There wasn't room for the man to slip between him and the pew in front of him because of Jake's long legs and the man's portly size. So he chose the only other option left to him. Jake shifted his legs sideways and motioned the large man who was about as round as he was tall to the other side of him.

More wrinkles lined the man's weathered face. His lips pursed and his eyes narrowed. With a quick jerk of his chubby thumb, he signaled for Jake to move. Then he moved his rotund body closer, until he towered over Jake, crowding him in.

Jake fought to keep down the rising panic in his chest. Not because the man scared him, but because he suddenly felt trapped. Every Sunday he came to church there and sat in his spot near the door, knowing he could leave at any time. But that wasn't the case now.

His eyes darted about the room that seemed to be getting smaller and smaller.

His fingers tingled, and his palms dampened.

Chilled sweats crawled up and down his spine.

His heart tapped rapidly against his ribs.

Air.

His lungs needed air.

And now.

Jake sent the man the most intimidating warning glare he could muster to get him to move out of his way. The old man's eyes widened and he stepped back. Relief barreled over Jake that it had worked. Jake stood and fought the urge to bolt from the church. He left the building as fast as he could without causing a scene or disrupting the ceremony. Once outside, he scrambled into the woods behind the church as far and as fast as he could, hoping and praying no one had noticed his leaving.

He stopped in the midst of a cluster of cottonwood trees and rested his back against one of the large trunks, wheezing in the cool air.

His arms ached. Felt heavy even.

Sharp pains pressed into his chest. He flattened his hand against his heart. In rapid successions it thumped, thumped, thumped against his fingers.

Closing his eyes, he groaned as the feeling of impending doom blanketed him. Thinking straight was beyond his ability.

He panted like an overheated mountain lion.

It was all he could manage just to stay standing.

"Jake?"

Leah.

Oh, no.

He yanked himself up from the tree but swayed dangerously with the sudden movement. Jake didn't want her to see him like this, so he turned his back to her and tried harder to right his breathing and regain control over his body. It wasn't working nearly as fast or as well as he would have liked.

A second passed and she came around to the front of him.

He turned, placing his back to her again.

"Jake?" She moved in front of him again.

He started to turn, but her hand clutched his forearm with a strength he didn't know she possessed. "Jake, look at me." She shook him not hard but enough to cause the swimming in his head to stop. "What's wrong? Do you need a doctor?" Concern warbled through her voice.

Jake wanted to comfort her, but he simply couldn't right now. He needed to concentrate on breathing.

"I'm going to run and get Doc Berg."

Jake grasped her wrist. He shook his head and held up his hand. "No. Don't," he said through gasping breaths. "I don't need a doctor."

Fear shrouded her face and darkened her eyes. "Jake, you're scaring me. What's wrong? Why are you clutching your chest? And why are you breathing so strangely?"

"Give me. A minute." He leaned over, placed his hands on his knees and coached himself like he had so many times before when this happened. *Breathe, Jake. Slowly. Relax. Breathe. You're okay. No one's going to trample you out here.*

"Can I do something?"

He shook his head and continued to pull air into his lungs. Moments later, his lungs were finally satisfied, his chest quit hurting and his arms returned to normal. "That's better." He stood, feeling more like himself. "Whew."

"What happened? Why did you leave?"

Before he answered her question, he needed to know something. "Did anyone else see me?"

"No. I don't think so. I just happened to notice you leaving from the corner of my eye. I wondered why, so I followed you. What happened back there, Jake? Why did you leave?" She tilted her head, and worry and confusion streamed through her eyes.

Did he dare tell her? Would she laugh at him? And could he bear the one person whom he admired most in the world thinking less of him?

"Jake." Her face hardened. "Remember when you said that if I ever needed to talk that you were here? Well, that goes both ways. I'm here for you, too. Talk to me."

Hearing those words, he wanted to pour out the whole sordid story, to bear his soul to her. But it was Phoebe's wedding, and Leah was missing it. "You're missing Phoebe's wedding."

"This is more important. *You're* more important, Jake."

His heart warmed at her words. He gave a quick nod and looked for a place for them to sit. An old bench by the church's woodshed would have to do. "Let's go sit over there, and I'll tell you."

Dust layered the bench. Not wanting Leah's fancy dress to get dirty, he removed his handkerchief and brushed it over it. Not clean enough, he removed his Sunday jacket, the only nice one he had, and moved to lay it across the top of the bench.

"Oh, Jake. Don't do that." She snatched it from him. "You'll ruin it." Before he could protest, she handed it to him and sat down on the smudged bench.

Seeing no way to argue, Jake slipped his jacket back on and sat on the wooden slab, leaving at least a foot of space between them, then faced her.

Leah rested her hands in her lap. Curious eyes roamed over his face, but he felt no pressure from her to rush. He appreciated that.

Drawing in a long breath of courage, he plunged forward. "I used to live in Atlantic City until the fire in 1864 broke out. When it started, everyone ran in different directions, screaming. No one paid attention to anyone else. They were all fleeing for their lives. Mama and I got caught in the middle of the confusion and were separated. Mama said she tried to get to me but couldn't break free from the crowd." The memory crammed in on him, and the air around him dissipated again. The scene played before his eyes as if it were happening all over again, right then and there. Unable to sit still, he stood and began pacing. Sweat broke out on his forehead and hands. His lungs burned as he tried to pull air into them.

"Jake."

When he said nothing, Leah grabbed his hands. "Oh, Jake." She must have seen the anguish he felt written all over his face and her arms came around him in pools of gentleness. She ran her hand over his back in a circular motion, cooing words of comfort. He drew strength from her soothing gesture.

His lungs filled again and the tormenting fear lifted. He backed up, grateful for her, and gazed into her eyes. "Thank you, Leah."

She nodded and let her arms fall back to her side. He wanted to snatch them back and put them around him, but he didn't. Instead, he put some distance between them, and Leah sat back down on the bench. "What happened next?"

"All I saw were legs and boots. I tried to roll into a ball, but people trampled over me anyway. Pert near killed me. If it hadn't been for Mama, I'd probably be dead. Somehow she broke free of the mob and found me. Took the bones in my arm and leg a long time to heal, though."

He heard her sharp intake of breath. "Oh, Jake. How awful."

Seeing her compassion and not repulsion gave him the courage to go on. "The bones healed. My mind didn't." He was ashamed to admit it. "Ever since then, anytime I feel crowded in, my hands sweat and tingle. My chest hurts. My arms feel heavy. It's hard to catch a breath. All I feel is fear. I have to run, get away, or I feel like I might lose my mind."

"I know exactly how you feel."

He opened his mouth to protest that she really couldn't and to ask her what she meant but didn't get to because Abby called her name from somewhere nearby. "Leah!"

"Here!" Leah called back and stood.

"There you are." Abby looked at her sister then over at Jake. "Hi, Jake. Boy, don't you look nice." She whistled.

Heat rushed up the back of his neck. "Thank you. So do you."

"I do, don't I?" She whirled. "It's my new dress. You like it? There's something about a new dress that just makes a gal feel better and prettier. Not that I'm saying I'm pretty or anything. I'm just saying..." Jake listened as she babbled on, smiling and laughing at her antics. The girl was such a character. "And now... I really hate to steal Leah away from you, Jake, but Mother sent me to find her. They're getting ready to head to Markus's father's house for the reception and dinner. Come on, Leah. Mother's waiting."

Leah looked up at Jake. Her silent question if he was okay showed through her concerned expression.

A short nod and a quick jerk of his head toward the direction of the church told her he was. "You two go ahead. I'll be there in a minute."

"You sure?" Leah asked.

"I'm sure."

Leah hated leaving him alone, especially after what she'd witnessed. She thought what she went through with the nightmares was bad, but now they seemed mild compared to Jake's experience. Torn between leaving him and going with Abby—and knowing there was no way she could tell Abby without betraying Jake's trust—she finally conceded. "Okay. See you later."

"Count on it." Jake smiled, and she returned his.

Leah and Abby headed to the white clapboard building where Mother and Mr. Barker were waiting in his carriage. Mr. Barker hopped down and helped her and Abby into the wagon. They headed down Main Street. Dust rolled from the parade of buggies and wagons in front of them.

In minutes they arrived at the estate of the richest man in town. Mr. Barker pulled his landau alongside the rest of the carriages and buggies and helped everyone out.

"Can you believe the size of this place?" Abby asked, linking her arm through Leah's. Then she leaned in so only her sister could hear. "I bet Mr. Darcy's is bigger than this, though."

"Mr. Darcy?" Leah looked at her sister as they headed up the wide staircase of the three-story mansion filled with windows and verandas. Wrought-iron benches, chairs and tables were situated precisely down the long, covered porch. "What made you think of him?"

"Well, last night I was reading *Pride and Prejudice* for the umpteenth time and thought about Mr. Darcy's wealth. Ours is probably nothing compared to his. I'm sure glad we don't have to live stuffy lives like that and that we can marry for love and not the size of someone's pocketbook like they did back then in England. Wouldn't that be awful?" Abby chattered on with her usual dramatic embellishment, using her arms to help aid with what she was saying. "I can't imagine having to consider my future husband's financial status or his connections or his station in life before even thinking about marrying him. Who cares about those things? Not me. But even worse than that would be having to be someone I'm not. Having to act all properlike. Ick. Can you imagine how boring that would be?"

"I don't think it sounds boring at all. We weren't bored in New York, and our lives were similar to Mr. Darcy's."

"I guess I was too little to remember. But Mother said Father told her that he wanted us girls to marry for love, not money, not for what the man did for a living or who he knew. And Father would have made sure the man loved us. That's the way it should be, Lee-Lee. Marrying for love. Not all that other stuff."

Abby's words struck a chord in Leah. She was right. Father would not have allowed his girls to marry without knowing they were in love and loved in return. If the man they loved didn't have money, Father would have made sure his daughters had a nice home and plenty of money to live on. He did make sure by seeing to it that she and Abby had sizable dowries. Still, was she settling for less by marrying just to move away from this place? If her father were alive, how would he feel about that?

She gave a silent snort. If he were still alive, she wouldn't even be thinking about marrying a stranger and moving away from those she loved.

Just when she and Abby had walked up the steps to the front door, Leah didn't know. She was so caught up in her thoughts that she hadn't realized the butler was waiting to take her wrap. "Oh. Um. Thank you, sir."

"You're welcome, miss." The slightly balding man held his chin up high. His white, pristine, high-collared shirt, white bow tie, black tailcoat and trousers were as stiff and starchy as he appeared to be. His black shoes sparkled, and when he went to receive her coat, she noticed his white gloves didn't have a speck of dirt on them. He draped their wraps over his arm, stepped back and stood stiff as a wooden plank until they passed. Only one word came to mind. Abby's word—stuffy.

"C'mon, Lee-Lee." Abby grabbed her hand and tugged her forward.

They strolled through the foyer. At the end of the vestibule, two men stood statue-still, one on each side of the doorway, wearing somber expressions on their faces and dressed the same way the butler was, only their ties were black.

Inside the massive main room, Abby told Leah she'd see her later and strode toward Phoebe, who squealed with delight at seeing her friend. Leah suddenly felt alone in the sea of strangers. Women who hadn't attended the wedding ceremony at the church stood talking and fanning themselves. Their bustle gowns were made of fine silk, brocaded tulle, crepe de chine and velvet materials. There were other styles and materials Leah didn't recognize, also. Leah glanced down at her new gown. It was nowhere near as fashionable as these ladies' dresses were. Suddenly she felt like an ugly caterpillar amid a swarm of beautiful butterflies.

She tugged on the collar of her dress. Spotting the open glass doors, she strode in that direction and stepped outside into a beautiful garden with tall, sculptured hedges. Bouquets of various flowers greeted her nostrils, mostly wild pink roses, white and lavender syringa bushes and a hint of the powdery, carroty scent of irises.

Trickling water lulled her toward the center of the garden, where a massive greenish-gray marble statue of a woman with one hand held above her head and the other next to her side holding a bowl stood on a pedestal in the center of what looked to be a large clamshell. Underneath the shell were large carved leaves that ran down the length of the fountain and touched the ground.

Leah's eyes drifted shut as she ran her fingers over the smooth marble, relishing the cool wetness of the slick stone.

"Sure is something, ain't it?"

"Sweet twinkling stars above!" Her hand flew to her neck as a gasp snapped through her. Jake's voice, along with his breath so very near her ear, nearly caused her to go toppling into the statue.

She spun toward him, but Jake stood so close to her that she couldn't, so she turned her neck and glanced up at him.

"'Sure is something' is an understatement. It's breath-taking," she whispered.

"This whole place is…it's…" He moved to her side.

"It's lavish. And so beautiful. Like something out of a fairy tale."

"Fairy tale, huh? Still believe in those, do you?"

"I sure do." She smirked at him. "I think every young woman wants to see her very own Prince Charming ride up on his white horse and swoop up and rescue his fair maiden."

"White horse, huh?" He chuckled.

Leah planted her hands on her hips. "You go ahead and laugh, but you'll see. I'll have my happily-ever-after. Mr. Darcy, I mean, Mr. Barrington, will come and take me away from all of this."

Jake's smile dropped and sadness took its place. "What you doing out here anyway? Why aren't you inside with everyone else?" He changed the subject, and she felt the relief of it. She didn't like him laughing at her dream of a fairy-tale ending.

Leah tilted her head and looked up at him. "Why aren't you?"

"Too crowded in there for me." He shrugged, but she saw how embarrassed he really was about his phobia.

She hated seeing him like that and wanted to make him feel better. She rested her hand on his arm. "It's okay, Jake. If you can't go in there, you can't go in there. It's nothing to be ashamed of. We all have something in our lives that we can't do. Besides, you have a good reason why you can't."

He nodded, but he didn't look convinced. "You never answered why you came out here."

Her hand fell from his arm and her gaze fell with it. "Well, if you must know, I came out here to think."

"About what?"

She'd gone that far, what sense did it make to stop now? "About Mr. Barrington."

"What about him?"

"I just wondered if this is the type of lifestyle he lives."

"How do you feel about that?"

Good question. How *did* she feel about that? Moments ago she felt underdressed and out of place. Did she still? A little. But she would overcome her insecurity. She'd learn to dress as fine as all the ladies in New York if need be. After all, she had before, when she was younger and living in New York. She could do it again. Of that she was certain. "I love the idea."

"You do?"

"Yes. Seeing all those beautiful gowns reminds me of when I was a young girl." She gazed out into nothingness as memories of her childhood wove through her mind. "I remember attending many elegant balls and wearing dresses as fine as, if not finer than, those ladies in there." And feeling every bit the princess, but she kept that thought to herself, especially after he'd laughed at her earlier.

"I can hardly wait to meet Mr. Barrington, to be whisked away to a life full of style and beauty. What girl wouldn't?" She couldn't keep the contentment or the happiness that idea brought on from curling her lips upward. Her very own Mr. Darcy would be coming soon. She would finally get away from this place and the nightmares to live the lifestyle she dreamed of living once again. Nothing would stop her from returning to where she had always been meant to be.

Chapter Seven

Three days later, Jake stood next to Leah at the front door of Michael and Selina's house. "Hi, Michael."

"Hey, what are you two up to?"

"Jake wanted to see the babies, so I told him I'd come with him. I haven't seen them for a while," Leah said, bouncing at his side. Yes, he had mentioned it, but he didn't think she'd drag him right over there right away like she had.

"That's right. It's been one whole day." Mischievousness sparkled through Michael's eyes. "And I'm sure this was all *Jake's* idea."

Jake chuckled.

Leah elbowed him in the side. "It's not funny."

He thought it was—in more ways than one.

"Don't just stand there, y'all. Michael, let them in." Selina's voice came from somewhere behind Michael.

Michael moved out of the way and Jake and Leah stepped inside. Jake hung his hat on a long peg near the door, feeling a little sheepish and very much out of place. He'd never been to the house of brand-new parents before, and truth be told, the babies scared him a mite more than he wanted to admit.

His attention went to Selina sitting on the couch, her legs stretched out before her and covered with a blue lightweight blanket. Two wooden cradles sat on either side of the rocking chair near her. "Sure nice to see ya again, Jake. Can I get y'all some coffee or tea or somethin' to eat?" Selina tossed her coverlet aside, but before she could even move her legs, Michael had sprung over to her and stood in the way of her moving.

"Don't you dare move. I'll get it," Michael ordered. The way Michael acted made Jake chuckle again and Leah, too, though she covered her amusement better than he did.

"Why don't you let me get us all something to drink?" Leah said from beside him.

"I can get it, Leah. I do know how to get refreshments." But the look on Michael's face said how much he'd appreciate her help.

"Oh, please. I'm surprised you managed to stay alive until Selina got here the way you cook. You two go sit down. I'll get it." Leah pursed her lips and narrowed her eyes at Michael. That threatening look would have made Jake obey.

Finally Michael shrugged. "Fine. I know better than to argue with you, sis. What would you like to drink, Jake?"

"Coffee, if you have some already made."

"Just made a fresh pot. It's there on the stove, Leah."

"Of course it's on the stove, Michael. Where else would it be, you silly goose?" She walked past him and tapped him on the arm.

"Watch it, or I'll turn you over my knee."

"You'd have to catch me first." She wrinkled her nose up at him.

"Don't tempt me."

Jake loved watching the interaction between the two siblings. He didn't have any family there to interact with.

His sister and her husband lived in Oregon and so did his mother and her husband, Jed.

"When y'all get done horsin' around, me and Jake here would like some coffee," Selina piped in with her slow Southern drawl.

"You lucked out, sister dear. Selina just saved your hide from a good tanning."

"Sure I did." Leah glanced at the ceiling and shook her head, then headed to the kitchen stove. With her back to her brother, she asked, "You want coffee, too, Michael?"

"Yes," Michael answered, then turned to Jake. "Shall we?"

They moved to the living room.

Michael sat in the rocking chair situated next to Selina and the babies.

Jake chose a spot on a chair across the way. Curious, he craned his neck, looking into each cradle to see the babies' little sleeping faces. Lottie's was round and Joseph's was square. Joey's hair was blond and Lottie's was brown. "They sure are cute."

Envy roped through him. Someday he hoped to have a wife and family, too. He glanced over at Leah, standing in front of the stove, looking every bit the part of the homemaker. If only she'd said yes to his proposal, she'd be at his place right now, making a home with him. He sighed. No sense wishing for something that would never be. She'd made it very clear she wasn't interested in that kind of relationship with him. She'd also made clear the lifestyle she wanted to live and the type of man she wanted to live it with. *Pride and Prejudice* popped into his mind. She said that Mr. Darcy fellow was the kind of man she wanted. He really had to read the thing to find out what sort of man did interest Leah. Not that it would make any difference. Still, he wanted to know.

"So how'd Phoebe's weddin' turn out the other day?" Selina asked, adjusting the coverlet that had slipped when she'd changed positions. Michael leaped up and immediately helped her with it.

Jake glanced over at Leah, wondering just how he should answer that.

Leah came into the living room carrying a tray with four cups of coffee each sitting on a small plate, spoons, a bowl with sugar and a creamer jar. "Phoebe looked fabulous," Leah responded with her back to Michael and Selina. She offered Jake a half wink of understanding, and his heart jerked when he realized what she was doing. She was protecting him. His admiration for her went up another notch. "Markus was so cute," she continued as she handed each of them a cup and waited while they added what cream and sugar they wanted to their beverage. "Markus couldn't take his eyes off of Phoebe the whole time. Especially when she walked down the aisle."

As she went on telling the details, Jake thought back to the reception and how he'd finally talked Leah into going back inside. It was sweet of her not to want to leave him out there by himself, but he didn't want her to miss out on a fun evening because of him. He'd said goodbye, told her he was going to leave but not until he saw her safely inside. He'd walked her to the double glass doors, and Leah slipped inside with her head held high, walking with the grace of a queen. Stepping back into the shadows, he watched her mingle with those high society ladies, looking every bit as if she belonged there. An ache filled his heart even now, knowing he could never compete with that.

"I sure do wish we coulda gone, but Michael wouldn't hear of it." Mercifully, Selina's voice pulled Jake from the deep, black hole of sadness his heart had started to fall through.

"Selina." Michael drew out her name. "We've been over this a million times already. It's only been a week since the babies were born. You know how fatigued you get. You need your rest."

"Sure, I get tired, but I'm about to shanty up the stair rail. I can't just sit around here doin' nothin' all day."

"You can and you will, sweetheart." Michael's order sounded like a request, too.

Selina hiked one brow. "You'd best be careful orderin' me about like that, Michael, or whenever I get stronger, I'll fix you up a mess a crawdad tails. Or snails."

Jake's attention darted between Selina and Michael. Was she serious? He'd heard about the crawdad tails before but not snails. Had she fed Michael those, too? Jake swallowed hard just thinking about how disgusting that would be. His wife had better never serve him anything like that. Once again, his attention slid over to Leah, sitting in the chair across from him, her attention on Selina.

"Would you really do that, Selina? Feed him snails and crawdads?" Her blue eyes blinked. She looked so cute and shocked.

Jake couldn't help but smile. He'd like to hear the answer to that one, too.

"Yes, ma'am. I would and already have." A look passed between Michael and Selina. They smiled at each other and the tension dropped. His hand slid over hers and caressed it.

"She sure did." He kissed Selina's hand and smiled at her again.

"You're kidding me, right?" Leah's forehead crinkled. She looked back and forth between them, blinking as she did.

"No, we're not kidding. In Kentucky they eat them all the time. The crawdads aren't too bad. I don't know about the snails. Haven't had those. No offense, sweetheart, but I hope I never do, either. And I refuse to get too worked up over it. It's part of who Selina is, and I love her for it."

Jake didn't know if love would ever be enough to make him eat fish bait. Just the thought of that stuff made him squirm.

They visited for about forty minutes and left.

Forest dirt, fern, kinnikinnick bushes and pine trees surrounded them as they walked side by side to the main ranch yard.

"So, what do you have to do now?" Leah asked.

"A few more chores before I head home. You?"

"Since Mother hired Veronique to help around the house, there isn't much to do anymore. We all pitch in and help with the cooking and laundry, so it doesn't take nearly as long as it used to. Sometimes Veronique's sisters, Colette and Zoé, come and help, too. Because of that, I'm able to go to town a lot more now."

"What do you do in town?"

"Visit with friends. Shop. Work on quilts. Stuff like that."

"I see." They reached the barn door.

After a few minutes of neither of them saying anything, Leah looked up at him and said, "Well, I think I'll go visit Rainee for a while. I'll see you later, Jake."

He gave a quick nod, and she headed in the direction of Haydon and Rainee's house.

He got to work filling a bucket with fresh, clean water and gathering everything else he needed to doctor the Palouse horse. Who'd-a thought the horse would have spooked at Kitty? That sweet little pig wouldn't hurt a leaf. Butterfly must not have agreed, though. When Kitty got too close to her, she took off running and ended up scraping her shoulder on a tree branch. Nothing anyone tried had helped Butterfly to get over her fear of pigs. Even getting her around Kitty hadn't worked.

Tethered outside, Butterfly pawed the ground and shifted her spotted rump around. She turned her neck and stared at Jake with those blinking doe eyes, probably wondering what he was up to.

Jake picked up the full bucket of water and a clean rag and headed to the front of the horse. He patted the mare on the neck. "Who names their horse Butterfly, anyway? This is one interesting family. I'll tell you that." His voice drifted into the midmorning void.

With one hand he held on to the lead rope and with the other he dipped the rag into the cool water and blotted the wide scrape across the horse's shoulder to soften the dried blood. On first contact, she shifted. "It's okay, girl." Jake patted her neck again and she stopped moving, so he continued to work at cleaning the wound.

"How's Butterfly doing?" From several yards away, Haydon dismounted his horse and came around to the front of the Palouse.

"Doesn't look too bad. Scraped the hide off is all it looks like."

"That's good. Hate to see her all scarred up."

"Don't think that'll happen. The hair should grow back just fine."

"From the looks of it, I agree." Haydon stepped away from the inspection of the animal. "When you get finished here, what're you going to do?"

"Was going to head home. Why? Need something?"

"Yes, actually, I do. Could I get you to do me a huge favor? Unless you have to get home right away."

"Nope. No rush. Got up earlier this morning and did everything I needed to. Wheat's doing fine. What can I do for you?"

"Can you run into town for me? I'd send one of the other hands, but Jess keeps them so busy, none of them have time to go."

"I can do that. What you need?"

Haydon pulled a list out of his pocket and handed it to him. "You'll need to take the wagon. Just have them put that stuff on my account."

Jake looked at the list and nodded.

"Well, I've got to get back out there." Haydon untied his horse and swung onto the saddle. "Thanks, Jake. I appreciate this. I'll pay you extra for your time."

Jake wanted to argue with him. But when Michael offered him the job, Jake had offered to help without pay, saying that's what friends do. He'd never wanted to take their money, but none of them would hear of it. They refused his help even unless he agreed to let them pay him. Jake had to admit, as much as he hated taking it, the extra money came in handy. Especially because he was looking to marry soon.

Leah knocked on Rainee's door. Children's voices and scuffling noises came from inside. The door flew open. "Auntie." Rosie threw her arms around Leah's waist. She returned her niece's hug and kissed her on top of her head. The girl released her and glanced up at Leah with those fawn-colored eyes that matched her mother's perfectly. Rosie even shared the same fawn-colored hair as Rainee.

"Hi, Auntie." Emily's arms slipped around Leah. Her hug wasn't as exuberant as Rosie's. It was more dignified. Emily might look more like Haydon with her blond hair and blue eyes, but she acted more like the Southern belle portion of her mother.

"Mother's feeding Haydon Junior. Want me to go tell her that you're here?" Emily asked.

Leah glanced toward Rainee's closed bedroom door, debating what to do. "No. I can come back later."

"Ah. Please don't go, Auntie," Rosie begged.

"Yes. Please don't go. Mother bought us a new book and we were reading it. Won't you please join us?"

"You could read to us." Rosie clapped her small fingertips, her eyes wide and expectant.

How could Leah say no to them? She didn't have anything planned, anyway. "Okay."

They each grabbed one of her hands and led her into the living room. Leah admired Rainee's new furniture. The old furniture was so worn out, yet Haydon couldn't convince Rainee to order a new set, so he had. The blue material with small, light gold roses, the button-tufted backs and mahogany-legged sofa and the matching chairs were beautiful. The pattern reminded her of the English tête-à-tête sofa they had back in New York. *New York.* Her heart flipped at the thought.

Rosie tugged on her sleeve. "Aren't you going to sit down?" Emily looked up at her from the couch. There was just enough space between the girls for her to fit.

Knowing she would be leaving soon, she wanted to spend as much time with her nieces as possible. She smiled and sat down between them. "Yes, I am. Now, who's going to read to whom?"

"You first, okay?" Rosie gave her that hopeful look that melted an aunt's heart into submission.

Leah took the book from Emily and read the title. "*Hans Brinker, or, the Silver Skates: A Story of Life in Holland* by Mary Mapes Dodge. I haven't read this before. This will be fun." She settled comfortably into the sofa and both girls tucked into her sides as she read.

"Oh. Hi, Leah. How long have you been here?" Rainee headed toward her and took the seat across from them.

"Not sure. Enough to read—" she looked down at the open book "—twenty-four pages."

"Did the girls offer you something to drink?"

Emily's eyes widened. "Sorry, Mother. We forgot."

"That happens. Would you care for some tea or something, Leah?" Rainee started to rise.

"No. I'm fine. I can't stay too much longer anyway. I need to help Mother and Veronique get lunch ready."

Rainee looked at the girls. "You two run outside and play. I want to visit with your aunt Leah for a bit."

"Ahhh," Rosie whined.

Emily stood and grabbed Rosie's hand. "Come on, Rosie. We'll go play hide-and-seek. You can hide first."

Rainee sent Emily a smile of approval, and the girls headed out the door.

Her sister-in-law shifted her body toward Leah. "So, how are you and Jake doing?"

"Me and Jake?" Leah tilted her head, wondering what she was talking about. Rainee knew she and Jake were only friends.

"You two have been spending more and more time together. I just assumed you were…you know…getting ready to make an announcement."

Leah's mouth widened along with her eyes. Her lips moved but no words came out.

"Oh. I am so sorry, Leah. I… Oh, my. I have really done it now. I have quite jumped to conclusions and embarrassed you."

Leah wondered if other people were thinking the same thing. She hadn't realized she and Jake had spent that much time in public together. And even though she'd gone to his house many times, it was only with Abby, and no one else knew of those visits. Did they? Surely not. "We're just friends, Rainee."

"I see." She didn't look convinced.

"I do enjoy Jake's company. He's a very nice man, but that's as far as it goes. Truly."

Rainee still looked unconvinced but said nothing further.

Leah chewed on her lip, wondering if she should confide in Rainee about her plans. All the years she'd known her, never once had Leah heard Rainee talk about others, unless it was to say something good about them. The decision was made. "Rainee, can I tell you something? If I do, will you promise me you won't tell anyone? Not even Haydon? That it won't go any further than this room, even?"

"Of course, Leah. You have my word it will go no further than you and me."

"Okay." Leah shifted in her seat. "I placed an advertisement in the *New York Times* for a husband." Leah waited for the shock to show on Rainee's face, but it never came. That gave her the courage to plunge forward. "I've already responded to a gentleman's post, and I'm waiting to hear back from him to see when he's coming for sure."

"I see. Where is he from?"

"New York City. Well, he's actually from England and has recently moved to New York. His name is Mr. Fitzwilliam Barrington."

"Fitzwilliam? As in Mr. Fitzwilliam Darcy from *Pride and Prejudice?*"

"Yes." Leah's insides played leapfrog. Excited, she scooted to the end of the couch and poured out the whole story. "So, you see, Jake and I really are just friends."

"Well." Rainee smiled. "I wish you both all the best. I know it works. That is how I ended up with Haydon, as you very well know." Happiness set its glow onto her sister-in-law's face. "I pray you will find a man as wonderful as your brother."

"Who do you hope will find a man as wonderful as me?" Haydon strode over to Rainee and kissed her on the cheek and said hi to Leah.

Leah's insides quivered from anxiety. Had Haydon heard their conversation? *Please, Lord, no.* "Hi, Haydon." She stood. "Well, I need to get home and help Mother. I'll see you two later." She turned and headed for the door.

"Okay. See you later." Haydon held up his hand and gave a quick wave.

"'Bye, Leah. Thank you for stopping by." Rainee stared after her.

Leah nodded and as fast as possible closed the distance between Haydon and the door.

"Who do you hope finds a man as wonderful as me?" she heard Haydon ask.

Leah listened for the answer as she reached for the brass doorknob.

"We were just talking, Haydon. Now, what are you doing home in the middle of the day? And to what do I owe this honor?"

Leah breathed a sigh of relief. She opened the door and closed it behind her. That was a close call. A little too close.

Chapter Eight

The list Haydon gave Jake included dropping a bridle off at the smithy; picking up grain, chicken feed and horse liniment; and getting the Bowens' mail.

Jake was surprised when the postmaster assumed that meant all of the Bowens' mail, including Leah's. On the top of the stack was a letter addressed to Leah from Fitzwilliam Barrington—New York, NY. If memory served him right, he was the man coming to possibly court Leah.

Outside the post office Jake looked around. The urge to yank the letter off the top of the pile and burn it was powerful, but he couldn't. Not and live with himself, anyway. Unable to bear looking at the thing, he tossed the mail under the wagon seat and headed to the Barker Hotel and Restaurant to grab a bite to eat before heading back to the Bowen ranch.

Annabelle Schmidt, one of Mr. Barker's waitresses, walked up to his table. "Hi, Jake." Dreamy eyes gazed down at him. The petite woman had made it clear she wanted to be his wife. He'd been flattered, but he couldn't see himself with her. A farmer needed a woman of strong constitution to survive that lifestyle. Leah could, but she didn't want to. Annabelle wouldn't survive a day.

Would the women who responded to his advertisement be able to? It was something he needed to make sure of before he sent for any of them. Good thing he hadn't sent that letter off to Miss Raquel Tobias yet. It sounded like she lived in comfort. What if she was a frail, delicate woman? That wouldn't do at all.

Jake hurried through his lunch of roast beef, mashed potatoes with gravy and apple pie. The best thing he could do was to get away from Annabelle, who kept coming by in between customers and flirting with him. Normally he was a slow eater, but this time he devoured his meal within minutes, paid his bill and excused himself. He all but ran from the place and to the wagon, thanking God he was able to get away.

Back at the Bowens' place, he hopped down from the wagon just as Leah stepped off Haydon's porch. She looked his way and gave him an exuberant wave, warming his heart with her sweetness. If only he didn't have to give her the letter that might very well take her away from him. But he did. He motioned for her to join him.

Her smile reached him before she did. "Hi, Jake. Did you need something?"

"Yep. The postmaster gave this to me." He handed her Mr. Barrington's letter.

Without looking at it she tilted her head, then gazed up at him with a frown. "Why would he give you my mail without my consent? Not that I mind or anything, but I'm curious."

"Haydon asked me to get the ranch's mail."

"Oh, I see." Leah's focus shifted to the letter. "Oh my, Jake. It's from Mr. Barrington."

He already knew that, but it wouldn't do any good to tell her that. "Didn't you just write him a few days ago?"

"Yes." She did a quick hop of excitement. "It must be

good news for him to have written back so quickly, don't you think?"

Now it was Jake's turn to frown. Barrington wouldn't have gotten her post already. Curious about what it said, he hoped Leah would share it with him. Then, as if she'd read his thoughts, she tore open the letter and read it aloud.

Dear Miss Bowen,
Forgive me my impatience, but I could not wait to see if you would respond to my post. I had to meet the woman who has intrigued me. Therefore, I have taken the liberty of booking tickets on the train forthwith. My sister Elizabeth and I will be arriving at Paradise Haven, if my calculations are correct, within a day or two after you receive this post. Please do not trouble yourself to make accommodations for us as we will book rooms in the nearest hotel.

All I can hope for is that you are not yet attached. If you are, I, of course, will be disappointed, but my sister and I will then use this time to take in the countryside out West.

When we arrive, I will send word where we are staying. If you would like to meet me, then send word back with the carrier. If I have been too presumptuous, then inform the carrier that you do not wish to meet me, and Elizabeth and I will be on our way.
Sincerely,
Fitzwilliam Barrington

Leah studied the envelope. "Sweet twinkling stars above. Judging from the postmark, and if his calculations are correct, he'll be here in three days. The fourth of June."

Leah slid her attention from the letter onto Jake. Joy, confusion and uncertainty crawled across her face.

"How do you feel about that?"

She looked around the yard with a blank expression before landing her attention back onto him. "I'm not sure. Of course, I'm excited and scared and apprehensive." All the things he'd seen on her face. "What should I do, Jake?"

"What do you mean, what should you do?"

"I know he said I didn't need to, but should I head into town and make accommodations for him and his sister? Should I invite them to stay here? Would Mother even allow such a thing? I mean, she did with Rainee, but that was different. Haydon had his own house."

Why was she asking him? He didn't know the answers. If he had his way, he'd advise her that as soon the carrier came she should tell him no.

"Oh, no."

"What?"

"I haven't even told Mother anything about him yet."

"You haven't?"

"No. I was waiting to hear back from him, then I was going to tell her. Of course, I've already been preparing for this day and made a couple of new dresses, but I had thought I would surely get into town for some more material to make at least one more dress before..."

New dresses? Jake was struggling to keep up with her. The topic had gone from what should she do to she hadn't told her mother and then on to new dresses.

He glanced at her simple yellow garment. "Why'd you make new clothes? What's wrong with the ones you have?"

She looked down at her dress as if seeing it for the first time. "What's wrong with it? Everything is wrong with it. I need to go. I have to tell Mother."

He'd never seen Leah this scatterbrained before. "Want me to go with you?"

She tilted her head and frowned.

"For moral support," he clarified. "That's what friends do."

"Oh. Oh." Understanding replaced the frown. "Of course. Moral support. Friends. Yes. Right." She pressed her finger against her lips and her eyes glanced around before landing back on him. "No. No. I better not. As much as I would love for you to, I need to tell her myself. But thanks for the offer just the same."

"You're welcome." He didn't feel all that welcoming, however. Panic gripped him when he realized she really was about to walk out of his life. "Oh, Leah, before I forget. I know you're gonna be busy with everything, but I was wondering something."

"What's that?"

He hated to ask because it was clear her mind was on other things. "Would you have time to go over another stack of letters?"

"Huh? I thought you were going to write Raquel Tobias. Did you change your mind?"

"Praying about that still. Need to ask her a few questions first, too. Meantime, I'll keep reading the posts I get."

"How many more did you get?"

"Eight."

"Eight!" Her eyes widened. "Sweet twinkling stars above. You sure are well liked."

"Nah. Just a lot of desperate women."

Her brows pulled together. "Is that how you see me? Desperate? Because I placed an ad looking for a groom?"

"What? No." He took a step backward, raised his hat and pushed his hand through his hair before placing the hat back on his head. "Didn't mean it that way. Just meant there are a lot of women out there desperate to marry."

Her head dipped sideways again, sending that spiraling curl down her cheek. How he wanted to brush it away, but when the palm of her hand rose, the urge skittered with it.

"Forget I said anything. So. Think you'll have time to come by? If not, it's okay. I know you have things to do."

"I can do it. No, make that I want to do it." She smiled. "This afternoon would work. I know Abby isn't doing anything. We can come to your place, if you want?"

Jake wondered why they didn't just go over them here, but he would do whatever worked for her. "Sounds good. Well, best get this wagon unloaded and get home. See you there."

The only way to describe the smile she flashed his way just now and how it affected him was sweet summer sunshine. "Looking forward to it."

So was he. So was he. And that wasn't good.

Leah ran to the house with more excitement about going over to Jake's than meeting Mr. Barrington. How strange was that? Nerves. It had to be nerves.

"Where are you running off to in such an all-fired hurry?" Abby caught up to her.

Leah stopped and had to catch her breath before she could get anything coherent out. "Boy, am I glad to see you."

"Why?"

"Because I need to see if you can go over to Jake's with me this afternoon." She hooked her arm through her sister's and nudged her forward but away from the house and any listening ears.

"Sure. I love it there. Besides, I don't have anything better to do."

"Thanks. You sure know how to flatter a girl."

"I didn't mean it like that." Abby nudged Leah with her hip, knocking her off balance.

"I know you didn't, but I have to tease you to keep you on your toes. Oh, and if you don't mind, I would really appreciate it if you'd be there with me when I tell Mother."

"Tell Mother what?"

"About my advertisement."

Abby stopped walking and unhooked her arm. "I don't want to be there when you tell her. She's going to be so upset with you."

"Surely you wouldn't abandon me now, would you, Abbs? Come on," she pleaded. "I really need you there for support."

"Why don't you ask Jake?" Abby did a little hop and a skip beside her as if she'd just given her the perfect solution, then she tugged Leah forward, resuming their walk.

Leah waved her off as if that wasn't even important , though her heart leaped with the sweet memory of Jake's thoughtful offer. "He already offered, but after my talk with Rainee, I didn't think it would be wise to have him there."

"What talk with Rainee?"

"Nothing of significance, really. But while I was there she wondered if I would be making an announcement soon about me and Jake."

"No." Her sister's blue eyes widened. "She didn't."

"Yes. She did. All because she said she saw us together so much."

"Well, yes. But I thought everyone knew you two were just friends."

Leah twisted her mouth and shook her head as if the whole idea was ludicrous. "Apparently not. And I know if

I walk in with Jake, Mother will wonder, too. She already basically asked me if I would marry him."

"She did?" Again with the wide eyes. "When did all this happen? You never said anything about it."

"It was the other day. Anyway, forget all that. It's really not important. Would you please be there with me when I tell her?"

"I wouldn't miss any of this for the whole wide world." She flung her arm out with a flair. "So, have you heard from any of the gentlemen yet?"

It was then that Leah realized they should have been walking much slower, but it was too late. The boards creaked under their feet as they made their way up the porch steps and into the house.

"I'll tell you more about them later."

"You'd better." Abby's warning look belied her smiling smirk.

"Mother! We're home," Leah hollered.

Mother stepped out from behind the laundry room door. Her dress was soaked, and some of her hairpins had come out. She ran the back of her hand over the sweat beads pooling on her forehead.

"What are you doing?" Leah asked.

"Laundry."

"Why didn't you say you needed help? Where's Veronique? Isn't she here?"

"*Oui*. I mean, yes. Am right here." Veronique peeked around from behind Mother. Strands of brown hair with gold highlights stuck to the moisture on Veronique's oval face. The five-foot-ten, stocky Frenchwoman was hardworking, honest and a great cook. A real blessing to have around.

"Do you need us to help?" Leah waved her pointed finger between her and Abby.

"No. I just got tired of sitting around so I thought I would help Veronique for something to do. What time is it?"

"Eleven forty-five. We thought we'd come in for a bite then Abby and I are going to go for a ride."

"A ride. That sounds like fun." Mother's face brightened.

Leah swallowed down the dread that rose up inside her. Was her mother hinting that she'd like to go? What would Leah do if she did?

"I wish I could go with you girls, but I promised Michael I would stay with Selina for a couple of hours this afternoon. He had some errands to run."

Whew. Leah let out the breath she was holding slowly and quietly so as not to draw attention. "You mean he's actually going to leave her for that long?"

They all chuckled.

"Tell Selina hi and kiss the babies for me," Leah said.

"For me, too," Abby added. "Hey, what's for lunch, Mother? I'm starving."

"You're always hungry," her mother teased. "Veronique made venison stew earlier."

Leah suddenly wondered if Jake had eaten. Maybe he ate in town. He did that sometimes. If so, had he run into Annabelle? The poor woman had a mad crush on Jake. Everyone in town knew it. Annabelle didn't even try to hide her feelings for him. Leah smiled at the thought. Of course, Jake had been gentle with her when he let her know he wasn't interested in marrying someone who was ten years older than he, but that didn't stop her. Poor Jake. The smile in her heart increased. He was such a kind man.

"Did you hear me, Leah?"

Leah snapped her attention onto her mother's. "What? Oh. No. I'm sorry, Mother. I didn't. What did you say?"

"I asked if you would get us some bowls."

"Oh. Um. Sure." She scurried to the cupboard and gathered the bowls. After they were all filled, she set them, glasses of tea, biscuits, butter and pear preserves on the table. She, Mother and Abby sat down, bowed their heads and prayed. Leah added her own silent prayer that her mother wouldn't be too upset and that God would give her the words she needed to say.

Leah buttered her biscuit, smeared a dollop of the homemade pear preserves on it and took a bite. Cinnamon and nutmeg filled her taste buds as she chewed slowly, enjoying the sweet fruit and putting off the inevitable. Knowing she didn't have much time before she headed to Jake's, she put her biscuit down and drew in a long breath. "Mother?"

"Yes?" Mother put a spoon of stew into her mouth.

"I'm not sure how to tell you this, so I'm just going to come right out and say it, okay?"

Mother stopped chewing and looked at her. She nodded.

"A while back I placed an advertisement in the *New York Times*."

Mother swallowed with a gulp and reached for her water. "What kind of advertisement, sweetheart?"

Leah looked over at Abby, who nodded to keep going. "For a husband."

"What?" The glass clattered to the table and barely stayed upright. Mother closed her eyes and shook her head in a jerky motion. She opened her eyes and stared at Leah. "Did I just hear you say you placed an ad for a husband… in New York?"

"Yes, Mother. That's what I said."

"Why? Why would you do that, Leah? And why wouldn't you ask me first?"

Abby picked up her spoon, suddenly finding interest in her stew. Leah wished she could do the same.

"Because I was afraid you'd say no, that's why, and I have my heart set on moving back to New York."

Her mother set her spoon down and wiped her mouth off with a napkin. "Why, Leah? Why would you do such a thing?" The anguish on her mother's face flooded Leah with guilt.

"Because I miss New York." She couldn't tell her that she hated this place and why. Mother wouldn't understand. No one would. So she dived into the other part of the story. "I knew the only way you and the boys would let me go is if I were married. So, I placed an ad, and I've received an answer."

Abby's spoon hit the table and she stared openly at her sister, soup forgotten.

"You—you have? From whom?" Mother's face paled and she suddenly looked sick.

Even more guilt assaulted Leah. She honestly hadn't thought her mother would take the news this badly. Yes, she knew she'd be upset but not to where it made her ill.

Bad as she felt, there was nothing she could do about it now, anyway. What was done was done. The man was already on his way. Besides, Leah didn't want to stop him from coming. She might be a tad scared and a bit apprehensive, but she still couldn't wait to meet Mr. Barrington and hopefully marry him. If she had to, she'd deal with consequences of that decision later. She squared her shoulders and lifted her chin. "His name is Fitzwilliam Barrington, Mother. And he's from England."

"England!" Mother gasped. "You're moving to England?" She waved her hand in front of her face, looking even paler.

"Mother? You okay?" Leah pressed her fist into her belly, which was twisting with torment for what she was putting her mother through.

"England?" Abby asked in horror. "You can't move to England, Lee-Lee!"

"Mother? Are you okay?" Leah jumped from the table to assist her mother should she pass out, which was looking like a very real possibility at the moment.

Mother raised her hand to wave her daughter away. "I'm—I'm fine. Just shocked is all."

Leah looked over at Abby, who didn't look much better than her mother but still managed to send Leah a sympathetic shrug.

"Don't worry, Mother. Abby." Leah eyed both of them for a brief moment and resumed her seat, thankful she no longer had to stand on her shaking legs. "I'm not moving to England. Mr. Barrington moved to New York City recently and saw my ad."

"So, you're going to New York to meet him?" Mother's words were spoken as if they were shards of broken glass.

Leah didn't think her mother's complexion could get any paler, but it had. More guilt dumped on her. "No."

The tension in her mother's face softened. "Oh, good. I'm so relieved to hear that." She patted herself above her heart.

"He's coming here with his sister. We're going to get acquainted first to see if we are compatible. Then we'll take it from there."

Mother remained quiet. She pushed her half-filled bowl away from her and rested her folded hands on the table.

Leah didn't know if she was praying or thinking. No longer hungry herself, she pushed her own bowl out of the way and laid her hands over her mother's. "Mother." She waited until her mother looked over at her. "Please don't be upset. I'm sorry I didn't say anything to you. I never meant to hurt you. But I am twenty-four years old. It's time I found a husband. Everything will work out. You'll see. I tell you what, Mother. If you don't approve of him, then I won't marry him. How's that?" Leah couldn't believe she was saying that. But she couldn't stand to see her mother so upset.

"Leah, I know everything will work out only because I have just now given it over to God. But I am hurt that you didn't discuss this with me first."

Leah opened her mouth to respond, but Mother held up her hand. "I understand why you didn't. I just don't understand why you would want to leave me. Leave your family."

She didn't want to leave her mother or her family—just this place. The idea of leaving them hurt, but when she considered the nightmares and the guilt that haunted her, leaving her family was her only option. "Mother, this has nothing to do with you or with the family. It has to do with me. I'm sorry if you feel I'm doing this to you. I never meant it to be that way. I'm doing this for me. It's something I've dreamed of for a long time. Besides, I'll come back often. Mr. Barrington wants to travel, too. I'm sure he won't mind traveling back here. Okay, Mother?"

Mother said nothing— She only stared at her. The minutes ticked by agonizingly slow until Mother finally spoke. "God's will be done." That was all she said. But it was the way she said it—with so much confidence and assurance— that made Leah nervous.

Judging from past experience, when her mother prayed, things happened—and not always the way her children had wanted them to. Mother prayed fervently for Haydon, and he'd done something he said he'd never do again—get married.

Mother prayed for Michael to love Selina, something he said he could never do, and then Michael fell deeply in love with her. Both were wonderful answers to prayer.

Still, Leah couldn't help but wonder how or what Mother was praying for her and why she had that knowing smile on her face.

"Oh, before I forget, girls—" Mother dropped a glance onto her and then one to Abby "—I won't be here for dinner this evening. Mr. Barker's invited me to dine with him."

"You sure have been seeing a lot of him, Mother," Abby said with a wide smile.

Her mother returned the smile with dreamy eyes. "Yes. Yes, I have."

"Do you like him?" Although Leah hated the idea of her mother with another man, she had to know the answer to the question.

"Yes, I do. Very much so. In fact—" her mother picked up her coffee and took a drink before setting it down again "—I'm hoping our relationship will develop into something more very soon."

Why did it suddenly feel like the situation reversed? Leah's head spun with the thought. "You mean marriage?"

"Yes. I mean marriage." Mother's face glowed.

"That's wonderful, Mother!" Abby jumped up and threw her arms around her.

Leah wished she could share her sister's enthusiasm. Seeing her mother on Mr. Barker's arm at Phoebe's wedding had been hard enough, but to actually hear her mother say the *m* word… That she couldn't bear.

Chapter Nine

Jake sat on his front porch listening for the sound of horse's hooves, but only the creaking of the rocker and an occasional bee buzzing by filled the quietness around him. That is, until Meanie started that frustrated bleating she so often did when he locked her in a stall to keep her out of trouble. Trouble. That was all the little critter had been since he'd taken her in. He could do nothing short of letting Meanie loose to fix that situation, but he'd never do that. Truth is, he'd grown kind of fond of the ornery goat.

He glanced at the copy of *Pride and Prejudice* sitting on his lap. Curious about what type of man Leah was interested in, he began to read. It was slow going, but determination prodded him on. The more he read, the more he wanted to slam the book up against the wall, to burn it, to do anything but read about some prideful, arrogant man who only cared about position, power and money.

All the things Jake despised in a man.

How could Leah be attracted to that? He shook his head in disbelief and bewilderment. Knowing Leah like he did, nothing about the kind of man she said she wanted or anything else was adding up or making any sense. Jake sent up a silent prayer for her, then glanced down the road to see if there was any sign of her yet. When there wasn't, he continued reading to see if Mr. Darcy had improved any.

Ten pages later buggy wheels crunched on gravel and Banjo barked. Jake turned his attention to the road. Leah. He glanced at the book in his hand. Not wanting Leah to know he'd purchased *Pride and Prejudice*, he darted into the house and shoved the book under his pillow. Outside and down the steps he dashed, arriving just as Leah pulled her carriage in front of his house.

"Hi, Jake." Abby greeted him with a smile and a happy wave. Before he had a chance to help her down, she jumped down from the buggy, crouched and rubbed her nose on Banjo's.

"Howdy-do, Abby." Jake turned his attention to Leah and offered her his hand. She shifted the reticule onto her wrist and laid her hand on top of his.

"Hi, Jake." Those dimples made an appearance again.

He helped her down and released her hand. "You ready for this?"

"I sure am." She looked pretty, all gussied up in her dress with the curly-tailed teardrop design. Paisley. That's what he'd heard someone call the pattern, though he didn't know much about material or dresses. It didn't matter what it was, she looked beautiful in it. Of course, as far as he was concerned, she'd looked pretty in just about anything. Even an old, worn-out grain sack. Leah was a beautiful woman. A woman any man would be proud to have on his arm.

Before he allowed any more thoughts of her to enter his mind, he reined them in like he would a runaway horse and anchored his gaze onto the porch. *She's here as a friend, Jake. To help you choose a wife.* Forgetting that again might be the death of him.

Side by side they climbed the steps. Leah stopped at

the top of them and turned around, her dress swishing at her ankles. "Abbs, do you want to join us?"

"No. If Jake doesn't mind, I'd like to go down to the barn and see Meanie."

"That's fine. Just don't let her out of the corral. She's a tricky one."

"I'll be careful." With those words Abby scurried toward the barn with Banjo prancing at her side.

"Sure sweet of Abby to accompany you here every time."

"It sure is. She says she does it because she likes your company, but I think it's the animals' company she likes most."

"Think you're right." They chuckled.

He gave a yank of his head toward the door. "Wanna go inside or sit here on the porch?"

"Out here would be great. It's too nice a day to be cooped up inside."

"I agree. Let me just grab us something to drink and the letters and I'll be right out." He disappeared into the house and peeked back to make sure Leah couldn't see him before he swiped his sweaty palms down the front of his jeans. What was with him today? Emotions he couldn't decipher were whirling through his brain like a destructive dust bowl.

Jake hurried to get everything he needed. When he stepped outside, Leah was sitting in the chair with her reticule resting in her lap, rocking, staring out into the trees, looking every bit like she belonged there. But she didn't. And never would. Not because he didn't want her to, but because she didn't want to be here. Her rejection still stung. But, no sense dwelling on that now— It was a well-traveled road that went nowhere.

"Here you go." He handed her the letters, set their drinks on the stand between the two rockers and sat down.

Leah took a long drink of her water.

"Must've been thirsty."

"I sure was. It's so dry that on the way over here I think I swallowed a bucket of road dust." She took another drink, then set the glass down.

"Jabber-jawed that much, huh?"

"Hey." She reached over and whacked his arm with the backs of her fingers.

He chuckled at the smile twinkling in her beautiful blue eyes.

"Oh, before I forget, I have something for you." She opened her reticule and pulled out three brand-new handkerchiefs and extended them toward him.

He glanced down at them and then his attention trailed to her face. "It ain't my birthday today."

"So." She shrugged with a grin. Then she grabbed his hand, laid the handkerchiefs in his palm, folded his fingers over them and pushed his hand back.

Jake slowly opened his hand.

The initials J.L. stared up at him. "Um-hm." He cleared his throat to choke back the rising emotion. He'd never had anything so nice before. He ran his fingers over the raised letters and was deeply touched not only by the detail, but also by the amount of time it must have taken her to make these. But how could he accept such a gift? He looked over at her. "I can't accep—"

"You have to take them, Jake." Leah stopped him. "There's no giving them back. It's your initials that are on them, so they belong to you. Besides, I don't know any other J.L.'s to give them to. Sorry, mister," she said, "but you're stuck with them." With a dramatic sigh that would rank right up there with one of Abby's, she sat back and crossed her arms over her chest, looking playfully smug.

Truth was, he really didn't want to give them back. He'd treasure them forever. There was only one problem with them— They were too nice to use.

"All joking aside..." Leah sat forward. "Please accept my gift and use them until they look as worn as your old ones."

His gaze flew to hers. Had she read his mind? "Not sure I can. Don't want to ruin them."

Leah wrinkled her nose. "Huh? But that's what I made them for, for you to use. It would mean a lot to me if you did, Jake. It isn't much, but it's my way of showing you how special you are to me. I've never had a friend as wonderful as you before. Now—" she shook her finger at him "—if you don't use them, I'm not going to help you with your letters. So, are you going to use them or not?"

Mischievousness snaked through Jake. Keeping his eye on her, with a quick snap of his wrist, he unfolded one of them, raised the kerchief to his nose and using his voice only, he pretended to blow into it. He folded it up, not so neatly either, then flashed her a smug smile. "Feel better?"

Leah tossed her head back and laughed. "I sure do," she said when she stopped laughing. "Thank you, Jake."

"No. Thank *you,* Leah." The humor had gone from his voice, replaced with gratitude.

"You're welcome."

They stared at each other for a few seconds, then Jake broke the connection. "Oh, how'd the talk with your mother go?" He picked up his glass and took a drink before setting it back down, being extra careful not to spill it.

Her dimples disappeared, and lines formed around her eyes.

"That bad, huh? Wanna talk about it?"

She nodded, then looked away, off down the road. "I felt so bad for Mother. I honestly didn't think it would affect her the way it had. I thought she was going to faint." She paused and drew in a deep breath. "I think Mother was mostly hurt that I didn't say anything. But, when I told her he was coming here, she seemed to feel better about it, although she doesn't understand how I could want to leave her or the rest of the family."

He heard the melancholy in her voice and dipped his head to get a better look at her face. "That bother you, Leah? Leaving your family?"

"Yes. But not nearly as much as the idea of staying here bothers me." She turned her attention back on him. "Know what Mother told me and Abby?"

He shook his head.

"That she likes Mr. Barker a lot and is in fact hoping for more than a friendship with him."

"As in marriage?"

"Yes. Seeing her with Mr. Barker has been hard enough. But to actually hear her say she wants to marry him. Well…" Her fingers fiddled with the strings on her reticule. "I know we talked about this the other night… And maybe you were able to handle your mother getting married, but I'm not sure I can. I'm trying. Honest I am. But—but…" She slammed her eyes closed and frustration ripped across her face. "Aaaccck! I can't stand this! I'm so tired of feeling this way. Tired of feeling guilty because of my emotions." She uncrossed her legs.

His heart softened for her pain and the confusion she was feeling. He'd been there once, too, and it wasn't a fun place to be. "It's a normal reaction, Leah. But I promise you, it does get easier."

She shrugged as if she had her doubts, which she probably did. All he could do was pray for her and be a friend for her. As long as he could, anyway.

"I'm just glad I won't be here when and if she does marry Mr. Barker."

Again he was reminded of her leaving, and it was like a gunslinger's bullet to his chest. "Does your mother know how you feel?"

"No, and I would never tell her, either."

"How come? Maybe it would help to talk to her about it."

"No. No, it wouldn't." She shook her head. "Nothing would help me feel better about this. Nothing." She raked in a breath and let it go. "Let's not talk about this anymore. It's just too upsetting. Now." She picked up one of the envelopes, slid her finger under the seal and pulled the paper out. "Let's find you a wife. I'll feel much better about leaving if I know my dearest friend is happily married." The smile she gave him was a forced one because no dimples showed up.

At that moment, Jake silently sent up a prayer that God would give Leah grace and mercy to help her to deal with whatever decision her mother made regarding Mr. Barker. Jake's attention shifted back to Leah when she started to read.

Dear Mr. Lure,

Your ad said, "When you write, tell me about yourself." Well, my name is Blossom Pearson. I'm twenty-five years old, five foot nine and weigh 145 lbs. My hair is brown and my eyes are green. You didn't say nothing about a picture, but I thought I'd send you one.

Leah stopped reading and peered into the envelope. "Sorry, Jake, I didn't even see this." She handed him a small picture without looking at it.

Jake's eyes trained in on the woman in the photo. He had to admit she was a beauty. Stocky, too. Looked like she could handle just about anything. Something about the softness in her eyes drew him. He'd like to hear more about her. "What else she say?"

"That pretty, huh?"

Jake snapped his attention over to Leah. "That doesn't matter."

"Sure it doesn't. If you say so." She giggled. The dimples were back.

If she wasn't a female, he'd smack her on the arm like she had done to him earlier. But she was definitely a woman. With all the right curves in all the right places. "Just keep reading, woman."

She giggled again. "Okay. Let's see."

I was born and raised on a farm, so I'm used to hard work. And I'm strong as an ox. I can manage a plow, milk cows, garden, do canning, cook and do just about any kind of farm work that needs done. I'm real good with animals. Especially horses. Broke a few myself. Well, that ain't exactly true. I think it was more like they broke me. Or maybe we broke each other.

Jake laughed. The woman had a sense of humor. That was good.

Well, don't know what else to say except hope to hear from you soon.

God bless you through Christ our Lord.
Blossom

P.S. Yes, Blossom is my real name. If you want to know why, you'll have to send for me to find out.

Leah folded the letter. "Jake, she sounds perfect for you."

"Think so?" He searched her face for any kind of doubt.

"Yes, I do. I think you should write her right away." A seriousness permeated her voice that hadn't been there before.

"You do?" He had hoped she would at least show some sign of disappointment at the idea of his getting married. After all, once he did, their friendship would have to end. Neither of their spouses would allow them to continue on like they had been. Jake wondered if Leah had ever considered that, and if she had, how did she feel about that?

"Did you want to me to read the rest of these?"

He flipped his mind back to the task of finding a wife. None of the posts he'd gotten so far intrigued him like Blossom's had. One thing was for certain—after hearing her letter, he knew he wouldn't write to Raquel. He wasn't even sure he'd write Blossom back, either. Or any other woman, for that matter. What he really wanted to do was to wait and see what happened between Leah and that Barrington fellow. Call him a fool, but somewhere deep inside of him, he still hoped for a chance for him and Leah to marry.

Not that it would ever happen, but he would hold on to that hope a little while longer. After all, Leah wasn't married yet. In the meantime, he'd concentrate on finding someone else just in case things didn't work out as he hoped they would.

Time and again, Jake had seen men and women marry for convenience, and somehow it had worked out. All he had to do was look at Michael and Haydon, who were both happily married. And although Jake would rather marry Leah, someone he knew and respected, rather than a total stranger, he knew better than anyone else that probably would never happen, so he needed to stop dwelling on it. Brooding on it would only lead to more heartache.

"Well, Jake," Leah said after four more letters that he really hadn't heard, "I've been here over an hour. I'd better go get Abby and be getting home. I need to get things ready for Mr. Barrington's arrival."

He nodded and they stood.

Leah picked up her reticule from the table, and side by side they walked down the steps and headed to the corral.

"Abby, are you ready to go?" Leah called.

Nothing. The barnyard was quiet.

"That's odd. Where could she be?" Leah asked.

"Don't know." Jake hiked a shoulder.

"Abby!" Leah hollered.

"Over here." Abby's voice came from the direction of the woods.

They headed that way. Abby met them halfway. Banjo followed close behind with her mouth wide open and her tongue hanging out the side of her mouth, panting.

"Have you seen Meanie?" Abby asked, puffing.

"Meanie?" Jake crossed his arms over his chest. "That ornery old goat escape again?"

"Yes. I'm really sorry, Jake," Abby said between gasps. "When I stepped out of the pen, I held the gate close to me so she wouldn't get out. But she rammed into my legs and knocked me down and took off running into the woods. I haven't been able to find her anywhere."

"It's okay, Abby. Told you she was tricky. I'll find her."

"We'll help. Then we really do need to go home," Leah said.

Abby went one way, Leah went another and Jake another.

Within minutes he heard Leah hollering, "Give me back my reticule, you ornery brat."

Jake glanced at the sky and rolled his eyes. "Oh, no." He bolted toward the sound of Leah's voice. When he got there, he saw Leah in an all-out tug-of-war with Meanie over her purse. Leah's hair was dancing around her head as curls came scrambling out of their holdings.

"Meanie!" Jake hustled to her.

Leah's attention flew to Jake and in the process she lost her grip on her bag. Meanie took off running with it as Leah landed on her backside in the dust. Jake darted after the goat as Leah scrambled to her feet and followed close behind them.

"Get back here!" he yelled, dodging and ducking through the trees. Suddenly, with no warning at all, his foot caught a tree root, and he tumbled to the ground. Only a half step back, Leah didn't have time to change course and with a thud she landed right on top of him.

Their faces were mere inches from each other.

They were so close their breaths mingled.

Neither moved.

Leah's wide eyes stared into his. She looked so cute, so disheveled and surprised. Even her lips were parted in shock.

The desire to kiss those lips barreled over him.

As if she'd read his mind, she blinked, yanking his senses back to where they belonged.

"You okay?" He shifted her off of him, careful not to hurt her.

"I'm...I'm fine." She brushed the tousled hair from her

face and the dirt from her dress. "I look like a mess, but I'm all right."

Jake stood and helped her up. Then he brushed the pine needles out of his hair and off his arms and legs while Leah brushed them off of herself.

Her cheeks were flushed. He wondered if his were, too. For sure they would have been if he had followed through with his desire to kiss her. Thank goodness he hadn't. Not because he didn't want to. Leah's outward and inward beauty, her love for the Lord and her fun, sweet, generous nature would be a temptation for any man. Including him. No, especially for him. But kissing her would have been a huge mistake.

Heat once again rose up Leah's neck and into her cheeks at the certainty that Jake had been about to kiss her. She tried to steer her thoughts a different way as she turned the carriage for home, but they clung to her mind and her heart.

"Why's your face so red?" Abby asked her in the carriage.

She wanted to lie but found she could not. "I'm not sure, but I think Jake was going to kiss me back there in the forest."

"What? Are you serious?" Abby shrieked.

"Like I said, I'm not sure—but I think so." Leah took her eyes off the horse clomping down the hard-packed road from Jake's place and looked over at his flourishing wheat field.

"Why? What did he do?"

"Well, when I fell on top of him, our—"

"You fell on top of Jake?" Abby interrupted with a gust of surprise in her voice.

"Yes, I—"

"When? How?"

"Abby, if you'd stop interrupting me, I'd tell you." No frustration came through, only a slight reprimand. For a brief moment, Leah's attention went to a pair of gray partridge birds flying above them before her focus returned to Abby.

"Sorry." Her sister didn't look one bit sorry. That was okay— Leah knew she was excited to hear the story. And Leah was glad she could share these things with her sister. Seven years separated them, but they'd grown close over the past year.

"Okay, so, I spotted Meanie near the cottonwood trees on Jake's property. You know the ones I'm talking about, don't you?"

Abby nodded, blinking, waiting expectantly.

Leah held her chuckle inside at seeing her sister like that.

"And?" Abby dragged the word out.

"Well, as soon as I reached for her halter, she snatched my reticule from me. I yelled at her to give it back. I'm surprised you didn't hear me."

"How could I? I was the opposite direction from you. Who cares about that, anyway? Keep going."

"Well, Jake heard me. He came right away. Meanie took off running. Jake ran after her, and I ran after Jake. He tripped on something. I think a tree root, or something, I'm not sure. Anyway, doesn't matter what he tripped on. Whatever it was, he fell and I landed on top of him." The memory burned through her like wind whipping embers into a blaze. "It was so weird. His face was so close, Abbs, and he had this look on his face…."

"Ooooh. How romantic. Then what happened?" Her sparkling blue eyes stared expectantly at Leah.

Leah jerked her head from side to side. "You've been

reading too many romance novels. Jake and I, we're not like that."

"But you could be." Was that hope on her sister's face?

"No, Abbs. We can't. I'm leaving, remember? And besides, I don't feel that way about him, and I know he doesn't feel that way about me."

"But he was going to kiss you."

"No." The more she thought about it, the more she talked herself out of it. "I said I thought he was going to kiss me, but I must be wrong. Jake doesn't think about me like that."

"How do you know that?"

"Because." She studied Abby's eyes a moment. "Look. If I tell you something, you have to promise not to say anything to anyone, okay?"

"You always ask me that. Do I ever?" Abby questioned her with not only her words, but also her looks.

"No. No, you don't. And I appreciate it more than you will ever know." She smiled at Abby. "A few months back, Jake asked me to marry him."

"What?" Abby's brows darted upward. "You're kidding? What did you say?"

"I said no."

"No." Abby's face scrunched. "Why?"

"You know why. Besides, he said it would be a marriage of convenience between two friends."

"Ouch."

"Ouch is right. But that's okay. It wasn't right—he and I. And now, with me leaving, I'm just glad I don't love Jake in that way or it would be too hard to move if I did."

"Do you think he loves you, Lee-Lee?"

Leah frowned. "Why would you ask that? I just told you his proposal was one of convenience, not love."

"Yes, well, you also said you thought he wanted to kiss you. And you two do spend a lot of time together."

"Yes, we do spend a lot of time together because we enjoy each other's company."

Abby's eyes brightened.

"As friends, Abbynormal, as friends. It's nice having a male friend. They're more rational and not so emotional. And Jake is easy to talk to. He says the same thing about me. As for him wanting to kiss me, well, perhaps I imagined it. Because as soon as I looked at his mouth, he couldn't get away from me fast enough. He jumped up and brushed himself off, and I had a hard time keeping up with him on the way to the barn."

Was the thought of kissing her that repulsive to him? The idea of him kissing her wasn't to Leah. How strange was that? She'd never thought about Jake kissing her before. Or what it would be like. Until this very moment. *Sweet twinkling stars above.* Her eyes widened on the thought. Not good. Not good at all. She swallowed hard and clicked on the lines. "Giddyup, Lambie."

Minutes later they rode into the ranch yard. "Uh-oh," Abby said.

Leah's gaze trailed toward the direction Abby was looking. She was so busy thinking about what had happened earlier, she didn't see her brothers standing in front of the barn with their arms crossed. For Michael to leave Selina's side, whatever they were up to could not be good. "'Uh-oh' is right. Mother must have told them about my plans."

Chin up, she guided Lambie toward the front of the barn, but before she could get close, her brothers were next to the phaeton.

Jesse grabbed the lines near her horse's bit and stopped her.

Haydon was the first to get to her. "We need to talk." He offered Leah a hand down, but it didn't feel very helpful.

"Hello to you, too." One glance at Haydon's face said he wasn't amused.

By that time, Jess and Michael had joined him like a wall in front of her.

Abby was at Leah's side in an instant. Two against three was better than one against three at least.

"What's this we hear about you placing an ad in the *New York Times* for a husband?"

Leah darted a glance at Abby, who looked pale as a dandelion seed. "Mother didn't waste any time, did she?"

"Never mind that," Haydon cut in. "I can't believe you did something like that without talking it over with us."

"What?" Leah bobbed her head forward with a tilt and scrunched her face. "Are you serious? I'm not a child any-more. I'm twenty-four years old and more than capable of making my own decisions."

"You might be twenty-four, but you're still our sister and under our protective care. There's no way I'm letting my little sister marry a complete stranger. I can't believe you did this. That you would go behind our backs like this." Haydon raised his cowboy hat and shoved his fin-gers through his blond hair. "Why, Leah? Why?" Nothing but concern filled his voice and eyes.

"Haydon—" Michael laid his hand on their oldest broth-er's shoulder "—we're all upset about this. But, we need to remember, we got wives like this, too."

"I don't care. This is our sister we're talking about here."

"Well, Rainee and Selina were someone's sister, too," Michael said as if he had all the calm in the world.

"Rainee's brother doesn't count," Haydon counteracted with a grunt.

"True, but Selina's does. Her brothers loved her as much as we love Leah."

Leah's heart melted at those words. They really did love and care about her.

Haydon stared at Michael, then looked over at Leah. She saw tender love for her along with confusion. She could tell he was torn, that a battle was going on inside him. Finally, he said, "Leah, would you promise one thing?"

"What's that?" Leah pushed away a strand of hair that had breezed across her eyes.

"If we don't feel right about this guy, would you take our advice and not marry him?" Up until this moment her brother Jess had been silent. "That's all we ask, Lee. We'll all be praying about this to see what God has to say about it. Fair enough?"

"I *did* pray about it, and I have peace about my decision."

"No offense, Leah, but you women let your emotions rule you," Haydon said, clearly wishing he could put a stop to it and that be that. "Besides, we're on the outside looking in. So would you trust us to pray about this and heed whatever God shows us?"

She glanced up at Haydon. As the oldest this had to be hard on him. He'd been the one to step in, to try to take her father's place when he'd died. This had to be killing him. A ghost she'd rather not deal with floated just behind his eyes. "Okay."

"Wise decision, Lee-Lee," Abby interjected.

"Hey, whose side are you on?"

"Both, of course." Abby wrinkled her nose at her, then smiled.

So much for secrets. She turned her attention to other pressing matters. "Oh, while everyone is here, I want to talk to you guys about something. What do you think of

Mother and Mr. Barker's relationship? Did she tell you that she was interested in pursuing a serious relationship with him?"

Haydon was the first to respond. "She did."

"And? What do you think about that?"

"We—" Haydon pointed at Jess and Michael "—think it's great."

Leah crossed her arms, not terribly happy with the answer. "You do? But what about Father?"

"What about him?" Jess asked.

She came uncoiled. "What do you mean 'what about him'? Am I the only one this bothers?"

"Leah." Michael put his arm around her shoulder and tucked her next to his side, a move that made her all the more angry. He glanced down at her. "Look, I know it's hard for you to think about Mother with anyone but Father. It is for all of us."

"It is?" She brightened, no longer feeling alone in her guilt-ridden thoughts.

"But..."

Her heart sank back into the abyss it dwelled in where her father was concerned.

"Father's gone. And he has been for a long time. We all see how lonely Mother is. We thought her and Mr. Svenson would get together until he decided to go back East. His leaving was hard on her. But now she seems happy again. Mr. Barker is obviously the one who is making her that way. He's a good Christian man who will take good care of her."

Leah looked away, annoyed to be the only one who was upset, and feeling guilty at the same time.

"It'll be okay, sis. You'll see." Jess tried to reassure her, too.

She couldn't even nod. Her heart was torn. She knew

Michael was right, but that didn't make it any easier. The only good thing about any of it was that she wouldn't be there to see her mother with another man. It would hurt too much.

Michael gave her a squeeze before releasing her. "Now, we need to talk about what to do with this fellow who's coming. When's he supposed to get here?"

They discussed Fitzwilliam and his arrival. Just thinking about his coming in three days stripped away the melancholy that plagued her moments before. She had so much to prepare—herself most of all.

Later that evening, Leah sat in her bed and pulled out her diary and quill.

Dear Mr. Darcy,
Today I think Jake wanted to kiss me. A part of me wonders what it would be like. Another part of me is really glad he didn't. That would change everything. I would be uncomfortable around him if he had. In fact, tomorrow I'm wondering if it will be awkward around him after that incident. I hope not, but I still wonder. Anyway, I just wanted to let you know that in three days I'll be meeting Mr. Barrington. I can hardly wait.

Leah continued to write about her day and all that had transpired with her brothers. A wide yawn brought moisture to her eyes. She wiped it away, signed off with a *Good night, Mr. Darcy,* closed the journal and locked it securely inside her nightstand. Another long yawn and she decided it was time to get some sleep. She had a lot to do before Mr. Barrington arrived.

Snuggling underneath her covers, she nestled her head

into the downy pillow and prayed that Mr. Barrington would like her.

Her eyes drifted shut.

"Father, where are you?" Leah hollered, running through the forest. Pine needles pricked her bare feet, stinging them, but she ignored the pain they inflicted. She had to find her father.

Deeper into the forest she ran, her shouts now filled with panic.

The sun settled behind the mountain and darkness shrouded everything.

Cedar, pine and cottonwood trees pressed in, encapsulating her and looming over her like the monsters they were.

Right before her eyes, their branches morphed into hands, and their knotholes turned into sinister eyes and mouths.

Evil now glared down at her.

Her heart slammed against her ribs with such force that Leah thought they would surely break.

With slow, menacing movement, the branches descended their arms downward toward her, straining closer and closer.

Leah ducked until she could duck no further. "Father, help me! I need you!" Her screams sucked all the air from around her. Breathing became difficult.

Long, spiky fingers dotted with leaves spread wide to take her into their grasp.

Leah pinched her eyes shut, waiting for the hand to grab her.

Seconds ticked by and nothing.

She slowly opened her eyes.

Her hands flew to the side of her head.

She screamed into the black void, "No! No!"

The monstrous tree had captured not her but her father, burying him underneath its mighty trunk. Only his legs, arms and head stuck out from underneath the massive beast.

Leah stared in horror.

Blood ran from her father's face in rivers.

"Lea—Leah. I—I love you, princess." Each word came out gurgled, slow, in painful gasps. Suddenly, his eyes rolled toward the back of his head and he went limp.

"Nooo! I'm sorry, Father! I'm sorry!" she wailed, her heart splintering from her chest.

Leah bolted upright and her gaze darted about the darkened room. Her heart beat so fast it throbbed in her ears as the images pursued her, even in reality. Blinking them back, she struggled to shake herself completely awake. With a toss, she yanked the covers back and swung her feet onto the cool floor.

The nightmare left her gasping for breath.

Tears slipped down her cheeks.

Those horrific dreams always ended the same—with her saying she was sorry. Sorry for what? She had no idea.

Exhausted, she wanted to lay her head back onto the pillow but couldn't. The gruesome image of her father might haunt her again.

Instead, she lit her kerosene lamp, lifted her Bible from the drawer and opened it to where her ribbon lay. *The Lord is my shepherd; I shall not want. He maketh me to lie down in green pastures: he leadeth me beside the still waters. He restoreth my soul: he leadeth me in the path of righteousness for his name's sake. Yea, thou I walk through the valley of the shadow of death, I will fear no evil: for thou art with me; thy rod and thy staff they comfort me.*

Thou preparest a table in the presence of mine enemies: thou anointest my head with oil; my cup runneth over. Surely goodness and mercy shall follow me all the days of my life: and I will dwell in the house of the Lord forever.

Two more times Leah read Psalm Twenty-Three before closing her Bible. She slipped her peach-colored muslin robe over her nightgown and walked over to her bedroom window. She tied back the curtain and lowered herself into the chair in front of her open window, resting her arm on the windowsill. Staring up at the stars, in the quietness of her mind she sang the song her father had made up. *Sweet twinkling stars above; there to remind us of our Heavenly Father's love. Each one placed by the Savior with care; as a sweet reminder that He will always be there.*

Too weak to battle the tears from coming, they streamed down her cheeks, and she ran a hand over them to wipe them dry. *Oh, sweet twinkling stars above. When my children gaze upon you remind them, too, of my love.*

She sniffed back the rest of the tears, but more replaced them.

Each twinkle is a kiss from me; a hug, a prayer, a sweet memory. Oh, sweet twinkling stars above. Sniffing as the tears continued to fall, she sang it over and over until finally a blanket of peace covered her. She could almost feel her father's arms around her. It was the one sweet memory from this place that held any sway over all of the bad. She sighed with the hard-fought contentment.

Insects hissed and clacked their wings.

Coyotes howled somewhere faraway.

Leah listened to them, enjoying the peace and quiet.

How long she sat there, she didn't know. Only when the grandfather clock downstairs chimed five times did she move from the window. With a heavy sigh, Leah went and washed up, got dressed and headed downstairs. She had a lot to do before Mr. Barrington arrived. Two days. It seemed an eternity.

Mr. Barrington. Her heart said the name again.

The man who might very well become her husband. At the word *husband,* Jake's face slipped into the front of her mind, and Leah shook the notion from her brain. As much as she enjoyed Jake, he would not be a part of her future. He couldn't be. She was leaving. And after that nightmare, the sooner she got away from this place, the better.

Chapter Ten

For the first time ever, Jake's insides squirmed like a restless snake at the thought of seeing Leah. He wasn't sure how things would be between them after he'd almost kissed her. Or if she even knew how, for that one brief second, he'd thought about doing just that. He had a feeling she did because her attention had fallen to his mouth. Truth was, he wouldn't mind seeing what it would be like to kiss her. To see if her lips were as warm and soft as they looked. *What are you doing? Stop it, buddy boy. Best get your mind off of her and get your work done. Thinking like that could get you in trouble, that's for sure.*

Jake haltered another cow and sat down with his back to the barn door. Streams of milk pinged into the bucket. A few squirts later, he spurt some of the warm, sweet liquid into his mouth. "Ah. Nothing better than fresh milk." He wiped his mouth and continued milking the Jersey. He had just finished when he heard someone coming into the barn. This early, it either had to be Jess or Haydon.

The familiar scent of roses reached his nose.

Leah.

His insides writhed with a mixture of excitement and uncertainty.

"Good morning, Jake." Leah's greeting and lighthearted step eased the tension inside him.

Whew. Leah was acting as if nothing was out of the normal. "Morning, sunshine." Jake continued milking, keeping his sight trained on Leah as she strolled up to him. To get a better view of her, he thumbed his hat off his forehead and stopped milking. Worry crowded in on him the second he got a good look at her.

Dark, puffy circles sagged underneath her eyes.

"You all right?"

"I'm fine. Why?"

"You look tuckered out." He moved the bucket behind him and stood.

"Oh, that." She smiled, but it was forced and drowsy. "I didn't sleep well last night."

"How come?"

"I had a lot on my mind." Her hands slid into the pockets of her light blue skirt and she fiddled with something inside them.

"Getting ready for that Barrington fellow, huh?"

"Yes. I have a lot to do to get ready for his arrival. But Mother asked if I would take care of the milk this morning because Veronique can't. With Mr. Barrington and his sister coming, Mother wants Veronique to make sure our house is sparkling clean." She looked around and stopped when she spotted the two covered pails he'd just finished. "Have you taken any milk to my brothers' houses yet?"

"Nope. Not yet."

"Would you mind if I go ahead and take those?" She pointed to them.

"Nope. Don't mind at all, but what's your rush?" He suspected he knew, and both reasons ate at him.

"I want to hurry and get done so that Mother, Abby and

I can head into town to buy some more material. I want to look my best when I meet Mr. Barrington."

He tipped his hat again and gazed the length of her. "You always look nice, Leah."

"Ah, that is sweet of you to say. Thank you, Jake." Those dimples appeared again when her lips curled. It was a friendly smile and cuter than a six-week-old kitten.

"Just a minute, okay? Don't go anywhere." He released the Jersey into the corral, where she'd stay until he finished milking the rest of them, then he'd shoo them back out into the pasture.

He haltered another one and moved the cow where the other one had been.

Leah stood on the cow's left, staring at the animal with inquisitive eyes. "This is going to sound strange, but I've never milked a cow before. I always wanted to, but my brothers always did it. Would you mind showing me how it's done?"

Jake looked at her clean yet simple dress. "You might get dirty."

"So?" She shrugged. "It doesn't matter if I do. This dress is old. I wear it when I help Mother and Veronique around the house. Besides, I'll change before I head into town so no need to worry about soiling it." She glanced at the cow and then back at him. "What do you say? Would you be willing to show me how it's done?"

Was he? Sure. Why not? Could be fun even. He gave a quick nod, grabbed the brim of his hat and lowered it back into place. "Come around to this side. Make sure you walk out and back far enough that she can't kick you."

She did as she was instructed to. Farther than necessary, even.

"Okay. Sit down." He motioned for her to sit on the stool.

She tucked her skirt under her and sat with her shoulder against the cow's right side.

He placed the bucket underneath the udder, squatted down next to her and rested his weight on the heel of his boot. "Okay. Here's what you do. Reach under here and grab the…um…grab the…uh…" Heat rose up the back of his neck. From the corner of his eye, he peeked at Leah. Her face reminded him of a ripened tomato.

God, help me out here, okay?

He roped some courage to himself and after a deep breath, he said, "Wrap your hand around…um…this right here." Jake demonstrated where she should place her hand. "Keep it close to the…um…" He cleared his throat. "The udder. Then squeeze." A stream of milk landed in the pail. "Okay. Now you do it."

He avoided looking at her face but watched as she did just as he'd told her to. Nothing came out.

She turned toward him with concern. "What did I do wrong?"

"Don't know. Try it again."

She did, and again nothing happened.

"You squeezing hard enough?"

"I don't want to hurt her." She blinked wide eyes at him as if what he'd said was the most absurd thing she'd ever heard.

Jake chuckled. "You won't hurt her. Here. Let me show you how much pressure to apply." He laid his hand on top of hers. Her small hand disappeared under his larger one. Gently, he guided her hand with his and the milk spurted out. A couple of tries later, he removed his hand. Milk continued to splatter into the bucket.

"I did it." The sound in her voice and the look on her face reminded him of a child who'd just learned to catch a ball for the first time.

"You sure did." He watched as she continued to milk the cow and even managed to get most of it into the bucket. "Hey, you're not doing too bad for a girl."

"What's that supposed to mean?" She cocked her head the way she did so often.

"You said your brothers never let you milk a cow. Figured they didn't 'cause you were a girl."

"Don't see what being a *girl* has to do with anything. Lots of *women* milk cows."

He noticed her emphasis on *girl* and *women*. Her way of letting him know she wasn't a girl but a woman. No need for her to point that out to him. That detail definitely hadn't skipped his notice. "Prissy little *women* like yourself don't," he teased.

"Prissy? Me?"

Just then drops of milk hit the top of his cheekbone.

She giggled.

"Hey." He jumped up, raised his hat and ran the back of his sleeve over his face.

Another round of drops splattered against his neck. She chuckled again.

"What is wrong with you, *woman?*" He grabbed the ratty handkerchief from the back pocket of his jeans and wiped off his neck.

"Nothing's wrong with me." She sent him a cheeky grin, then dipped her fingertips in the milk bucket again and flicked the liquid toward him. This time it landed near his mouth. After a quick swipe to remove the splatters, before she could hit him again, he dropped to a squat, dipped his hand in the bucket and tossed it at her. The milk landed in her hair.

She squealed, then nailed him again in the ear with a handful before he had a chance to block it.

He scooped another handful, and this time the milk landed on her cheek.

She shrieked and started to shove the stool out of the way, but one of the three legs caught on the dirt floor, and the stool tipped over. Her arms shot out in front of her. He tried to catch them but couldn't. She landed on her rump, then her back, and ended up with her legs draped up and over the stool.

"What's going on in here?" Michael strode in the barn door and right up to them, where he put his hands on his hips to survey the mess.

In one fluid motion, Jake rose and helped Leah up. He faced Michael, expecting to see anger but instead saw a face spiked with humor. Jake knew what Michael was thinking, but he needed to set that right and fast.

Leah wiped her soiled hand on her skirt and brushed the dust and hay particles from her dress. Stems of hay hung in her hair, but he wasn't going to remove them and give Michael any more wrong ideas to speculate over. He quickly used his handkerchief to wipe the milk from his hand.

"Uh. Hi, Michael," she said before Jake got anything out. "I, um, I asked Jake to show me how to milk a cow."

"Oh. Is that what you were doing?" Michael rubbed his chin.

"Yes." Leah slammed her hands on her slender hips. "I've always wanted to learn, but you would never teach me how. So I asked Jake to. And I'm pretty good at it, too." Leah gave her brother a smug look filled with pride.

"Yes, real good." Michael peered into the nearly empty pail and then at the two of them. "Looks like you got more on yourselves than in the bucket."

Her eyes narrowed. "What are you doing here, anyway? Don't you have something better to do? Seems to me you've been leaving Selina a lot more often lately. You sure that's wise?"

Michael shrugged as Jake assessed Leah out of the corner of his eye. He didn't dare do more. "Abby's there. And I don't leave her for long periods. Besides, they were all sound asleep when I left." He frowned at Leah. "What are you doing here so early?" Michael eyed Jake and Leah suspiciously.

"If you must know, Mother asked me to come get the milk." She looked over at Jake. "May I have those two?"

Jake snatched up the two cloth-covered buckets sitting on high shelves off of the dirty floor. "I'll carry these up to the house for you."

"You don't have to do that. I can get them. But thanks anyway." She reached for the buckets, but Jake refused to hand them over to her. They were heavier than they looked.

"I said I would carry them for you." He sent her a look that left no room for argument, then turned his focus onto Michael. "Did you come down here for a reason?"

"Yes." Michael looked at Leah. "Would you excuse us for a minute?"

She glanced at Jake and the pails.

"I'll bring them up to the house in a minute, okay?"

Leah nodded, then picked up the milk pail he and Leah had dipped their hands in. "I'll take this and give it to the pigs." She left the barn with a quick glance over her shoulder.

Jake faced Michael and waited.

"I was wondering if you'd do me a favor."

"What's that?"

"Leah posted an advertisement in the New York paper for a husband." Michael stared at Jake, waiting for his reaction, no doubt.

"I know."

"You do?"

"Yep." And that was all he was going to say about it.

Michael's mouth twisted. "Well, some man answered it and he's coming out here in a couple of days. I... We... That is, Haydon, Jess and I were wondering if you'd take Leah into town to pick him up. Jess and Haydon can't, and I don't want to leave Selina that long. Would you mind? We'd feel a whole lot better if we knew you were with her."

Jake wanted to ask why they'd feel better about him being with her, but he didn't. He would do it to protect her and keep an eye on her—and to meet this dandy who was about to take his place. His place. Listen to him—as if he had a place in Leah's life. "Be happy to."

"Thanks, Jake." Michael laid his hand on Jake's shoulder. "I'll feel a lot better knowing you'll be there."

So would he. So would he.

Leah paced the kitchen floor, wondering where Jake was and what was taking him so long. She couldn't wait to get the milk. The sooner she did, the sooner she could take care of it so they could head to town.

"Leah, would you sit down? You're going to wear a path in the floor. Pacing isn't going to get that milk here any faster." Mother added another uniformly diced potato into the large cooking pot filled with cool water. She wanted to have everything ready for when they got back from town to fix pyttipanna, better known in America as Swedish hash.

Veronique normally did most of the cooking, but with all the extra housecleaning she had to do, Leah and Mother would take care of the cooking and baking for the next couple of days.

The sound of heavy boots climbing up the steps to the

kitchen stopped Leah's fretting. She darted toward the door and swung it open.

"Where do you want these?" Jake had a bucket in each hand.

"On the table will be fine."

"Good morning, Katherine." Jake's muscles bulged beneath his shirt when he hoisted the pails onto the table. The man sure had nice muscular arms.

"Good morning to you, too, Jake."

He smiled then looked at Leah. "When you're ready to head into town just let me know and I'll get the buggy ready."

"Thanks, Jake." Leah watched the broad-shouldered man walk out the door and down the steps. Jake was the sweetest, gentlest man she knew. Someday she hoped he would find a nice woman to marry. She tilted her head, wondering why that thought pinched her soul.

"Leah, are you listening?" Mother asked from only inches behind Leah.

Leah whirled and blinked. "Sorry, Mother. I didn't hear you. What did you say?"

"I said, are you going to stand there gawking at Jake all day or get that milk taken care of?"

"I wasn't gawking at Jake," she murmured under her breath after she brushed past her mother. She snatched up the pails of milk and headed to the creamery room. The heavy buckets weighed her arms down as she trekked through the pantry and into the room farthest away from the heat of the kitchen. Inside the cool room, she continued to murmur. "Sweet twinkling stars above. First Michael and now Mother. Can't a woman admire a man without everyone assuming they're a couple? Or that they're in love? Jake and I have fun together. So what?" She thought about their playful encounter. Jake had such a playful side to him and was so much fun. Too bad Michael had to show up and ruin it.

Leah set the buckets down and tugged at her lower lip, pondering over what Michael could possibly want to talk to Jake about that she couldn't hear. Something about that bothered her.

She quickly finished taking care of the milk, set the table and helped her mother finish dicing the ham and onions. Thankfully this time they wouldn't be adding any bacon or eggs to the pyttipanna or it would take them even longer to finish. Leah could hardly stand it now. She couldn't wait to head into town.

"Those babies are so cute," Abby said, bursting through the kitchen door. She flopped down into one of the chairs with her legs sprawled in front of her and her arms draped at her sides. "I can't wait until I become a mother."

Leah couldn't picture her baby sister a mother, although Abby was growing up fast and becoming a beautiful, outgoing woman. When had that happened?

"That's the last of the chopping." Mother stood. "Shall we put this up and get ready to head into town?"

"Yes." Leah jumped up and loaded her arms with bowls of chopped food. "Abbs, would you go down to the barn and see if Jake is still there? If he is, would you ask him to get the phaeton that seats four people ready, not the buckboard one?"

"Sure." Abby breezed out the door as fast as she'd breezed in.

That night, after a long day of shopping, Leah wrote about the events of the day in her Mr. Darcy diary. She read the new letters she'd received in response to her post. Not one of them intrigued her like Mr. Barrington's had. She slid them in the drawer and readied herself for bed, praying the nightmares wouldn't come. She needed sleep. Tomorrow would be another long day of preparations to meet Mr. Barrington.

Chapter Eleven

The day before had gone by in a blur of activities, including attending church. Today Mr. Barrington would arrive.

Leah studied her reflection in the mirror.

"You look beautiful, Leah." Mother stepped up behind her.

Leah glanced in the looking glass at her mother's reflection. "Thank you, Mother. And thank you for helping me finish this gown. It's beautiful." Leah turned her attention to the soft-pink satin gown.

The gathered, short sleeves and swooped neckline made her cameo necklace stand out against her sleek neck. She and mother had made a sash that hung below her waist and swept around to form a bustle in the back with a row of pink roses holding it together on the sides. Underneath the sash in front were layers and layers of delicate white ruffled lace that ended about a foot from the bottom hem of the dress. Directly underneath the lacy ruffles they'd sewn a four-inch-wide piece of pink lace all the way around the dress and bustle, leaving the last foot of the gown to match the top. Long, white gloves finished the ensemble.

Earlier, Mother had helped her sweep her hair back,

leaving Leah's long curls flowing down in the back. She had even woven beaded ribbons through her blond tresses.

"I haven't lost my touch," Mother whispered.

"What do you mean?" Leah peeled her eyes off of her reflection and onto her mother's.

"Back in New York, we used to dress like this all the time. There was always a grand ball somewhere. Or someone was hosting a party. You remember going to them, don't you?"

"Yes." She turned to face her mother. "Do you ever miss it? I mean New York and the balls?"

"Sometimes yes. Most times no."

"What do you miss about it?"

"I miss being able to wear beautiful dresses once in a while. Not the corsets, though." They laughed. "I especially miss feeling feminine and pretty."

"But you are pretty, Mother."

"That's what Charles, I mean, Mr. Barker, says." At the mention of his name, especially his first name, Leah stiffened. "If he and I do marry, I'll be able to wear more gowns again. You know how elite his establishment is. Almost everyone who goes there dresses up," Mother continued, oblivious to Leah's discomfort. She was trying to be happy for her mother, she really was, but she couldn't help but wonder if anyone even cared about her father anymore except for her.

"Well, enough of that. You need to go or you'll be late meeting…" She paused. "What was his name again?"

"Fitzwilliam. Mr. Fitzwilliam Barrington."

"Oh, that's right. Well, run along now. I'll be praying for you."

"I'll need it. My insides are shaking so badly. I just hope I don't faint."

"You won't. Just remember to breathe."

"Who can breathe with one of these things on?" Leah squirmed in the uncomfortable corset that Rainee had loaned her, saying she didn't care if she ever got it back. She'd only worn the thing two or three times before. No wonder Rainee refused to wear them. Corsets really were the most uncomfortable contraptions ever made.

Mother walked her downstairs and out the door. Standing on the porch, she pulled Leah into a hug and then let her go with a smile and an unshed tear.

With the grace of a lady, Leah stepped down the porch stairs. At the grass, she turned and waved at her mother, then she raised the pink parasol that matched her dress and glided toward the barn, feeling prettier than she'd ever felt before.

Her heart skipped when her eyes landed on Jake, standing near the phaeton with the fringed parasol top, dressed in the same suit he had worn to Phoebe's wedding and looking every bit as handsome as he had that evening.

She strolled over to him, and he removed his black cowboy hat, pressed it over his midsection and, with a slight bow, he made a sweeping gesture toward the carriage. "Your chariot awaits, my lady."

She laughed at his antics, then cocked her head and eyed him. "What are you doing here?"

"I'm your driver."

"My driver?"

"Yep. You don't think your brothers were going to let you meet this man without a chaperone, do you?"

"Well, no. We discussed it the other day, so I knew that someone was going with me. I just didn't know who. I figured it would be one of them."

"Well, Michael asked if I would take you. I told him I'd be happy to."

Truth be known, she was happy he was taking her, too.

"By the way. You look beautiful."

"Thank you." The compliment meant a lot coming from him.

"Shall we?" He stood at the backseat of the carriage and offered her his hand.

"What are you doing?"

"Can't have you sitting up front with the chauffeur, now can we?"

"You're not my chauffeur, Jake. You're my friend." She snapped her parasol shut, brushed past him, stopped at the front seat and perched her gloved hand toward him. "Now, I'll take that offered hand up if you don't mind, kind sir."

His smile of approval caused her heart to flip.

He reached for her gloved hand and steadied her as she rested her foot on the step and climbed aboard. She gathered her skirt inside and placed her parasol next to her.

Jake ran around and climbed in on the other side.

Although she knew it wasn't proper for her to be seated next to him like this, she didn't care. She was proud to be sitting next to him instead of in the back like some spoiled rich girl, treating her friend like a hired servant. As for what the townspeople would think when they saw them riding into town together like this, well, she didn't care about that, either. Nor did she have to worry about it. After all, she was going to pick up her future husband, so that should keep the tongues from wagging about her and Jake.

Maybe it hadn't been a good idea to let Leah sit next to him on the way to town. All the way there, Jake struggled with her intoxicating scent of roses and soap. Not only that, Leah looked even more beautiful than she normally did. However, seeing her dressed like that reminded him once again of how different their lifestyles were and how it was a good thing she had turned down his proposal. The two of them marrying would be like mixing fire and water.

Leah squirmed in the seat for what seemed like the millionth time.

"Pretty nervous, huh?"

She nodded and sighed.

"Try not to get too worked up. You'll make yourself sick."

"I know."

The train depot came into sight at the edge of town.

"Jake, could you stop here a moment?"

"Sure. Whoa." He halted the perfectly matched black and white spotted horses. Lines firmly in hand, he gave her his undivided attention. "What's wrong?"

"I wondered if—" her eyelids lowered, then rose back to look at him "—I wondered if you would pray with me now."

She looked so hopeful there was no way he could refuse her. "Sure." He reached for her hand. They bowed their heads, and when he finished praying, he realized his prayer hadn't only been for her benefit but for his, too. He knew this was going to be hard, but he hadn't realized just how hard until that moment. If Leah and this Barrington fellow got along or, worse, fell in love, then he would lose the best friend he ever had. Pain clawed at his heart. If only she would have said yes to him before. But knowing it was a good thing she had turned down his proposal and living with that decision were two very different battles.

"Thank you." Leah's voice was soft.

Jake nodded, clicked the lines and headed into town. In the distance, the train wheels clacked against the iron track. Within minutes it would be here. Now it was his turn to be nervous. But, for Leah's sake, he wouldn't let it show. He needed to not only be strong for her, but also for himself. His sanity depended on it.

At the front of the depot, Jake helped Leah down. Their boots tapped side by side against the wooden planks as they walked down the plank board platform to meet the train.

The train whistle pierced the air. Smoke billowed from the black stack, and the clanging of the wheels grew louder as it neared.

Leah's hand touched on his arm. A range of emotions battered across her face.

"Relax. Everything will be okay. You'll see." Brave words coming from a man who was as nervous as she was.

They turned their focus to the passengers now disembarking. The conductor helped a lady wearing a green dress every bit as fancy as Leah's from the train. Behind her was a man in a tail suit, holding a cane in one hand and gloves in another and wearing a top hat. A proud peacock showing off his feathers came to mind.

That dandy had to be Mr. Barrington and the lady with him, his sister.

The man stepped beside the woman, stopped and looked around.

Jake decided to take matters into his own hands. "Wait here," he said to Leah.

She nodded.

Jake strode over to the couple. "Excuse me. Are you Mr. Barrington?"

The man turned dark, condescending eyes and surveyed Jake with disdain.

Jake pressed his shoulders back. No man, rich or otherwise, would make him feel bad about himself. He'd suffered that sting enough to last a lifetime. "I asked if you..."

"Yes. I heard you. And yes, I am Mr. Barrington. Who might you be?"

"Jake Lure." Jake offered the man his hand.

All the fellow did was glance at it as if it were poison.

Jake let his hand fall to his side. What he really wanted to do with it was rearrange the haughty man's face.

"Jake." Leah's confused voice sounded from beside him.

He glanced down at her, then shifted his attention to the Barrington fellow. "Leah, this *gentleman* is Mr. Barrington." Gentleman. Ha.

Barrington's face brightened. "Ah. Capital. I see you've received my post."

Capital? What was that supposed to mean?

The rascal removed his hat and bowed. Then he fastened his hand onto Leah's fingers, raised her hand to his lips and kissed it. When he straightened, his eyes raked up and down Leah's body approvingly.

Jake's fists clenched at the audacity of this man. To avoid embarrassing Leah, he restrained himself from ramming his fist in the man's eyes for disrespecting her like that.

"You are every bit as lovely as I had imagined. Quite striking, actually. It is a real pleasure to make your acquaintance, Miss Bowen. I am sure we will get along quite famously."

A smooth talker this one was. Jake was determined to keep his eye on this fellow who portrayed himself to be a gentleman but was nothing more than a shed snakeskin.

Heat rose into Leah's cheeks at Mr. Barrington's compliment. Judging from the admiration on his face, his study of her must have met with his approval. "It's a pleasure to meet you, too, Mr. Barrington." Leah gave him a small

curtsy and a smile, relieved that she remembered the social graces from her childhood.

He returned her smile. His teeth, although white, were slightly crooked. His brown eyes, hair and long sideburns reminded her of the chocolate squares she indulged in every now and again.

"Miss Bowen, may I present my sister, Miss Elizabeth Barrington?"

The woman, who looked identical to her brother, curtsied, and so did Leah. "It's a pleasure to meet you, Miss Barrington."

"Please, call me Elizabeth. May I call you Leah?"

"Yes. Yes, you may." The woman's silk, royal-blue bustle gown must have cost a small fortune. As had her matching parasol, reticule, ribbon sash hat and matching slippers.

Those slippers won't last long out here.

"May I call you Leah, as well? I know it is highly improper unless we are courting, but I feel it is just a matter of time before we shall be." Mr. Barrington smiled.

"Of course. Leah's fine."

"Capital. And you may call me Fitzwilliam."

"Thank you, Fitzwilliam." Leah loved listening to his British accent. The man was extremely handsome. And tall, too. Not as tall as Jake, but taller than she at least. "I hope you don't mind, but I've made arrangements at Mr. Barker's hotel. It is the finest hotel in town." Leah had done that the day she, Mother and Abby had gone to town to get the material for the dress she was now wearing.

"That was most considerate of you, Miss Bowen. I mean, Leah." He hooked her arm through his.

Leah looked at their linked arms, then over at Jake.

Jake shrugged.

"You, sir. Get our bags." Mr. Barrington's tone boasted with authority aimed at Jake.

Her mouth fell open and her eyes widened. "You mean Jake?" Leah asked.

"Jake? You address your servant by his first name?"

"Servant? Jake is not my servant." Annoyance rolled inside her at that, but she would not let her face show it—She'd let her voice instead. "Jake—" she emphasized his name "—is my friend. A very dear, very close, very special friend." She smiled at Jake.

"I see." Mr. Barrington's eyes narrowed at Jake, and he looked like he'd just tasted sour milk.

"Brother, I'm sure Mr. Lure or Leah might know someone we may hire to take our belongings to the hotel." Elizabeth smiled at Leah and Jake with a hint of an apologetic smile if Leah wasn't mistaken. Elizabeth's eyes lingered on Jake rather than on Leah, a fact that Leah did not miss. She found her own gaze going to him and sticking, too.

"No need, Miss Barrington. I'll see to them," Jake said, swinging a large bag to his hip.

"Jake, you don't need to do that." Leah slipped her arm out of Mr. Barrington's and stepped beside Jake. "I'll see if Mr. Barker will send someone over to get them."

"I don't mind." He shrugged.

"*You* may not, but *I* do." She sent him a look to let him know she really didn't want him carrying them.

He stared at her for a moment, then set the bag down. Leah sent him a smile, letting him know how relieved she was he'd followed her silent request.

Another nod from Jake. She turned toward Fitzwilliam. "If you're ready, we can take you to the hotel now. If you haven't eaten, we can eat lunch there." Leah's attention slid to Elizabeth. "You must be exhausted from your long journey."

"I am."

"If you'd like, you can have a hot bath and rest awhile."

"That would be lovely, Leah. Yes. You are quite right. A hot bath and a soft bed sound most agreeable. Thank you."

"That's very thoughtful of you to consider my sister's needs, Leah. I must admit, I could use a bit of a rest myself. Perhaps after we've done so, we could hire a carriage to take us out to your ranch?"

"Brother," Elizabeth said. "May we do that tomorrow? I am in need of nourishment and a good night's rest."

"Very well, sister. Even though I am quite anxious to spend time with Leah, I can see you need your rest. We shall wait until the morrow then." Fitzwilliam smiled at Leah. "Though it shall be an interminable wait."

What a sweet man to think of his sister's needs, even above his own wants. "Very well, let's go get you two settled in then. Would you like to walk to the hotel or ride?"

"If it's not too far, I would prefer to walk. I have been sitting much too long," Fitzwilliam answered.

"Yes, we have. Taking a turn would do us good." Elizabeth smiled up at Jake.

She sure seemed to do a lot of that.

"Shall we?" Leah glanced at each one. When Leah turned toward the direction of the hotel, Mr. Barrington looped her hand through his arm again and tugged her forward, away from Jake's side. She glanced over her shoulder at Jake and was about to mouth *sorry* when she felt another tug on her arm.

Jake gave her a quick nod to go on ahead.

"Miss Barrington, may I?" At the sound of Jake's voice, Leah turned her head enough to see Jake offer Elizabeth his arm and smile warmly at her.

Something about that didn't sit right in Leah's belly.

But she'd think about the why of it later. Right now she wanted to concentrate on Fitzwilliam.

The walk to the hotel was pleasant enough except for the fact that Leah spent more time listening to the conversation behind her than she did to the one she was a participant in.

"Here we are." She stopped at the large three-story hotel.

"Impressive. Quite impressive. Allow me." Mr. Barrington turned the brass knob on the large mahogany door.

Leah smiled at him and stepped far enough inside to let the others in. She quickly studied the room, trying to see it from the Barringtons' viewpoint.

Crystal chandeliers loaded with fresh candles hung from the high ceiling. Light and airy, white swag curtains covered the three big windows in front and the three big windows on the sides. The white drapery material dotted with dainty pink and blue roses matched the fabric on the mahogany Chippendale chairs and the tablecloths that covered the matching tables.

On the far end of the room were two long, curved staircases, one on either side of a long mahogany registration desk. Next to the bottom of the stairs were entryways into the kitchen, one door for going in, the other for coming out.

"Don't worry, Leah. Even they would have to agree it's a fine establishment," Jake whispered near her ear from behind her.

He knew her so well. She went to respond to him but never got the chance because Mr. Barrington clutched her arm and propelled her forward.

Fitzwilliam was obviously jealous of Jake, and Leah completely understood why he might be. After all, he didn't know how it was between her and Jake. If he did, he would know he had nothing to be jealous about.

"Leah."

Leah stopped and turned to find Mr. Barker heading her way. "Mr. Barker, how nice to see you again." She really did like the man, she just didn't like the idea of he and her mother married. But she was trying. And she would be polite.

"It's nice to see you again, too, Leah."

Leah glanced over at Jake. "You know Jake Lure."

"Yes, I sure do. How are you doing today, Jake?" They shook hands, and Mr. Barker's smile radiated his respect.

"Fine, sir. And you?"

"Never better." He glanced at Leah. She knew what he was referring to. Her mother and their relationship.

She didn't want to think about that now so she turned to introduce Fitzwilliam to Mr. Barker. Once again, his eyes were narrowed in Jake's direction, but he recovered quickly.

Poor Jake. He didn't deserve Fitzwilliam's disdain.

"Mr. Barrington," Leah said, liking how refined and dignified he looked there.

Fitzwilliam turned his head toward Leah and the frown disappeared, replaced with a smile that didn't quite make it to his eyes.

"I'd like you to meet Mr. Barker. He's the owner of this establishment."

Fitzwilliam's eyes brightened considerably then. "Pleasure to meet you, sir."

Mr. Barker extended his hand, but Fitzwilliam didn't take it. He bowed.

Mr. Barker did a quick glance in Leah's direction, then let his arm fall slowly to his side.

"And may I present my sister, Elizabeth?"

"Nice to meet you, ma'am." Mr. Barker gave a quick nod.

Elizabeth curtsied. “Thank you, sir. It is a pleasure to meet you, as well.”

Seconds of awkward silence passed until Leah spoke up. “Mr. Barker, we’ve come to have a bite to eat before my guests retire to their rooms. I’ve reserved two rooms here for them.”

“I’ll take good care of them, Leah.” For an older man, Mr. Barker was very handsome. She could see what her mother saw in him, still… *Not now, Leah,* she silently scolded herself. “Follow me and I’ll show you to your table.” Mr. Barker led them to the best spot in the dining area and seated them.

“I’ll send Carina over to take your orders. And now, if you’ll excuse me, I have business to attend to. If I can be of service to you for anything, just ask Carina to send for me, okay? It was a pleasure to meet you all.” He glanced down at Leah and smiled. “Tell your mother hello for me.”

Although her insides cringed, she said, “I will.” She watched him walk away.

Jake leaned close to her and whispered, “Remember. It gets easier. I promise.” Like a butterfly alighting on a branch, his hand brushed hers under the table and he squeezed it gently. Gratefulness for his solid presence in her life drifted over her heart.

Their gazes locked for a moment. Leah willed her eyes to show him her gratitude. Jake gave a quick nod, shifted back into his chair and removed his hand.

Leah pulled her focus off of Jake and slid it onto Fitzwilliam, who was once again glaring at Jake. She needed to explain the friendship to Fitzwilliam. Not now, though. And not in front of Jake.

“Hi, Leah.” Carina stepped up to the table, dressed in a light green gown. “Hi, Jake.” Her smiling green eyes lingered on Jake as did her generous, full-lipped smile.

"Carina, this is Mr. Barrington and his sister, Elizabeth."

"It is a pleasure to meet y'all." Their pretty waitress glanced at Elizabeth and stared at Fitzwilliam.

Fitzwilliam sat in his chair like a statue. Leah waited for him to say something to Carina, but he didn't. How odd. First Fitzwilliam didn't shake Jake's or Mr. Barker's hands and now he didn't respond to Leah's introduction to Carina or even acknowledge her presence. Is that how things were done in England? Or was the man just nervous or shy? Leah hoped it was the latter—that at least she could understand. The other, she couldn't and wasn't sure she wanted to try.

"It is a pleasure to meet you, as well." Elizabeth didn't seem to have a problem acknowledging Carina. "Carina is such a lovely name."

"Thank you, ma'am." Carina pressed a finger to her lip. "I don't recognize the accent. Where y'all from?"

"England. But we live in New York now," Elizabeth answered.

"Really? What are y'all doing here?"

"Carina, I'm sorry to interrupt, but my guests could use a drink and something to eat." Leah gave her a small smile. Carina was a sweet girl, but once she got wind of something, the whole town eventually did, too.

"Oh, of course. How thoughtless of me." Carina smiled a half smile. "What would y'all like to drink? We have tea, coffee, water, milk or wine."

"Leah, what would you care to drink?" Fitzwilliam asked with a smile.

"Tea with cream and sugar."

"The lady would like a spot of tea with cream and sugar," Fitzwilliam told the waitress as if she hadn't heard Leah.

"'A spot of tea'? What's that?" Carina's face wrinkled.

"A cup, madam. It means a cup full of tea." There was no condescension in his voice, which pleased Leah.

"Oh." Carina shrugged and looked at him like he was nuttier than a walnut grove.

"I'll have the same, Miss Carina," Elizabeth said when Carina looked at her.

"Jake, what'll you have?"

"Milk."

"Milk? How very odd." Fitzwilliam frowned at Jake, who looked completely unfazed by it.

But she was.

"And you, sir? What would you like?" Carina gazed down at Fitzwilliam with admiration in her eyes. Leah rolled hers at Carina's obviousness.

"Wine. White if you have it."

Wine? The man drank wine? At a few minutes past twelve, even. Was that something the British did? Leah made a mental note to ask Rainee about that. If it wasn't, she didn't want someone who drank, no matter how desperate she was to leave this place.

"What's on the menu today, Carina?" Jake asked as Leah threaded her way through the questions.

"You have your choice of roasted pork with mashed potatoes and gravy and glazed carrots." She ticked the choices off with her fingers. "Beef stew. Chicken and vegetable pie. Or fried trout with fried potatoes and green beans."

They all placed their orders and Carina brought their drinks.

"So, did you have a nice journey?" Leah asked Fitzwilliam, then took a sip of tea.

"Yes, we did. The countryside was quite to our liking."

Leah tried to think of something else to say, but nothing came to mind. She picked up her tea again, hoping Fitzwilliam would say something. Without looking directly at them, Leah noticed that Elizabeth and Jake weren't having any trouble with conversation. She would join in with theirs but it looked like they were engrossed in whatever it was they were talking about. In fact, Jake looked completely enraptured in what Elizabeth was saying. A twinge of jealousy brushed across Leah.

"Leah."

She looked over at Fitzwilliam. "Yes?"

"How far is your ranch from here?"

The conversation picked up then as did the passing of time. Leah found herself completely engrossed as Fitzwilliam regaled her with one interesting story after another, and her excitement about getting to know him grew. Fitzwilliam turned out to be an interesting man whose travels had taken him to exotic lands—many of which she could hardly pronounce. Each sounded more fascinating than the one before. They were all lands she couldn't wait to see.

When lunch was over, Jake made arrangements for their luggage to be sent over. Leah helped them get their room keys and invited them to come to the ranch the following afternoon and stay for dinner. Goodbyes were said, and with that, she and Jake headed down the boardwalk to the buggy.

"So, what did you think of Fitzwilliam?" Leah asked Jake as they walked slowly down Main Street. Fitzwilliam's antagonism toward Jake made the whole ordeal miserable. Elizabeth was nice enough. Easy on the eyes, and Jake enjoyed talking with her, but that Fitzwilliam fellow…

Jake wanted to tell Leah exactly what he thought of Fitzwilliam, but he held his tongue. "Haven't been around him long enough to know just what sort of fellow he is yet."

"But he seems really nice, though, don't you think?"

Jake shrugged. She didn't want to know what he really thought.

Her boots tapped against the boardwalk as they made their way toward the train depot. At the carriage, Jake helped Leah up and then climbed aboard beside her. "What did you think of Elizabeth?" she asked.

Now that he could answer and be honest about. "She's a very nice, interesting lady." An attractive one at that. He turned the horses toward the Bowens' ranch.

"What all did you and her have to talk about?"

"She asked me what I did and where I lived. I told her. She sure surprised me."

"In what way?" Leah asked as they headed onto the dirt street out of town.

"The woman wants to live on a farm. Said she hates city life."

"Has she ever lived on one before?"

"Said she did. She loved being around the animals. Getting her hands dirty. Something she said English ladies never do. Especially one of her social standing. Didn't seem overly impressed with her own social status." Jake could see why, if she had to live a stuffy, boring life like that Mr. Darcy fellow in the book he'd finished reading. He had to admit, though—in *Pride and Prejudice* Mr. Darcy turned out to be a nice guy. Jake hoped that would be the case with Fitzwilliam Barrington. But he had his doubts. He'd seen the ugly, evil glint of jealousy in the man's eyes.

Years before, Jake's uncle Urias killed a man in a fit of jealous rage. Before they'd hanged his uncle, he'd warned Jake of the evil of venomous jealousy. Said no woman was worth killing someone over. If looks alone could kill a man, Jake was certain he'd be dead right now. Thinking about that Fitzwilliam fellow turned his blood to stone. He just hoped that Leah would see it before it was too late.

Father, there's something about that man that doesn't sit right with me. If he's not the man for Leah, would You drive a wedge between them? And please do it before Leah gets hurt.

The ride had been quiet. Each of them was lost in their own thoughts. He dropped Leah off at her house, put the horses and buggy up and glanced at his pocket watch. Time to head to the designated meeting place. Michael, Jesse and Haydon wanted to hear his opinion about the man before meeting him. He'd tell them exactly what his first impression of the man had been. After all, that's what they wanted.

Chapter Twelve

Leah pressed her hand into her midsection, willing it to calm down. In twenty minutes Fitzwilliam and his sister would be arriving for dinner.

Colette and Zoé, Veronique's younger sisters who Mother hired on occasion to help Veronique out with household duties, hustled about in the kitchen.

Veronique charged into the room.

"Is everything ready, Veronique?" Leah asked for the tenth time.

"*Oui,* Leah. All is ready." Sometimes Veronique's French accent was hard to understand. Wearing her best black dress and white apron, both pressed to perfection, Veronique reminded Leah of the maids they'd had back in New York.

Leah may have been young then, but those delightful, fun-filled memories had never left her. Ballrooms filled with the elite of New York society wearing elegant gowns and exquisite jewelry and men dressed in fine suits. Footmen and maids dressed in black-and-white who scurried about waiting on their guests, making sure they had plenty to drink and finger foods to eat.

How Leah longed for those days. She most remembered

the days spent with her father. Where he proudly waltzed her around the floor and introduced her to people she'd never met before. Leah could hardly wait to get back to New York and that lifestyle. Fitzwilliam reminded her of those times, just as she had hoped he would. The man was handsome, and his manners were to her liking. Exciting tales of his travels intrigued and excited her. And the way he tended to his sister's needs, well, if that was any indication of what he would be like as a husband, then she had found herself a real gem. And that gem was due to arrive any minute now.

Leah hiked up her skirt and rushed upstairs to check herself in the mirror. The light blue gown wasn't as elegant, nor did it have the lace or ruffles or a bustle like the one she'd worn to meet him had, but, then again, she'd worn her best gown yesterday because she'd wanted to make a good first impression. Hopefully she had.

She wound her finger around the side curls she'd left down in front of her ears and replaced the few pins that had slipped.

The sound of voices downstairs caught her attention. Her family had begun to arrive. In a way she wished they weren't coming, but they wanted to meet Fitzwilliam. Leah couldn't blame them. They were concerned about her and wanted to get to know the stranger their sister might marry. She made her way downstairs, sending up a quick prayer that all would go well.

The house buzzed with people. At the bottom of the staircase, Leah stood undetected for a moment, smiling and watching the family she loved so dearly. Her brothers stood on one end of the vast living room talking while the women congregated to the other end, passing around the babies.

"Some gathering, isn't it?"

Leah turned to find Jake dressed in brown pants and cowboy boots, a tan shirt with brown buttons and a brown vest. His hair was neatly combed, his chin and upper lip were shaved clean, and the air around him bespoke of masculine, woodsy spices. Her heart waltzed knowing her best friend was there. "Hi, Jake. I'm so glad you decided to come."

"Wasn't going to. But couldn't resist that pouty look on your face."

"Hmm." She placed her fingertip on her lips. "From now on, I'll have to remember to pout every time I want something." She cut him a brief smile before turning somber. "Seriously, Jake. I really am so glad you came. I feel a lot better *and* calmer knowing you're here. Thank you."

"Hey, you two, get in here," Haydon ordered with not one ounce of authority.

"We're being summoned." Jake smiled down at her.

They walked side by side into the living room, where Jake headed to the group of men and she to the women. Leah said her hellos, ending with Selina. "I'm so glad you came. Are you doing okay? Do you need to sit?"

"All I done lately is sit even though I'm feelin' finer than frog's hair."

"Yes, but you must not overdo it, sweetheart," Michael said from behind Leah.

Leah glanced at him, then back at Selina.

"He's a bossy one, ain't he?"

"He sure is," Leah agreed, then winked at both of them. She looked around for Lottie and Joey.

Seated on the sofa were Mother, Abby, Rainee and Hannah.

Abby cooed to Joey. Seeing her nephew dressed in the blue cotton pants and shirt she'd made for him brought a pleased smile to Leah's lips.

Hannah cradled Lottie in the crook of her arms. Lottie looked like a princess in the lacy pink dress Abby had sewn for her.

Mother dangled eleven-month-old Haydon Junior in front of her and rubbed noses with him. His dark blue pants covered his tiny feet and the light blue shirt Mother had sewn fit him to perfection.

Rainee bounced Hannah's eighteen-month-old giggling Rebecca on her knees. With each bounce, the white ruffles on her red dress went up and then down, up and then down.

Contentment hovered on each glowing face. Leah couldn't wait to become a mother.

She felt a slight tug on her skirt and looked down.

Her nine-year-old niece Emily gazed up at her with those same blue eyes as Haydon's. "I think they're here, Auntie."

Seven-year-old Rosie scurried up behind Emily. "I got a peek at them, Auntie. Boy, is she ever pretty. And he's handysome just like my daddy." Rosie's fawn-colored eyes sparkled up at her.

"Handsome," Emily corrected.

"That's what I said." Rosie put her little hands on her hips and jutted out her chin.

It amazed Leah how Rosie was a little miniature Rainee and Emily a miniature Haydon.

"Never mind that now," Emily said. "Auntie, did you hear me? They are here."

"Yes. Yes, I did. Thank you." She tapped Rosie on the tip of her nose. "I'll go greet them now. You girls want to come?"

"Can we?"

"No. You may not," Rainee said.

"Sorry, girls." Leah kissed each one of their cheeks, then floated like a graceful swan to the door.

* * *

Jake slipped away from the men, went into the parlor away from the noise of the living room and stood near the open window closest to where Fitzwilliam and Elizabeth disembarked. He stood back far enough to remain undetected and watched and listened.

Jake overheard Fitzwilliam say the house wasn't very large and that they must not have as much money as he had hoped. Was the man after Leah for her money?

"Who cares about that, brother?" Elizabeth's tone came with a rebuke. "I certainly do not. And neither should you. We lack neither fortune nor consequence."

If they had more than enough, then Jake didn't understand why it mattered to the man. Unless Fitzwilliam was like those characters in that novel he'd read. Where money was all that mattered to them. That and position.

The porch steps echoed with footsteps and the front door squeaked. Leah met Fitzwilliam and Elizabeth at the top of the stairs. "Good evening, Fitzwilliam. Elizabeth. Welcome to my home."

"Thank you for inviting us." Elizabeth's kind voice drifted through the window as she gave a small curtsy.

"Good evening, Leah. You look rather lovely." The man peered at Leah and then around her. "Where are your footmen and butler? Why did they not greet us and answer the door?"

"Footmen? Butler?" Leah tilted her head and her curl slipped across her cheek. "We don't have footmen or a butler. Not out here."

"You don't? How very odd."

"I don't think it's odd at all." Jake detected a hint of insecurity and uncertainty drizzling through Leah's words.

How dare that man make her feel inferior. Jake wanted to step outside and put the pompous rogue in his place.

"Brother, you must remember we are not back in England. This is the West. They do things differently out here. And I for one love it."

No need to. Elizabeth just had. Jake wanted to hug the woman for it and for saying something he knew would put Leah at ease. It was hard to believe those two were related. Miss Barrington was nothing like her brother.

"Quite right, sister. Forgive me, Miss Leah. As my dear sister said, I am used to things done a certain way. Please bear with me as I try to adjust to your customs."

"Will Jake be here?" Elizabeth asked, peering over at the house. They had yet to make it to the porch.

It warmed Jake to know she asked about him.

"Jake." His name spoken from Fitzwilliam held only disdain. Jake wondered if Leah noticed it, too. "Sister, dear. Why would the hired help be invited to a formal dinner?"

Hired help? When was the man going to get it through his thick skull that he was a friend of the family and only working for them to help them out?

"As I said before, Mr. Barrington. Jake is *not* the hired help." Leah sounded miffed, and Jake wanted to hug her for it. It must be an evening for hugs, Jake thought, grinning to himself. "He has been kind enough to help my brothers out when they desperately needed him. He has put his own affairs aside to do so. Jake has his own farm to run. And a nice one at that." Jake heard the pride in Leah's voice. Her words meant a lot to him. They warmed his insides clear down to his toes. "Most importantly, Jake is not only my dear friend, but he's also a close friend of the whole family." She turned to Elizabeth. "To answer your question, Elizabeth. Yes, Jake is here."

"How delightful. I cannot understand why you haven't

captured him for yourself. He's such an agreeable, handsome man."

"Sister!" Fitzwilliam boomed the word.

Jake chuckled quietly and found himself flattered by Elizabeth's comment about him. There was a lot more to her than he had first guessed.

"Well, 'tis but true, brother."

"I am quite delighted Leah hasn't. For then I would not have the pleasure of making this lovely woman's acquaintance."

"Thank you, Fitzwilliam." Jake heard the pleasure and blush in Leah's voice.

The man was sure slippery. Knew just how to charm a woman. Surely Leah saw right through it, though. Didn't she?

"Shall we go inside?" Leah asked.

Fitzwilliam offered his arms to both women and disappeared toward the front door.

Jake moved away from the curtain and slipped back into the living room.

Michael stepped up to him. "I appreciate you keeping an eye on them for me."

How did Michael know what Jake had been doing? Jake opened his mouth to say he didn't do it for them but for himself, but Leah chose that moment to enter the living room on the arm of the snake.

"Excuse me." Leah's voice rang out loud and clear. She gazed up at Fitzwilliam, whose eyes widened for a brief moment, but he quickly masked his shock. The highfalutin snob probably didn't approve of Leah raising her voice.

Jake eyed Fitzwilliam up and down. The other men present all wore nice suit jackets, pressed trousers and cowboy boots. Not Fitzwilliam. How out of place the man looked in his starched white shirt with a silk neck cloth, gray waistcoat with his gold watch fob chain showing, his black tail suit, gray top hat and gray shining shoes. Like a peacock in a goat show.

Jake's eyes landed on Fitzwilliam's. Disapproval sneered through those brown eyes of his, but once again the man quickly covered up his disapproval before Leah saw it.

Leah introduced him and Elizabeth to everyone in the room.

Rainee and her daughters curtsied and the men offered Fitzwilliam their hands, but he refused them and instead bowed. Jake watched each interaction. Leah's brothers didn't look overly impressed.

After his brush with royalty, Michael walked over to Jake and leaned close. "A little on the pompous side, don't you think?" Michael spoke in a tone meant for his ears only.

Jake nearly bit his lip off to keep from laughing.

"Among other things."

"He sure doesn't like you, does he?"

"You noticed that, too, huh?"

"I'd say it's probably a badge of honor myself."

They chuckled, and Michael left to stand at Selina's side.

Minutes later, Leah's mother announced, "Dinner is ready. Shall we all head into the dining room?"

The men dispersed and gathered their wives and children.

Rainee's red-headed maid, Esther, and Ruth, the petite brunette who worked for Hannah on occasion, came to gather the babies.

"If you need anything or have any trouble, I want you to come get me immediately. And if Joey and Lottie start fussing—"

"Michael," Selina interrupted her husband. "These women will take good care of the children. Rainee wouldn't-a hired them iffen she didn't trust 'em. Lottie and Joey will be just fine. So come on. Let's go sit down and eat and enjoy ourselves. It won't be long before they'll be needin' their mama to feed them again."

Jake watched uncertainty waltz across Michael's face.

"Michael, your babies are in good hands. I promise," Rainee interjected.

"We all know how hard it is leaving them with someone for the first time." Jesse hit his younger brother's shoulder. "But they'll be fine. I promise."

"They'll be right there in the next room, Michael. You can check on them whenever you want." Haydon added his two bits, too.

"I'll go check on them for you, Uncle Michael." Thomas, Jess's oldest son, pressed his shoulders back and stood up tall. Tall for an eleven-year-old anyway.

"We will, too," Rosie and Emily both said.

"Me, too," Jess's other son, William, tossed in. It was obvious the six-year-old didn't want to be left out.

Jake smiled, taking it all in. This loving family supported one another and cared for one another. Watching them made him wish he had brothers and a family like this one. Homesickness for his own family drizzled through him. He wondered what they were doing now.

"Okay. Okay." Michael handed Joey to the maid, but his attention stayed riveted on the babies until they disappeared into the next room.

Leah hooked her hand through Mr. Barrington's. "Shall we?"

His feet remained in place. "Pardon me, Leah, but it is highly improper for us to go in before our host."

"Huh? Oh." She waved him off. "We don't care about stuff like that out here. Out here, guests go first."

His forehead wrinkled. "Highly improper. Most disagreeable to be sure."

Jake scanned the Bowens' faces, hoping the man hadn't offended them, but no one seemed to have heard him but Leah, Elizabeth and himself.

"Brother." Elizabeth laid her hand on his arm. "Please, do not make a scene," his sister whispered, her cheeks a dark shade of red.

Jake stared at Fitzwilliam with one brow hiked and sent the man a warning glare that he'd better fall in line.

Fitzwilliam sent a disapproving look back at him, one that turned into a challenging, smug look, then he looked at his sister. "You're right, Elizabeth dear. Thank you for pointing out my own faux pas."

Faux pas? What in the world was a *faux pas?*

Fitzwilliam turned his attention to Leah. "My apologies to you, Leah. My sister is correct. Again, I must beg you to bear with me. I am quite used to things done differently, but this is your home and we are your guests. Please accept my sincere apology."

Leah's smile showed her relief and her pleasure. "Of course I accept your apology. Now, let's head into dinner." She glanced at Jake. "You coming?"

"Wouldn't miss it." Jake sent his lazy grin her way, the one she enjoyed. Then it was his turn to send Fitzwilliam a smug look. Narrowed eyes stared back at him until Leah turned toward him. Immediately Fitzwilliam's glare changed to a smile. That man was phonier than a fifteen-cent piece.

"May I?" Elizabeth offered her hand to him.

Jake smiled down at the woman who was inches shorter than he. "You may." He looped her hand through his arm and followed Leah into the dining room, thinking how interesting this evening was going to be.

Leah glanced at Elizabeth's hand draped over Jake's arm and his hand patting it in a friendly gesture. Her gaze slid to Elizabeth's face. Miss Barrington stared up at Jake with stars in her eyes. Leah wished she could see Jake's eyes, but from where she stood, they were hidden from her view.

A throat cleared. Leah's gaze slid to Michael, who nodded for her to head into the dining room. Oh. She stepped inside and thanked God that her mother knew how to entertain the wealthy and elite society. From what she'd seen so far, Fitzwilliam was both. That both excited and intimidated her.

She raised her chin and proudly led Fitzwilliam into their formal dining room. Surely he couldn't find fault with anything in here. Two years before, her brothers had added on to Mother's house a large parlor, a library, an office and a formal dining room. For Christmas that year they had all gotten together and surprised Mother with a solid oak Queen Anne dining set, including chairs, table, china hutch and serving table, along with a blue, gray and maroon Victorian rug that gave a nice ambience to the room. Last year they'd bought her two silver candelabras and a crystal chandelier laden with fresh candles, which went great with Mother's bone Limoges china with delicate purple and blue roses and gold trim.

Little by little they were restoring what Mother had left behind to move here. And little by little the place was starting to look like their home back in New York. Except this home wasn't as large, and Leah had to admit, it was much homier.

Mother strolled to her place at the head of the table, and

Haydon pulled out her chair. After all the women were seated, the men took their places.

Haydon sat at the other end of the table, opposite his mother. Rainee sat on his right, then Emily, Rosie, Jess, Hannah and two of their children, Thomas and William.

Michael sat on Haydon's left, then Selina, Fitzwilliam, Leah, Jake, Elizabeth and Abby.

"Let's pray."

Leah closed her eyes and bowed her head. She felt Fitzwilliam shift next to her. She slatted one eye and peered at him. His gaze traveled around the room and landed on her. He slammed his eyes shut and quickly bowed his head.

Leah smiled. He'd been caught. She couldn't blame him for being curious. She would be, too. For a brief moment, her attention touched on Elizabeth. Unobserved, Leah watched Elizabeth as the woman stared moon-eyed at Jake until Haydon finished the prayer and everyone said amen. Uneasiness stroked Leah's soul. Later on she'd ask herself why that bothered her.

Veronique and Zoé came in and served the first course.

Fitzwilliam picked up his spoon, tipped it away from him and took a sip. "This is quite delicious. What it is it?"

"It's ärtsoppa." At his frown, she explained. "Pea soup."

"I see." He took another sip and so did she.

Leah reached for a slice of kavring—dark rye bread—dunked it into her soup and took a bite. She turned to ask Fitzwilliam if he'd like some but didn't because he looked aghast. "Something wrong?" she whispered.

He leaned toward her and spoke quietly. "Is this another American custom? Eating with your fingers?" His gentle tone belied the shock plastered on his face.

"Yes. Is something wrong with that?" Rather than take offense, Leah reminded herself that Fitzwilliam had asked her to bear with him.

"Brother, would you please pass me that delicious-looking bread?" Elizabeth made direct eye contact with Fitzwilliam, and his face unpuckered instantly.

"No. No. Not at all." He smiled, and she smiled back at him, relieved that everything was okay.

He picked up the plate and handed it to Leah. She passed it to Jake, and he handed it to Elizabeth. Their hands lingered longer than necessary. Leah frowned, then shook herself mentally, driving the image from her mind.

During the whole time they ate their meal of mashed potatoes, Swedish meatballs, cream sauce, carrots with parsley sauce, kavring bread with lingonberry jam and apple pie with sweet whipped cream on it, her brothers bombarded Fitzwilliam with a million questions. Mr. Barrington answered each one graciously. He also politely pointed out what he considered to be a faux pas in dining: using the wrong fork.

Eating with her fingers.

Not using a knife to gather her food onto her fork.

Talking when her mouth wasn't empty and so on.

She paid close attention, knowing she would need to learn those things if they were to marry. After all, she wouldn't want to embarrass him or herself.

By the time the meal ended, however, Leah was torn. She enjoyed Fitzwilliam and found him extremely handsome and loved his accent, and she was grateful he showed her the correct way to do things, but being around him and talking to him wasn't anything like being around or talking to Jake. With Jake she could just be herself. She didn't have to worry about what fork to use or anything else. Now she was worried about everything.

Leah looked over at Jake. He and Elizabeth were engrossed in a conversation. Elizabeth's eyes lit up and she held on to Jake's every word. Was it her imagination, or was Jake leaning closer to Elizabeth than necessary? Leah stared. Feelings she'd never experienced before stirred inside her. Feelings she didn't understand.

Thankful her brothers occupied Fitzwilliam, Leah continued watching Jake interact with Elizabeth. Then, as if he sensed her watching him, his ear turned her way, and then his head, until those gunmetal-gray eyes that reminded her of a beautiful gray tabby cat locked onto hers. He offered her that lazy grin of his, and her heart tripped.

Jake turned to Elizabeth, "Excuse me a moment, Elizabeth." He shifted his focus back onto Leah. "Everything okay?"

"Sure." She nodded. "How about you?"

"Yep. Having a great time."

Was he having a great time because of Elizabeth? If so, why did that bother her?

"I'm here with you and your family, Leah. How could I not have a great time?" That lazy grin of his showed up again.

The heaviness lifted from her heart. Jake always had a way of making her feel better.

Jake sat on the porch swing, rocking his heels back and forth. Leah's brothers and their families had gone home hours before, and Fitzwilliam and his sister had finally left, too. The man didn't want to until Jake had assured Fitzwilliam he, too, was leaving as soon as he finished up a few evening chores for the Bowens. Truth be known, he'd had every intention of doing that very thing until Leah had invited him to stay for some Swedish bird nest cookies and milk.

Leah stood at the door holding a tray. Jake jumped up and opened the door for her. She set the tray on the table next to the porch swing and sat down. The swing creaked when he lowered his tall frame next to her.

She handed him a saucer of cookies and a glass of milk and grabbed the same for herself. He took a guzzle of milk and a bite of a cookie, which had strawberry jam in the thumbprint center hole and walnuts surrounding it. "So, how do you think dinner went?" he asked, brushing the crumbs off his lips and trousers.

Her hand froze midair. She placed the cookie back onto her plate and looked at him. "It was okay. I know one thing, though."

"What's that?"

"I can see why Rainee despised all those rules. There's so many of them. Who cares what fork you use or if you eat with your fingers? Fingers were here before forks, anyway. Even though I know I need to learn all those things…" She shrugged and left her sentence hanging.

"What are you talking about?" Jake continued to eat his cookies and drink his milk.

"Well, during dinner Fitzwilliam pointed out things I was doing wrong."

"Doing wrong? Like what?"

"Oh, that I ate with my fingers, that I used the wrong fork, that spouses never sat next to each other at the table. That children were to be seen and not heard and never should have been allowed to sit with the adults at the dinner table. I know he's only trying to help."

Jake didn't agree, but he'd keep that thought tucked inside. Leah needed to decide for herself if that Barrington fellow was the man for her.

"He also thought it was strange that we had a French maid who served Swedish food."

Jake frowned. "What's wrong with that?"

"I don't know. I didn't ask. To tell you the truth, I didn't care why." She giggled.

"What's so funny?"

"I was thinking about the look on his face when Haydon told him we raised pigs. He couldn't believe anyone would want to be around those 'smelly, filthy animals.'" Leah imitated his British accent. "Then Rainee chimed in about how before she'd come here she was scared to death of them and now she loved them. I thought he was going to choke on his food, he gasped so hard."

Jake laughed over that one. "All joking aside, what do you think of Fitzwilliam? You think he might be the one?" He slowly raised the last bite of his cookie to his mouth and popped it in. Leah did the same. Waiting for her answer was pure torture.

"I'm not sure," she finally said several swallows later. Her answer did nothing to alleviate his fear of losing her forever.

Chapter Thirteen

Leah stretched in bed and glanced at the clock. 7:45. Last evening had been a long night. Jake hadn't left until after eleven. She yawned and wondered if he was as tired today as she was, especially because he had to get there even earlier than normal so he could finish his chores in order to go on their ride this morning. Before he'd left, Leah had invited Jake to go along with her and Fitzwilliam and his sister on a horseback ride around the ranch, and Jake had readily agreed. Had his readiness been because of Elizabeth? After all, he didn't seem to care for Fitzwilliam. He hadn't said as much, but she saw it in his eyes when he looked at the man.

She herself still wasn't sure how she felt about Fitzwilliam. He made her laugh, but not as much as Jake did, of course. Then again, he wasn't Jake, and she needed to remember that and give Fitzwilliam a chance. After all, she'd only known him all of two days.

She glanced at the clock again and sighed. 7:52. If she was going to get ready by the time they got here, she'd better get going.

Leah bathed in a tub of rose water. After drying off, she slid into a brown, split riding skirt and a tan blouse before lacing up her brown brogan boots. Today, she didn't have to worry so much about her appearance as she had the first two times she'd been around Fitzwilliam. And she knew Jake didn't care what she wore.

Down the stairs she skipped. She didn't know if her excitement stemmed from the idea of seeing Jake or because she was about to spend more time getting to know Fitzwilliam. Either way, happiness brightened her heart like the sunshine that now filled the clear blue skies outside.

"Morning, Mother," she chirped. Leah kissed her mother's soft cheek and grabbed a biscuit, two slices of bacon, and a cup of coffee and sat down at the table. "Thank you for letting me sleep." She folded the two slices of bacon between the biscuit and took a bite.

"You're welcome. I knew you didn't get to bed until late. Did you and Jake have a nice visit?"

She and Jake? Why didn't she ask about her and Fitzwilliam? "Jake and I always have fun. So—" she leaned forward with her elbows on the table "—what did you think of Fitzwilliam?"

Mother set her coffee down and looked at her. "He seems nice. Rather formal, though. It seemed like all he did was correct you. You sure you want to marry someone like that, Leah? Are you ready for a lifestyle filled with necessitates?"

The sunshine in her spirit dropped a notch. No. She wasn't sure. All she knew was that she'd craved it all her life. It would take some getting used to again, of that she was certain. Who better to help her and mentor her than the well-traveled, handsome Mr. Barrington? "Yes. I think I am."

Mother pursed her lips and nodded. "I hope so. And I hope you know what you're doing."

"I do, Mother." She scooted her chair out.

"Aren't you going to finish eating?"

"No. I'm not hungry. I'm too excited to eat." She looked around the tidy kitchen. "Where did Veronique put the lunch I asked her to pack?"

"In the pantry."

"Where is Veronique, anyway?"

"I sent her home. She needed a rest after last night."

"She sure did. Veronique and her sisters did an amazing job. They are such hardworking people. And so sweet. I really like them."

"Me, too."

"Well, I'd better run, Mother. I'm meeting Jake down at the barn at nine."

"Jake?"

"Yes, Jake. I invited him to go with us."

"I see."

Leah didn't like the look on her mother's face. "It's not like that, Mother. I invited him to come along to keep Elizabeth company."

Mother just smiled. A smile with a slight smirk to it, one Leah wasn't sure she liked. "Well, run along and have fun, dear. I'll see you later. Oh, I almost forgot. I'm dining with Charles, I mean, Mr. Barker, this evening."

Leah forced a smile. Just hearing those words made her cringe. This was so hard. She wanted her mother to be happy. She truly did. But the struggle was too much for her. She looked forward to getting to know Fitzwilliam better in hopes that he would want to marry her and take her away from this place and all its troubles as soon as possible.

"Okay." She gave her mother a quick kiss again, grabbed the food and a wrap, then flew out the door and down to the barn. "Jake." She swung the door open. Disappointment met her instead of Jake. Where was he?

She checked all the outbuildings and couldn't find him. Worry pounced on her. Surely he made it home safely last night, hadn't he? Leah saw Jess near the woodshed and hurried over to him. "Have you seen Jake?"

Jess leaned on the ax handle resting on a tree stump they used to split wood. "Good morning to you, too."

She tsked and rolled her eyes. "Morning, Jess. Now, have you seen Jake?"

Jess laughed. "Yes. He's standing right behind you."

Leah whirled. Behind her stood Jake with his arms crossed and a smile on his face. His horse grazed in a clearing in the trees.

"When did you get here?"

"Been here and back home already."

"You have?" She took in his freshly clean appearance.

"Yep."

"What time did you get here this morning?"

"Five."

"I told him he didn't have to come in at all today, but he wouldn't hear of it," Jess interrupted. "Guess he can't stay away from this place. Can't imagine why." Jess shot her a cocky grin, then looked at Jake with an approving nod.

Jake didn't seem at all fazed by Jess's comment. Perhaps he didn't get her brother's meaning. She sure did. Heat flooded her cheeks. She couldn't believe her brother would imply something like that. When was everyone going to get it through their brains she and Jake were just friends?

"Me, neither." Jake winked at her.

Jake winked at her! And right in front of her brother. What was he thinking? Her whole neck and face warmed this time. To cover her embarrassment, she turned and strode to the barn, calling over her shoulder, "You coming?"

"Yep." His chuckle followed her and continued when he caught up with her. "Why are your cheeks so red?"

She stopped and planted her hands on her hips. "Jake Lure, don't you ever do that again." Her eyes narrowed in a way she hoped looked menacing and angry.

He looked at her with all the innocence of a newborn lamb. "Do what?"

"You know very well what you did."

He raised his palms upward. "What?"

"I can't believe you winked at me. And in front of my brother, no less. What is wrong with you? You'll give him the wrong idea about us."

"He already has the wrong idea. Or...maybe not." Jake walked away, leaving her standing there with her mouth open and her eyebrows buried under her bangs.

Jake couldn't believe what he'd just said. He had to leave before he saw her reaction. He grabbed three halters and headed to the corral. Just as he reached the corral gate, Leah caught up to him. "Which horses do you want for Elizabeth and that fellow?" he asked.

"That fellow has a name. *Fitzwilliam.* And don't think you can say something like that to me and just walk off, either. What did you mean 'or maybe not'?"

He gazed down at her, chastened. "Was just teasing, Leah. You should know me by now."

"I do. But I thought you quit all that heckling stuff long ago."

"I did. That wasn't heckling. That was teasing. There's a difference." He didn't dare tell her he'd really meant it. The truth was he'd started to develop feelings for her. Real ones that went beyond friendship. And that scared the liver out of him. Especially since she was leaving. *Get a grip,*

Jake. Act normal, and she'll take a hint to drop it. "Okay. What horse you want for Fitzwilliam?"

She looked on the verge of giving him another tongue-lashing, but at the last second she sighed and the anger dropped. "Thank you for helping me get them. How about Moose for Fitzwilliam and Magpie for Elizabeth? I'm not sure how much riding either of them have done, but Moose and Magpie are the gentlest ones we have. I'll have to get out the sidesaddle for Elizabeth, though. Oh, no— It hasn't been used for so long. I hope it's clean. I didn't even think to check."

"It's clean. I rubbed all the saddles and tack down the other day."

"Oh. Okay. Thank you, Jake. I don't know what I'd do without you."

If only she meant that literally. With an inward sigh, Jake gathered two of the horses while Leah haltered Ginger, a horse named after Abby had outgrown naming the Bowens' animals.

Inside the barn, hay dust floated in the air. Horse, grain and cleaned leather smells intertwined with Leah's rose scent.

Jake went to work readying the animals. "You excited about today? Or nervous?"

Leah tugged on the cinch and glanced at him. "Both. I'm just glad you'll be there."

"Me, too." But not for the same reason she was, he was certain. He wanted to spend more time with Leah and keep an eye on that phony dandy. If only Leah had noticed all the times Fitzwilliam had shown disdain over the way she and her family did things. The man not only hid it well, but also masked it before Leah caught him. She thought he was trying to help. *Lord, open her eyes to the truth.*

"Did you enjoy your time with Elizabeth?" Leah

grabbed the saddle strings and tied the food sack onto her saddle, then gathered the reins.

"Yep. Sure did. She's lots of fun. Interesting and easy to talk to. And she isn't concerned like her brother is if something ain't done properly."

"She isn't, is she? From what little I've seen, she's the complete opposite of Fitzwilliam."

That's for sure.

They finished readying the rest of the horses in silence. When the task was complete, they led them outside, looped the reins around the hitching post in front of the barn and sat on the bench together, waiting for the Barringtons to arrive.

Minutes passed and still no sign of them. "What time is it, anyway?"

Jake pulled his pocket watch out from inside his vest and clicked it open. "Eight forty-five."

"They should be here any minute now."

"Yep."

Another moment slipped into the sunshine.

"Jake, do you miss your family?" She didn't look at him when she asked it. Her attention was riveted on her lap.

"Yep. A bunch."

"How come you left them to move out here?"

"My farm here belonged to my real Papa's parents. When my grandparents died, they left it to me. Mama wanted me to sell it. Couldn't do it. I wanted to keep Papa's legacy going. So, I moved out here."

"Was your family upset that you did?"

"Not upset so much as sad. I was, too, for a while, but it was the right thing for me."

Leah sat there in the sunshine, head down, her gaze going nowhere other than her lap. "I wonder if my family will be sad when I move, too."

He knew he would be. His heart said so. "Sure they will. Will you miss them?" *Will you miss me?* That question remained locked inside his heart.

"Sweet twinkling stars above! Are you kidding? Of course I will. I'll miss them more than a hot fire in the dead of winter."

"Then why are you leaving?"

Hooves pounding on the hard ground and rattling tack entered the silence that followed. Jake forced his attention from Leah onto the ranch yard. Annoyance slid through him at the sight. *Oh, joy.*

"Oh. They're here." Leah pushed herself off the bench and scurried toward the buggy.

"Whoa," the driver said from up front, covering Leah's boots with dust when the horses stopped.

"Hey, George. Nice to see you again." Jake smiled at the sixty-five-year-old man who helped Bartholomew, the town smithy. Jake reached up and shook hands with the man.

"Nice ta see you, too, Jake. How's that farm of yours doin'? You sure do have a nice spread." Envy filled George's eyes.

From the corner of his eyes, Jake noticed Fitzwilliam heeding George's words. "Doing good. Wheat's growing like weeds."

"Glad to hear it. If ya ever want to sell that place, you just let me know. I'd love to have it. Me and half the people in Paradise Haven, that is." He cackled.

Jake knew George could never afford it, but it made him feel good the man thought so much of his place. "Not selling, George. I'm here to stay."

"Kinda figured that."

Elizabeth stood in the buggy. Jake hurried to her side and raised his hand to help her down. "Morning, Elizabeth." The woman made a pretty picture dressed in a light blue riding jacket, dark blue skirt and dark blue riding hat. Still, Leah in her plain brown-and-tan riding outfit made an even more splendid picture. Leah could wear a rag and outshine any woman around.

"Good morning, Jake. 'Tis a pleasure to see you again." Every time Elizabeth looked at him, admiration and a look he could only describe as dreamlike softened her large brown eyes.

"What's he doing here?"

Jake glanced over at Fitzwilliam, who was once again scowling at him. He was starting to see a pattern here. This time Jake was flattered by it. It meant Fitzwilliam thought he was a threat to his and Leah's relationship. But he wasn't going to let the man think his look bothered him. So, just for the sake of doing it, Jake sent him an intimidating glare and was pleased to see the momentary shock on Fitzwilliam's face.

"I invited him." Leah tilted her chin like a proud filly. That look said Fitzwilliam had better not say another word about it.

Fitzwilliam must have gotten the hint because he said nothing more but shot Jake a look that could have melted steel. Then, like dew evaporating from the flowers, Fitzwilliam plastered on a phony smile and angled it toward Leah. "Capital idea. I'm sure Elizabeth will enjoy having him about." He sent a smug look of his own back to Jake.

Jake closed his eyes. The two of them were acting like two roosters fighting over the same prized hen. Someone had to lose, and unfortunately it would probably be Jake.

"How are you this morning, Fitzwilliam?" Leah didn't have to look up as far to see Fitzwilliam's face as she did Jake's. She loved Jake's massive height.

"Very well, thank you. And you?"

"Great." Leah looked up at the pale blue sky that smothered her face with warm kisses. "It sure is a beautiful day for a ride."

"Yes. Yes it is. Shall we get to it, then? I'm quite anxious to see how large this ranch of yours is."

What an odd thing for him to say. Why did he care how big her family's ranch was?

"Driver." Fitzwilliam turned to the man still seated on the buckboard. "You may take your leave now. But be back by here by half past six. Do not be late."

George nodded, reined the horses around, gave a quick swat on their rumps and mumbled that his name was George and something else Leah couldn't hear plainly about people who thought they were better than other folks.

"Well, let's get going. We have a long ride ahead of us." Leah looped her arm through his and started toward the horses. "You two coming?" She looked over her shoulder at Jake and Elizabeth.

"Right behind you," Jake answered as he gathered Elizabeth's hand, tucked it through his arm and sent Elizabeth a lazy smile. The same one he gave Leah. Again jealousy snaked through her. She needed to get a grip on it, and soon.

Mere feet from their horses, Fitzwilliam stopped and glanced around.

"What's wrong?" Leah followed his trail of vision.

"Where's the horse I shall be riding?"

Huh? Did the man need glasses? Right in front of him stood four horses tied to the hitching post. "Uh. Your horse, Moose, is right here." She patted the gelding's white-spotted rump.

"Moose?" One of Fitzwilliam's eyebrows rose and the corners of his mouth fell.

"Yes, Moose." At his look of confusion she went on to explain. "When my sister Abby was younger, she begged my brother Haydon to let her name the animals on the ranch. He couldn't resist her sweet, angelic face so he agreed. I'm afraid you will discover we have many animals with very strange names."

"Ah. I see."

Leah could tell by the low pucker of his mouth that he didn't, but that was okay. Everyone in her family now found the bizarre names humorous. They were just part of what made her family her family.

Fitzwilliam walked up to Moose's side and eyed the saddle. "I've never ridden a saddle like this before."

Leah's countenance fell with her shoulders. Not another faux pas. How long would it take her to learn his ways? And did she really want to? A question to definitely ask herself later.

"But—" he held up one finger "—I shall find it a challenge. And I am quite fond of a good challenge." His gaze slithered from the horse to Jake.

Leah wondered what that was all about. "Oh good. I'm so glad. What kind of saddle do you normally use?"

"One without this thing." Fitzwilliam rested his hand on the saddlehorn.

"It's called a horn," Jake said as he passed them and untied Elizabeth's horse. "This is your horse, Elizabeth. May I?"

Leah watched as Jake placed his large hands around Elizabeth's petite waist. His muscles bulged as he hoisted her effortlessly onto the saddle.

"Thank you, Jake." Did the woman have something in her eyes? She sure blinked them often enough.

Jake smiled at Elizabeth then mounted his horse. His gaze landed on Leah as she stood on the ground among the horses. Their eyes locked. Leah smiled, and so did Jake.

"I do not see another horse with a sidesaddle. Where is your horse?" Fitzwilliam's breath brushed against Leah's ear. She wanted to swish it away and tell him not to talk so close to her ear.

"Oh. This one's mine." She untethered her horse, gathered the reins near the bit and pushed backward on them. "Back, Lambie. Back." Her horse did as she asked it to.

Fitzwilliam followed Leah around the horse, examining as he went. "Where's your sidesaddle?"

"I don't use one. I tried it once and hated the thing." She slipped one rein under Lambie's neck and tossed it over the horse's mane. The other she held in her hand while she placed her boot in the stirrup and swung up and into the saddle, then gathered the other rein.

She glanced down at Fitzwilliam. His expression went from a gaping mouth and bulging eyes to narrowed eyes and a wrinkled nose. Now, what had she done wrong this time? Her sigh was barely contained. "What's wrong *now?*" She hadn't meant for the frustration to fly out of her mouth, but it had anyway.

"Brother." At the sound of Elizabeth's voice, his features softened.

"Just another American custom to get used to is all." With a shake of his head, he mounted his horse.

Leah heard him mumble about how the saddle was the most uncomfortable thing he'd ever sat on.

She wanted to laugh at the awkward picture he made up there, but instead she rode up next to him and said, "I thought you loved adventure."

Jake's chuckle nearly sent her over the edge of her own laughter, but she caught it just in time.

Fitzwilliam snapped his neck in Jake's direction. "I do." He narrowed his eyes at Jake and then turned a forced smile on her. "Make haste, my dear. And let us go."

To hide her frustration at Fitzwilliam's open display of abhorrence toward Jake, Leah nudged the heels of her brogans into her horse's side, leaving the others to trail behind her.

It was going to be a long day.

As they headed out of the ranch yard, Jake pulled alongside her and Elizabeth next to him. Fitzwilliam rode on the other side.

They rode through the sparse fir trees past several blooming bushes.

"Those are quite lovely. What are they?"

"Syringa bushes," Jake answered Elizabeth.

"They smell divine. And those? What are they, please?"

Leah followed Elizabeth's pointed finger.

"Kinnikinnick shrubs," Leah answered this time.

Leah breathed deeply the strong citrus scent of the ground-hugging kinnikinnick shrubs with their leathery leaves and pink blossoms mingled with the sweet scent of the syringa bushes.

"I must say, it's quite handsome up here." Fitzwilliam's compliment warmed Leah.

Branches resting on top of the green forest floor crunched under the horses' hooves. Over the lush green rolling hills they rode. Fields of red poppies waved in the breeze that was ever-present.

They headed toward the forest at the base of the mountain. The spiked flowers of Indian paintbrushes dotted the grassy hilltops and field edges with their bright orange and yellow.

Leah explained to Fitzwilliam what they were and about the rich volcanic ash soil and how it came to be there.

Fitzwilliam appeared to be interested, but he was more intrigued with where their property line ended.

"Fitzwilliam, what's it like in England?" Leah asked.

"It depends on what part of England one is at. Some places are quite similar to here, very lush and green. Some are not. One obvious difference is that there are no castles or brick mansions in America. Not that I've noticed in my travels, at least."

"You told me about some of your travels, but where all have you traveled to?"

"As I said when we were dining, I have journeyed the world. I've been to France, Ireland, Italy, Germany, Switzerland, Greece..." Fitzwilliam went on and on about where all he'd been, telling her nothing exciting about any of the places, even though she'd asked him questions. Instead, he talked about his many accolades, and all he'd accomplished and his great wealth.

Sorry she had asked him now, Leah kept riding, waiting and hoping the man would stop talking. She knew he was trying to impress her, but for some reason his voice was starting to grate on her nerves. Strange, Jake's voice didn't have that effect on her. She loved listening to him and could for hours and hours without wishing he'd be quiet. Even though Jake was a man of few words, he was a great conversationalist, and not chatty like Fitzwilliam. Maybe Mr. Barrington was just nervous. Tillie, a widowed woman at church, chattered like a magpie when she got nervous. At least she hoped that was the case with Fitzwilliam.

Long, grueling minutes later, Fitzwilliam finally stopped prattling and pulled a long drink from his canteen. Leah took the opportunity to focus on Jake. Leather rasped as she shifted in her saddle to talk to him, but he and Elizabeth were laughing and talking. Leah envied Elizabeth. Jake always had something interesting to say.

Hours later, they stopped and dismounted at a clear spring that ran year-round on the top of the ancient cedar grove mountain.

Jake walked up behind her. "So, how was the ride up here?"

Leah leaned back to make sure Fitzwilliam wasn't close enough to hear her. She blew out a long breath when she saw him and his sister at the base of one of the cedar trees that was at least ten feet in diameter. They gazed up at it, completely engrossed and talking animatedly about it.

Leah turned her attention back onto Jake. "The man never stopped talking. Some of what he had to say was interesting, but most of it was about himself. What do I do?"

"I'll pay more attention and try to help you out, okay?"

"You'd do that for me?"

"Yep. That's what friends are for."

"Oh, Jake, you must make haste and come see this." Elizabeth hooked her arm through Jake's and led him to the base of one of the mammoth cedar trees.

Jake glanced back over his shoulder. Even though he was being led away, Leah knew he would be there for her when she needed him to be. That's just the way it was between the two of them.

Fitzwilliam strode up to her and laced her hand through his arm. "You are quite a handsome woman, Leah. I'm blessed you have chosen to respond to my post. I think we shall get along quite famously. Oh, and as my dear sister so kindly pointed out to me, I must apologize for talking so much. A case of nerves, I fear. I will try to contain myself from here on in."

"Well, if you get to talking too much, I'll let you know, okay?"

He took a step back with shock, then chuckled. "Yes. Fair enough, madam."

"I'm hungry. How about you?"

"Yes. I am quite famished."

"Jake. Elizabeth," Leah hollered and tugged herself away from Fitzwilliam's grasp. "Time to eat." She headed to her saddle and untied the food sack. Jake grabbed the blanket he'd brought and spread it out in a clearing near the spring.

Making sure Leah and Elizabeth were seated, the men sat down. Fitzwilliam sat so close their legs touched. Uncomfortable with the intimacy of that, Leah grabbed the food out of the sack and, as indiscreetly as possible, positioned her body closer to Jake, without touching him.

Leah placed roasted pork sandwiches, cheese slices and the Swedish rye crackers she'd made onto four napkins. She pulled a butter knife from the bag and set it on the blanket, then reached inside the sack and pulled out the small jar of lingonberry jam. Grasping the preserve jar lid, Leah twisted the lid hard but it wouldn't budge.

"Allow me." Fitzwilliam took the jar from her. He strained to open it but again it wouldn't open, so he discreetly set it down on the blanket.

Jake picked it up, and opened it with one try.

Leah smiled at him. Pride oozed from her.

"Aren't you glad we loosened it for you, my man?" Fitzwilliam said.

Leah curved her face toward Jake. Making sure no one could see her, she rolled her eyes.

Jake's eyes twinkled in acknowledgment. "Couldn't of done it without you, Fitzwilliam," he said, and Leah hid her grin.

With all the food out and settled, Leah gazed at them.

"Shall we pray?" Fitzwilliam frowned, then nodded. "Jake, would you do us the honors?"

"I can." Fitzwilliam chimed in.

"Oh. Uh. How about next time since I've already asked Jake? After all, it would be rude, would it not, to tell him I've changed my mind?" she asked as if Jake wasn't right there to hear. Which he was, and she knew he'd get exactly what she was doing.

"Oh. Yes. How rude of me. Go ahead, Jake," Fitzwilliam said it as if it were his idea.

"Thank you, Fitzwilliam." A knowing look passed between Leah and Jake.

One thing was for sure—Jake could pray. His prayers were short, sweet and filled with gratitude. The man loved Jesus. Did Fitzwilliam? She had never thought to ask him about his faith. That should have been her first question. She'd been so desperate to leave she hadn't even thought about that. Shame swept over her heart. Everyone started to eat, so Leah made a mental note to ask him later.

Four gray-and-white camp robber birds swooped down from the trees, begging for food. Leah, Jake and Elizabeth tossed morsels of the crackers to the birds, but Fitzwilliam sat watching, his face scrunched. Where was the man who said he loved adventure?

All through their meal, Fitzwilliam talked nonstop. Jake tried to interrupt him several times and had even managed to get a few words in. No longer able to bear his prattling, Leah blurted, "Are you nervous again?"

Fitzwilliam stopped and looked at her, eyes blinking.

Jake chuckled.

Fitzwilliam shot a glaring look Jake's way.

"I'm sorry," Leah said. "I must be getting tired. Forgive my bluntness." Truth was, she was neither sorry nor tired. She was just ready to get this day behind her.

* * *

Jake had enjoyed every minute of their outing, mostly because Leah was getting a glimpse of the pompous Mr. Magpie. At the rate the man was going, with any luck at all Leah would send him packing before sundown. Even then, it wouldn't be soon enough for Jake.

"Hate to break up the party, but if we're going to get you home in time for George to pick you up, we'd best head on back now."

"Oh, yes," Leah chimed in. "I forgot about that. Thank you, Jake." Her gratitude sparkled through her eyes. Eyes he'd come to read very well.

Jake stood and offered her a hand.

Fitzwilliam was on his feet faster than it took to pull the trigger on a gun and snatched Leah's hand before it ever reached Jake's. Jake wanted to yank his hand off of Leah's, but he had to remember that he wasn't the one courting her. He was there to be a chaperone. A chaperone with a motive.

They rode into the yard and tethered their horses to the hitching post.

George was already there.

"I'll take care of the horses, Leah."

"Thank you." For Jake's ears only, she said, "When you get done, come up to the house, okay?"

He gave her a short nod.

Elizabeth strolled toward him, looking as fresh as when she'd first arrived. "Thank you, Jake. I don't remember when I've had a more lovely time."

"Didn't do anything."

"Yes. Yes, you did. You allowed me to be myself. I didn't have to perform." She looped her arm through his and led him away from everyone. "If my brother heard me say this, he would have a fit of apoplexy, but I cannot bear being around the people in our society any longer. Every move you make is watched and recorded. Everything is judged by who your family is and how much money they make.

"And of course you must marry someone of good breeding and of good fortune. I care not one whit about those things." She glanced around, and peace settled in the depths of her eyes. "I love it here. It's so peaceful. There's no one you have to impress. Well—" she giggled "—unless you consider my brother. But him, I can manage." She smiled.

Jake nodded, wondering why she was telling him all of this.

"Elizabeth, come. We must away," Fitzwilliam said from across the other side of the buggy.

"'Must away'? What does that mean?" Jake asked Elizabeth.

"We must take our leave now."

"Oh. Evening, George. See you made it back with plenty of time to spare." He glanced at Fitzwilliam, who once again glared at him. If Fitzwilliam knew how much Jake enjoyed annoying him, the man wouldn't glower at Jake so much. The old heckler in Jake wanted to rise up, but he worked hard at keeping that part of him controlled and refused to stoop to the slimy snake's low level.

Like the gentleman he'd been raised to be, Jake helped Elizabeth into the buggy. She pulled her skirt in and gazed at him. "My brother is inviting Leah to come to the hotel for a spot of tea tomorrow afternoon. Please say you will come as well?"

"I'll come," he agreed. Anything to keep his eye on Leah and to keep that man from bamboozling her.

Seeing Elizabeth's eyes brighten, Jake hoped she wasn't

getting the wrong idea about the two of them. There was no "them."

"Thank you. I am in need of a good friend right now."

Friend? The word yanked his smile down. Why did women only want to be his friend? What was wrong with him that they couldn't get past a friendship? Not that he was interested in anything more than friendship with Elizabeth, but she didn't know that.

"Capital. I shall see you on the morrow then. I am indeed looking forward to it."

Jake looked over at Fitzwilliam. The man beamed, but Leah didn't. Jake knew her well enough to see that she wasn't at all pleased. He hid his grin. With any luck at all, Fitzwilliam would soon be history.

Leah stood next to Jake and watched the buggy pull out of the yard. When it was safely out of earshot, she let out a long breath. "Am I ever glad that's over."

Jake chuckled.

"What? Aren't you?" Leah asked.

"Yep. Sure am."

Leah's relieved laughter surrounded him.

"Hey, I have an idea. You want to stay for supper? Don't know what we're having yet, and it'll be just me and Abby this evening, but I would love it if you would join us."

Jake wouldn't miss it. It was more time spent with Leah. Something he needed to take advantage of while he still had the chance. "Sounds good."

"Great." Her face brightened all the way. That brought a smile to Jake's heart and melted his insides like wax in the hot sun.

"I'll take care of the horses and see you inside."

"Okay. See you in a few minutes." She took a few steps and stopped. "Hurry up, okay?"

"Yep." He sure would.

Chapter Fourteen

"Abby, I'm home." Leah dashed into the house. "Abbers," she hollered as she went about checking the house for her sister only to find she was nowhere around. Knowing she would be home soon, Leah donned her apron and scrounged around for something to fix. Inside the warmer was a tin plate with a browned pie crust. She pulled it out and took a whiff. Swedish meat pie. One of her favorites. She shoved it back in the warmer and set the table with three place settings.

Heavy footsteps sounded on the porch.

Jake.

Her heart skipped a few beats. Leah ran to meet him at the door.

"Look what I found down at the barn."

Abby peeked around him and flashed a cheeky grin her way.

Leah shook her head. "You, Abbynormal, are a nut."

"I know." Her sister brushed past Jake. "Sorry I wasn't here to help with supper. I just got back from Phoebe's."

Jake stepped inside.

"How is Phoebe? And how does she like married life?"

"She loves it." Abby sighed. "I can't wait until I marry."

"You? You won't be eighteen for three more months."

"So? I still can't wait."

Leah sighed. "If I didn't want to leave here so badly, I wouldn't bother getting married."

"I don't understand you, Lee-Lee. Why do you want to move to the city when you have everything you need here? Including love." Abby yanked her head toward Jake.

"Abigail!" Leah gasped. Heat rushed up her neck and into her face. She swung her attention to Jake, standing near the table and wearing his lazy grin. He seemed nonplussed by Abby's comment. Leah spun around. "Er, um. I need to get dinner." She scurried to the stove.

Leah had no idea how to react to Abby's implication that Jake loved her. Oh sure, she knew he loved her as a friend, but the man wasn't *in* love with her. He couldn't be. She wouldn't let him. She was leaving. And love would get in the way of her plans to escape the nightmares that were almost a nightly occurrence now and to flee the place that took her father's life. She had to stay focused on her mission—to marry someone from New York. Mr. Barrington, to be precise.

Leah brought the pie to the table and set it down. "What would you like to drink, Jake? Milk? Tea? Coffee?"

"Milk sounds good. I can get it."

"No. No. You are a guest. Sit down and I'll get it." Leah returned with a pitcher of milk and some cheese.

Jake rose from the table, pulled out her chair and waited until she was seated before he sat down again.

While Abby was busy slicing the pie into five pieces, Leah filled their glasses with milk and set the pitcher on the table, then reached for Jake's plate.

"Two pieces, Abbs."

"Hungry, are we?"

"No. This is Jake's plate."

"I know that." Abby scooped out two large pieces.

With everyone's plates filled, Leah looked over at Jake. "Would you mind praying, Jake?"

"Nope. Not at all."

They bowed their heads.

"Father, thank You for this food. For the hands that prepared it. For great friends. And for Leah."

Leah frowned. Wasn't she a great friend?

"Bless this food. Amen."

"Amen." Abby picked up her fork and dived into the ground meat pie. "I'm so hungry I could eat a whole pig," she said around the food in her mouth, but Leah barely heard her. She was still wondering about Jake's prayer.

Jake took three bites and a drink of milk. "This is good. Did you make it?"

"Huh?" Leah glanced at Jake.

"I asked if you made this."

"No. Mother or Veronique did."

"Don't you cook?"

"She sure does. She's a great cook, too," Abby answered for her sister.

"That right?"

"Yes. She does all kind of things really well. She can cook, clean, sew, crochet, knit. Just about anything a person would need to make a good wife."

"Abby!" Leah nearly came out of her chair. "What is wrong with you this evening? You're making our guest uncomfortable."

Abby looked over at Jake. "He doesn't look uncomfortable to me. And he isn't a guest. He's family. Or hopefully he will be very soon."

"That's enough!" Leah shot her sister a you'd-better-stop-it-now glare before turning to face Jake. "I'm sorry,

Jake. You'll have to excuse my sister. I don't know what's come over her."

"Doesn't bother me." His shoulder hiked. He cut off a chunk of his pie and put it in his mouth as if nothing had been said.

Leah didn't know what to think or say. Nothing he said or did tonight made any sense.

"So, how did your day go with Fitzwilliam?" Without waiting for Leah's answer, Abby asked, "You aren't serious about that man, are you, Lee-Lee?" Abby wrinkled her nose in disgust before taking a bite of cheese.

"I'm not serious about anyone, Abbs. I'm just trying to get to know Fitzwilliam to see if we can make a marriage work. That's all."

"Whatever you say, Lee-Lee." Abby turned to Jake. "What do you think of Elizabeth, Jake? She doesn't seem anything like her brother. She's nice."

"Fitzwilliam is nice," Leah jumped in quickly, but her voice didn't sound too convincing even to her own ears.

"I was asking Jake, Leah."

"She's nice enough. Must admit. She isn't anything like I thought she'd be."

"What do you mean?" Leah tilted her head in Jake's direction.

"She hates the city. Wants to be a farmer's wife. To cook and clean and raise animals."

"Probably yours, no doubt," Abby mumbled, but Leah heard her nonetheless and was certain Jake had, too.

"Does she know how hard farm life can be?" Leah picked up her glass and took a drink of her milk.

"Don't know. She didn't say. Only said she loved it out here and preferred it over her lifestyle."

Leah pondered Jake's words. Surely she must attend balls and dinner parties all the time. The woman got to travel all over the world to exotic places meeting people from all sorts of cultures. Something Leah only dreamed about doing. How could Elizabeth prefer this lifestyle to her perfect one?

"There's more to life than parties and balls, Lee-Lee." Abby's voice popped Leah's thoughts.

"I know that, Abbs." She allowed her hot annoyance to drift through her voice. "But you've never been to them. You don't know how fun they are. Or how special it was to have Father whirl you around the dance floor." Leah closed her eyes. Her heart ached afresh at the memory of her father dancing with her.

The backs of her eyes stung.

Unable to keep the tears from coming, she scraped her chair back and bolted out of the house. Dodging willow bushes, syringa shrubs, cottonwood trees and pines, she fled deep into the forest. She came upon a felled log amid a batch of ferns, where she plopped down, placed her face in her hands and sobbed.

Minutes later, the log moved, and without looking, she knew it was Jake.

Jake sat on the log and slipped his arm around Leah. "Come here."

Tear-soaked eyes gazed up at him. Seeing her like this, so sad and so shaken, broke his heart. He wished he could take her pain onto himself. Gently, he pressed her head into his chest. "It's okay."

"It hurts so badly. I miss him so much."

"I know. I still miss my papa, too."

"You—you do?" She pulled back, her eyes questioning him.

"Yep."

"But you said..."

"Know what I said about the papa I have now, and I meant it. It did get easier seeing my mama with him, but I never said I didn't miss my flesh-and-blood papa."

"What do you miss about him?" Tears shimmered on her lashes.

Jake brushed them away with his thumb and wiped them on his pant leg. "Everything."

"Everything?"

"Yep. When he first died, I thought the pain would never end. Felt about as alone and lost as a wayward sheep." He tucked his finger under her chin. "Leah, we all need someone who understands how we feel. Someone that'll listen to us. You know I'm here for you, right? That I understand what you're going through."

Leah's chest heaved in choppy breaths and the floodwaters came gushing out again.

He pushed himself off the log and pulled her into his arms. His heart wept with her.

"It hurts so badly." She'd already said that.

"I know."

"I miss him." She'd already said that, too. But it was okay. All of it.

"I know. Believe me, I know."

Moments later her tears let up again and, with a sigh, she backed out of the circle of his arms. They now felt empty without her. Alone even. He wanted to pull her back to him, but didn't. "Tell me. What are some of the things you miss about your father?"

"Father always made me laugh. I miss that. I miss our talks. I miss how he used to tuck me into bed every night and pray with me. He made me feel so special. Treasured, even. Like a real princess. That's what he used to call me, you know."

"That's important to you? Feeling like a princess?"

"Yes."

"Why?"

Her shrug was a lazy, off-handed one. "Mostly because it reminds me of my father. It makes me feel like he's still here with me. And I need that. Especially when—" Suddenly she sat straight up and shook her head. "Oh. Um. Listen. I'd better get back to the house. Abby's probably worried sick about me." She scurried ahead of him through the trees, her feet and skirt whooshing and crackling as she did.

"Leah, wait!" It took ten steps before Jake caught up to her and stopped her, turning her toward him. "What were you going to say, Leah?"

"I don't want to talk about it anymore, okay? It hurts too badly." That was the third time she'd said that.

The loss of a parent was something one didn't get over easily, but Leah should have healed far more than this by now. It had been a long time. Many, many years. Something was wrong with this whole situation. Jake really wanted to know what was tormenting her. To press the issue. But her pleading, bloodshot eyes kept him from probing further. He frowned, keeping his questions inside with a hard fist of control. "Can I pray with you?"

Leah nodded. "I'd like that."

Jake gathered her hands in his and bowed his head. "Father, You know how much Leah misses her father. Comfort her as only You can. Wrap Your arms around her. Let her know that while she may no longer have her earthly father here with her, that, You, her Heavenly Father, will always be with her, that You never leave her nor forsake her. Help her to find comfort in those words for they're Your words. And Father, this thing that is hurting Leah so deeply, touch that area and heal it as only You can. Surround her with Your love and Your grace. In Jesus's name. Amen." Jake raised his head and his gaze touched Leah's.

"Thank you, Jake." She sniffed, never removing her eyes from his. Instead they searched his, probing deeper and deeper. For what, he didn't know, but he allowed her to keep prying until she found whatever it was she was searching for. Her blue eyes went from hurt to grateful then to… To what? He didn't know. He only knew they held a soft warmth he'd never seen before.

Something in that moment changed in her. He wanted to ask what it was, but deep in his gut, he knew now was not the time. Now was the time for him to be still and let her have her way. Her hands remained buried in his, and he didn't release them because something was going on between them. Something spiritual. As if their souls were connecting on a deeper level.

"Leah!" The desperation in Abby's voice caused them both to blink.

Leah slipped her hands out of his, but her eyes kept meeting his until Abby arrived. "We're over here!"

In his heart, he knew the connection that had begun hadn't been severed, just put on hold.

"Finally. Where'd you go? I was so worried about you, Lee-Lee." Abby threw her arms around Leah. "Are you okay?"

"Yes, Abbs. Everything is fine." Her gaze touched on his again and the connection was back. When the time was right, he'd find out just what had happened.

Abby looked at him, then at Leah. "Good. Now that I know you're okay, I'm going back to the house and finish eating." She glanced between them again and scuttled away.

Bless her heart.

One more glance into each other's eyes, and they

headed back to the house in silence, but it wasn't uncomfortable. Their minds were intertwined with thoughts and words that had yet to be spoken.

Dear Mr. Darcy
Something happened in the forest today. My feelings for Jake have changed. I'm not sure just how, but during the whole time we were talking, when he prayed for me, and even afterward, something happened between us. I feel somehow closer to him. Which scares me. I don't want to care about Jake in that way. It will ruin everything. All my plans. I have to go now. I need to pray about this. I will talk to you later, Mr. Darcy.

Leah shut her diary and locked it in her nightstand. She lay down with her hand above her head and closed her eyes, letting her heart say the prayer she didn't have the words to utter.

When she woke up the next morning, she rushed through her toiletries and hurried into the kitchen. "Morning, Mother." Leah kissed her cheek. "Morning, Abbs."

"Good morning," they both replied.

"What's for breakfast? I'm starving."

"Äggröra and bacon."

"Scrambled eggs sound good." Leah fixed her plate, grabbed a cup of coffee and sat down at the table.

Leah dived into her food. Not having eaten much last night, she was famished this morning.

"Leah, I hope you don't mind, but there's been a change of plans today."

"What do you mean, Mother?"

"Well, Charles and I ran into the Barringtons at the

hotel last night, and we invited them to sit with us. Mr. Barrington seems like a nice man. A bit too talkative for me, but he's very informative and highly intelligent. And he is an extremely savvy businessman. Anyway, Charles invited them to a gathering he's having at his home this evening."

Leah noticed Mother didn't bother to correct calling Mr. Barker by his first name this time. That meant she really was serious. Leah sent up a quick prayer about moving away from there faster and for the strength she needed to be tolerant for her mother's sake. "Oh? What kind of gathering?"

"Well, it's more than a gathering, really. A friend of Charles is passing through Paradise Haven and is staying at Charles's hotel. Mr. Martonella and his company have agreed to perform for Charles. Charles thought your friends might enjoy it, so he invited them along with several other prominent business acquaintances. Mr. Barrington said you had plans to meet for tea." Mother reached into her apron pocket and pulled out a post, then handed it to Leah. "So he asked me to give this to you."

Leah took the envelope and gazed at the waxed seal with the embossed letter *B.* She slid her thumb under the red circle and opened the letter.

My dearest Leah,

I hope you do not mind, but there has been a change in plans. Rather than tea this afternoon, Mr. Barker has been kind enough to invite us to his home this evening to attend an opera. I have taken the liberty of accepting his invitation on your behalf. Also, Elizabeth has requested that you ask your friend Mr. Lure to join us. If this is not agreeable to ei-

ther one of you, please send a post straightaway to let us know.
With fond regards,
Fitzwilliam Barrington

Leah folded the letter. She'd never been to an opera before. What did one even wear to such a thing? She'd already worn the two new bustle gowns she'd made, and there was no time to make a third.

"Well, what do you think, dear?"

Leah looked over at her mother. "I'm not sure. I'll talk to Jake and see what he thinks."

"Why do you care what Jake thinks?" Abby joined in the conversation, although her question was pointed.

"Because, Abbs. He was invited, too."

"So? What's that got to do with you? Elizabeth invited him."

Leah sighed. "I just meant I need to ask him if he wants to go. If not, then I need to send word to Elizabeth."

"Oh." Abby tossed the last bite of her toast with apple butter on it into her mouth. "If you say so." A twinkle sparked through her eyes.

The comments Abby had made the night before about Leah and Jake flittered through her mind again. Abby was up to something where she and Jake were concerned.

Well, Leah wasn't going to take the bait dangled in front of her. "Mother, I'll go see if Jake wants to accept Elizabeth's invitation. I'll be right back."

"Finish your breakfast first. Then go." Mother pointed to her loaded plate.

Paying no attention to her manners, Leah downed her food in record time and placed her dishes in the sink.

"Tell Jake hi for me. And give him a kiss for me, too. Or better yet, make it from you." Abby winked at her.

Leah sent Abby a warning look, glanced at her mother with a what-can-I-say shrug and made a dash for the door. When she stepped onto the porch, she heard her mother ask Abby, "What was that all about?"

Despite her wanting to know what Abby's response was, Leah didn't wait to hear it. She shuddered just thinking about what it would be.

Down at the barn, Leah searched for Jake, but he wasn't there. She checked the corrals, the chicken coop and the hog barn, but she couldn't find him at any of those places, either. She glanced over at Michael's house, wondering if he went there. Leah rushed over and knocked lightly on the door.

Michael stepped into view holding one of the twins. "Morning, Leah. Come on in."

"Good morning, Michael." She stepped inside and froze. By the fireplace stood Jake, holding the other twin. The baby looked tiny against Jake's giant form. What an image he made. One that made her heart flip.

Jake looked over at her and smiled. "Morning."

"Oh. Um. Good morning to you, too." The words fumbled from her mouth. Embarrassed by her stammering, Leah looked around for her sister-in-law. "Where's Selina?"

"Taking a nice, hot bath."

"Oh." Why had she come again? Her brain was no longer filling her in on such important details.

Michael raised his eyebrows with concern. "Did you need something?"

"What? Oh. Yes. I was looking for Jake, actually."

"Well, looks like you found him."

Leah took the baby from Michael. "How's Auntie's

Joey doing?" she cooed and played with his chin until he smiled. She tore her attention from the baby. "When you get a minute, Jake, I need to talk to you."

"We can talk now. I was just getting ready to leave."

"You can't leave yet," Michael blurted.

"Why not?" she asked.

"Because. Who's going to help me with the twins? I can't take care of them myself." Her brother looked absolutely horrified.

Leah cleared her throat to stifle her laugh. "You don't need any help, Michael. Every time I've been over here, you've done just fine with them."

"Yes, but Selina wasn't in the tub then. And you, Mother or Abby was here. I've never been alone with them before."

"Well, it's time you start." She handed Joey back to him. "They won't bite. I promise. Come on, Jake."

Jake looked at her then at Michael, who looked as lost as a puppy in the woods.

"Come on, sis. Don't leave me like this. Please."

She couldn't stand seeing the look of desperation on Michael's face or indecision on Jake's, so she quit toying with them. "Okay. Fine. You win. What I have to ask Jake can wait."

She walked over to Jake. "May I?" She motioned toward Lottie. In a heartbeat, Jake handed her to Leah as if she were a hot coal.

Leah chuckled. Men. They wanted children but couldn't handle them for more than five minutes.

Minutes ticked by. Leah changed both the baby's diapers, put them in a pail inside the laundry room and went back into the living room. When her bustling was finished, Selina was already out and in the rocker with a baby in each arm. Her face glowed. "Mornin'."

"Good morning to you, too. How are you feeling today?"

"Happier than a squirrel with a sack full of hickory nuts."

Leah laughed. Her sister-in-law came up with the funniest sayings.

"Well, I'd better run along." Jake moved to the door. "Still have a couple of things to do before heading home to get ready for this afternoon."

Leah's attention went from Selina to Jake.

"Whatcha doin' this afternoon?" Selina set the rocking chair in motion.

"Going to some tea party." Jake rolled his eyes and shook his head.

"You? Going to a tea party? This I've got to see." Michael chortled.

"Can't picture you at no tea party neither, Jake."

"Yeah, well, somehow I got roped into one."

"Well, you don't have to go," Leah interjected with just a touch of annoyance.

"There's where you're wrong." He lowered his gaze at her, and it held no levity. "I do."

"Why? Nobody's making you go. If you don't want to, don't."

"I have my reasons for going." He took a quick glance at Michael and then back at her.

Leah frowned. What was that all about? "Well, the plans have changed, anyway."

"Oh, yeah?"

"Don't look so relieved, Jake. If you didn't like the idea of a tea party, you're not going to like this one, either."

Chapter Fifteen

Dread pitted into Jake. He couldn't imagine anything worse than a tea party with a pious, arrogant man who was out to steal his best friend. "You can tell me on the way to the barn."

They said their goodbyes and headed out the door and through the pine trees. *Yak yak yak yak*—the fast sound of a magpie greeted them along with an earthy scent of foliage and forest floor.

"So what's this change of plans?" Jake glanced down at her as he kept walking.

A twig snapped under Leah's foot. Her ankle twisted, and she lost her balance. Jake's hand shot out and steadied her. "You okay?"

"Fine. Thanks."

He gave a quick nod and a short frown.

"At breakfast this morning, Mother gave me a note from Fitzwilliam." Hopefully the note said he was leaving town. A man could wish, anyway.

"Mr. Barker's friend is in town with his opera company. They're going to perform for a group of Mr. Barker's friends and business acquaintances this evening. They invited the Barringtons and us to come."

"Us?" Jake throat constricted. A group of people? In a crowded room? His heart raced and his palms started to sweat just thinking about it.

"Jake?" Leah's hand rested on his arm. "You okay?"

He stopped and tried to force a smile on his face, to act like everything was fine, but it wasn't. He struggled to breathe.

"Take a deep breath, Jake." Her eyes locked on his, and he searched them for more direction.

"Come on, Jake. Take in a deep breath. You can do it," she coaxed.

He continued to follow her instructions until his breathing returned to normal. Because of Leah, this time it hadn't taken long.

"Thank you, Leah."

"You're welcome. I'm just glad you told me what happens to you. If you hadn't, I wouldn't have known what was wrong or how to help you."

He nodded, grateful that he had shared his embarrassing problem with her. This was the first time the panic attack lasted only a minute or so. They resumed walking toward the ranch yard.

"I'll send word that you won't be going."

This time he grasped her arm and stopped her. "Didn't say I wasn't going."

"But how can you?"

"Is it indoors or outdoors?"

"Um. I don't know. Mother might. Let's go ask her."

"No. You ask her. I'll be down at the barn. Have to finish mucking stalls. Then I'll be done."

"I don't understand why my brothers give you such dirty jobs. Why don't they have the hired hands do it?"

"They didn't give them to me. I offered."

"Why would you do that?"

"Why not? I'm a farmer, remember? Not some highfalutin man who thinks he's too good to scoop manure. It's what I do. It's how I make my living."

"I didn't mean to offend you, Jake. I know you're not like Mr. Barrington."

"How'd you know I was talking about him?"

"Because I've noticed you don't like him."

"That obvious, huh?"

"Yes, it is. And it's okay. You don't have to like him. I'm not sure I do, either."

"Does this mean you're not gonna marry him?" Hope pounced on him.

"I didn't say that."

"I'm confused."

Leah stopped and turned those beautiful sky-blue eyes up at him. "I'm not marrying for love. I'm marrying so I can leave."

"You'd really marry someone you didn't like? Or love?"

"Why's that so strange to you? It happens all the time. Besides, you asked me to marry you, and you don't love me."

"True. But you and I are good friends. We get along great."

"It still would have been a marriage of convenience."

"Well, yes. So, what's that got to do with what we're talking about?"

"I'm just saying that not everyone is lucky enough to find love. Some people have to marry for convenience's sake."

"True again. But you ought to at least like the person you're thinking about marrying. If you're not sure you even like the fellow, why would you consider marrying him, even out of convenience?"

"Because staying here bothers me more than marrying a man like Fitzwilliam does."

"You really hate this place that much that you would marry a man you didn't like just to leave here?"

"I didn't say I didn't like him. I said I'm not sure how I feel about him. Besides, there's more to it than that, Jake."

"Like what?"

"Like… I don't want to talk about this or Fitzwilliam anymore. Let's get back to what we were originally talking about."

He let out a frustrated breath. "You always do that."

"Do what?"

"Leave or change the subject when it gets too much for you."

"No, I don't."

"Yes, you do."

"Well, even if I do, so what?"

"Look, Leah. I don't want to argue with you, okay? I need to get busy. So if you would go ask your mother, I would appreciate it." He turned on his heel. "I'll see you later."

"Now who's walking away?" Her question bounced off his back.

He didn't answer but kept on walking. Jake couldn't believe she was willing to marry someone just to get away from there.

At the barn, he slid the double doors open and stepped inside. Soiled straw scent lingered in the air. He snatched a hay fork off the nail, picked up the wheelbarrow handles and headed to the first stall. While he cleaned, he thought about Leah and her comment about mucking. That comment only served to remind him that she was out of his league. He had thought maybe they would have a chance, especially after last night, but now he knew there would never be a chance for him. But that wouldn't stop him from doing whatever it took to keep her from marrying Fitzwilliam. His gut had warned him time and again about the man.

Jake tossed the last of the soiled straw into the wheelbarrow, grabbed the handles and wheeled it out of the stall.

"There you are."

He set the wheelbarrow down and faced Leah.

"Mother said Mr. Barker invited about forty people. He's going to have it at his house in the ballroom. I asked if she'd seen the room before and she said she had. I asked about how big it was, if it had doors. She said it was huge and that there were several double glass doors. She wanted to know why I asked, but I didn't tell her."

"Thanks. I appreciate that."

"Do you think you'll be all right in there?"

"Should be fine long as I sit next to the double doors." Jake hated he even had to think this way. That he couldn't defeat this demon that plagued him whenever he was stuck in large crowds.

"Okay, then. I'll make sure you do."

"Look, Leah. I don't want you saying anything to anyone. It's embarrassing enough that you know."

"I won't tell anyone. I'll figure out some way to work it out. Trust me, okay?"

He set his jaw. "Thought you didn't want me to go."

Leah tilted her head. A lone, curly strand slid across her cheek.

Without thinking, he reached for it and tucked it behind her ear. His fingers trailed along her jawbone as he retracted his hand.

Questions lingered across her face and eyes. Questions he had no answers to. Like why he'd allowed his hand to follow the soft contour of her jaw. Why he enjoyed the feel of her soft skin. Or why he had the urge to take her in his arms and taste her sweet lips. *What are you doing? Those kinds of thoughts can only lead to heartbreak.*

He let his hand fall to his side. "Sorry." It was all he could manage before he clutched the handles on the wheelbarrow and headed out the barn and into the dumping area.

"Jake." Leah stood behind him as he raised the wheelbarrow handles and let the soiled straw fall into the pit. "What made you think I didn't want you to go?"

Relieved she hadn't mentioned the incident in the barn, he set the wheelbarrow down and faced her. "Earlier you said I didn't have to go. That nobody was making me. I figured that meant you didn't want me to."

"Sweet twinkling stars above, Jake. That's not it." She shook her head and the soft curls he'd touched moments ago kissed her cheeks, something he wished he could do. This time, however, he roped in his urges before he did something foolish again. "You sounded like someone was making you go. I didn't want you to think you had to for my sake. I know you said you'd help me, but you really don't have to do this if you don't want to."

"Do you want me to go?" His eyes touched on hers.

She lowered her lashes. "Yes. I really don't want to go if you're not there."

"Why, Leah?"

She looked up at him. "What do you mean, 'why'?"

"Why is it so important for you to have me there? To help you? Is that your only reason?"

"I don't know what you're asking me, Jake." Wide innocent eyes frowned at him.

"Never mind." He had hoped for something more. What, he wasn't sure, but something that said he mattered. That their friendship mattered. Anything.

Who was he kidding?

He wanted to hear she couldn't live without him. But that wasn't going to happen. At least not the way he wanted it to. He shoved his hands through his thick hair.

Why did he keep torturing himself with something that was never going to be?

Even if he was in love with her, he didn't think that would be enough to sway her to stay. Good thing his heart wasn't fully engaged. His feelings for her were growing, but he wasn't in love with her. Or was he? He didn't know. He only knew this whole thing about her leaving battered his heart with bruises he thought would never heal. "I'll go."

Leah blinked. "What?"

"I'll go, Leah. I'll be there to help you. But this is the last time."

"What do you mean 'this is the last time'?"

"I mean, you'll probably be getting married soon. It's best I back out of the picture after this. You don't need me hanging around while some man is trying to court you."

"Court me? Fitzwilliam and I haven't even talked about that."

"Isn't that why he's here? To court you? To see if there can be a future between you two?"

"Well, um, yes. But nothing's been said yet."

"Just the same. After today, I won't be going with you anymore."

"What about Elizabeth?"

"What about her?"

"She needs an escort." He could tell by the look on her face that she was grasping at anything to keep him with her.

"This whole thing was your idea, Leah. Not mine."

"Yes, but you like her, don't you?"

"She's nice enough. What's that got to do with anything?"

"Jake." Leah laid her hand on his arm. "Please. Please don't leave me alone with him. I need you there."

"Why?"

"Because I feel protected when you're there."

"Do you need protecting?"

She shrugged. "I don't know why it's important to me. But it is. Please. Please say you'll go with me."

Her pleading eyes stared up at him. How could he refuse his best friend?

Friend.

He was growing to hate that word.

Leah glanced at the clock. Time to head downstairs. She took one last look in the full-length mirror. Today, she didn't take as much care with her attire. She put on a modest blue silk dress that hung around her shoulders. Her hair was rolled at the sides and gathered into a spun bun at the back of her head. No combs or flowers adorned it. Her joy at going this evening had diminished with her talk with Jake.

When he'd told her that she was on her own after this evening, a million needles pricked her heart. She didn't want to think about what the pain in her heart and soul meant. She had an idea, but admitting it, she would never allow.

"Lord, have mercy on me" was all she could manage before descending the stairs.

"You look nice, Lee-Lee."

"Thanks, Abbs. So do you." Her voice was monotone.

"What's wrong?"

"Nothing."

"Leah, something's wrong. I can tell."

"You girls ready to go?" Mother stepped into the room.

"Yes, Mother." Leah forced herself to respond in a normal tone. She didn't want any more questions.

They grabbed their wraps and headed to the landau carriage Mr. Barker had sent. The driver opened the doors and helped them inside. Leah kept to herself and her gray thoughts. Even Abby gave up trying to talk with her, and Leah couldn't blame her sister. Her heart just wasn't in this.

The landau rolled to a stop in front of Mr. Barker's pristine white, three-story mansion with four white pillars in front. Bay windows sparkled on the right and left sides of the house. White and lavender blooming syringa bushes filled the air with their sweetness. Manicured shrubs formed a barrier wall to the backyard. Wild pink roses climbed the outside walls. Their scent mingled with the syringa bushes.

Even though Mr. Barker's house was enormous, it was only half the size of the mansion she'd been born in back in New York, and she wondered for a second what Fitzwilliam would think of it.

The driver helped them out and a footman escorted them into the house.

Inside, they were led to a large oval room with light brown and tan floors so shiny they looked like glass sparkling in the sunlight. Gold and white chandeliers dangled from the ceiling. Ceiling to floor, reddish-brown brocade curtains with gold scarf swags and tassels hung over the three evenly spaced windows at the end of the room. Fine gold and glass sconces centered each one.

At the front of the room a Bösendorfer grand piano stood on the right. Rows of white Chippendale chairs with padded seats covered in the same material as the curtains were centered in the room, leaving plenty of space on each side, down the middle, and even more space behind. Large white pillars like the ones outside Mr. Barker's house surrounded two sizable glass French doors on each side of the chairs.

Leah's chest expanded with relief, knowing Jake would be fine in this room. It certainly was large enough not to feel closed in. Even better, the doors were open and there were several ways of escape.

She glanced around to see if Jake had arrived yet, but she didn't see him. She did spot Mr. Barker, however, amid a group of elegant men and women. The men wore an array of gray, blue and black frock coats with matching trousers, white starched shirts and bow ties. The women wore silk and tulle dresses, satin and lace, faille and lace, and even crepe de chine and velvet, and all were bustle gowns with bows and flowers made from satin ribbons. Exquisite diamonds, rubies and sapphires inlaid in gold adorned their necks and gloved wrists.

Her heart skipped a happy beat. This was the beautiful sort of people she would be associating with once she moved to New York.

"I'll see you two later." Abby let go of her and headed over to Phoebe.

Mother pulled Leah's arm through hers. "Let's go say hello, shall we?"

Leah didn't have a chance to refuse her mother's request because she tugged her along, and the two of them glided toward the group.

When they arrived at the small party of guests, Mr. Barker's attention drifted to Mother's and stopped. His eyes brightened and a huge smile split across his face. "Hello, my dear." He looped Mother's gloved hand through the crook of his arm. "Gentlemen, may I present to you my special lady friend, Katherine Bowen."

They all greeted her with cordial smiles.

"And this lovely young woman is her daughter Leah." Mr. Barker gently pulled Leah into the fold.

Men she'd never seen before greeted her warmly, staring at her approvingly even, but the women only nodded and raked their eyes up and down the length of her.

Seeing their looks of disapproval, heat rushed into her cheeks. At that moment, she wanted to crawl under the floor and pull it over her.

She glanced at her mother to see if she noticed, but Mother only had eyes for Mr. Barker.

Whispers behind gloved hands about her attire reached her ears. How could they be so cruel?

If only she'd taken more time with her appearance and worn her bustle gown and the jewels Father had given her. Elaborate jewels that had belonged to Father's mother. If she had, they would not be looking down their noses at her.

"Miss Bowen." Fitzwilliam's icy tone from beside her caused her gaze to jump to him. No smile or any warmth of feeling ingrained his features. And he'd called her *Miss Bowen* instead of *Leah.* That couldn't be good. What gross faux pas had she committed this time?

His gaze discreetly ran down the length of her and a scowl marred his face. Without even excusing them from the crowd, he cupped her elbow and led her away from the small gathering of people near the French doors.

"Leah, my dear, this is a formal affair with men and women of great prominence. Why did you not dress appropriately for it? How could you embarrass me this way?"

Her heart sank. She had a lot to learn. The only problem was, would she ever? "I'm sorry, Mr. Barrington. I didn't know it was going to be this elaborate or I would have taken more care in dressing."

"Did you not know that this was to be an operetta?"

"Well, um, yes. But…" She shrugged.

"But what?"

"Well, I, um… I've never been to one before."

His line of vision trailed to Abby, then to her mother. "Your mother and your sister are appropriately dressed." One brow hiked.

He didn't believe her.

He was right not to. She'd been so hurt by what had transpired between her and Jake that she didn't care. Nothing mattered if Jake wasn't in her life. She loved him.

Leah froze, and the blood drained from her face. It was as she feared. *Dear God, no. I can't love Jake.*

Jake's handsome face, lazy smile and soft tabby-gray eyes invaded her mind. As did thoughts about how he accepted her just the way she was, how he didn't even try to change her, how he made her laugh, made her feel special. Her knees went weak at the thought and very nearly pitched her to the floor.

"Evening, Leah." Leah stiffened at the sound of Jake's voice.

Drawing in a deep breath, she turned to face him and forced a smile onto her face, forced herself to act as if everything were normal. "Evening, Jake."

Jake's smile slipped, replaced by a concerned frown.

She hadn't fooled him at all. He knew her well. Well enough to know something wasn't right. His eyes never left her face. Seeing him through different eyes, she tried not to notice how handsome he really was inside and out.

Or how his broad shoulders, powerfully built arms and wide chest filled out the light blue shirt he wore under a dark blue vest.

Or how strong his muscular legs looked in the new dark blue pants that covered them.

Leah yanked her attention off of him. Those were things an unmarried woman should not be noticing.

She peeked a glance at Fitzwilliam.

His arms were behind his back and he stared at her with brown eyes of steel.

Her heart didn't care, but her mind did. He was still her way of escape from this place and the nightmares. She couldn't risk his disapproval. But what about Jake? What about her newly discovered love for him? Confusion infused itself into her heart and soul. Desperately she tried to think of a way to stay, to rid herself of the nightmares, of her strong hatred for the place that had ripped her father from her. Every coping strategy she'd tried since his death had failed. Nothing had worked. No. She had no choice. She had to go.

"Leah, can we talk?" Jake said.

"Excuse me, sir." Fitzwilliam pulled himself up straighter, and his tone practically dripped with ice. "But Leah is with me. There are some people I want her to meet. So if you will excuse us."

Before Leah had a chance to protest, she found herself all but being dragged toward the same small group of people who'd made her uncomfortable earlier.

Leah glanced over her shoulder. Jake started to follow her, but Elizabeth stepped in front of him. He peered around Miss Barrington. That was all Leah noticed because Fitzwilliam's yank on her arm forced her to look forward or stumble.

They reached the small group, who were engaged in a deep conversation of some sort. Mother and Mr. Barker were no longer standing among them. They were talking to another small group of people on the other side of the room.

Fitzwilliam forgot all about introducing her and joined

in with the men's conversation. In the midst of the small crowd, Leah suddenly felt alone.

One of the women looked at Leah. "Mr. Barrington says your family came from New York City and that your father was a prominent businessman there. What do you think about the wholesale corruption? Do you think William Tweed should have been appointed commissioner of public works?"

Leah had no clue what the middle-aged woman with brown hair, green eyes and a long pointed nose was talking about. "I, um. We moved out here years ago, so I'm afraid I don't know what that is."

"You don't?" The woman ran her disgust-filled eyes up and down Leah's face. "That man purchases things for a pittance and sells it at an outrageous amount, and the Tammany society supports him. Why, that political machine runs all of New York City."

Tammany society? Running New York City. She didn't remember Father ever talking about anything like that.

"My husband thinks it's wonderful."

"He does?" asked a woman with shock on her face. "It's pretty corrupt if you ask me."

"What do you think, Leah? Do you think it's right to do that?"

Leah couldn't believe these women were talking politics. It was something she knew nothing about. Nor did she care to. "Oh. I, um…" She didn't know how to answer that. If she told them the way she really felt, which was, no, she didn't think it was right, then the lady whose husband thought it was a great idea would sneer at her. And if she said yes, it would go against what she believed—that the thing sounded like nothing but greediness to her—then the others women would scoff at her.

"Well, surely even way out here you've heard about

the high assessment land value in Manhattan over the past twenty-seven years?" Another beautiful woman with dark black hair and striking blue eyes close to Leah's age joined in the conversation.

"No, I haven't." Heat filled Leah's cheeks at the disapproving looks that woman sent her way. Suddenly, the woman no longer seemed beautiful to Leah. In fact, she and the rest of the ladies who were sending her their scowls appeared ugly to her. Amazing how a person could look lovely on the outside until you got to know them on the inside. The ugliness in them caused even their pretty outsides to appear ugly.

"Does your family invest in stocks?"

How was she supposed to know if they did? Her brothers didn't discuss finances with her. They believed women shouldn't have to carry that burden—that it was a man's burden alone to bear. Her father had felt the same way. She hiked a shoulder in response to her question.

"What do you think about *Le nozze di Figaro?*" the same woman asked.

"I don't know what that is." Leah's eyes dropped in shame.

"Don't you know we've come tonight to hear selections from it?" Ugly shrouded this beautiful woman even more so now.

Knowing she would feel even stupider, she said, "Selections?"

"Yes, selections. I saw the entire opera at la Monnaie when we went to Brussels last year."

"La Monnaie?" *Floor, open up now. Please.*

The lady's laughter held only degradation. "Why, of course, la Monnaie. Surely you have heard of la Monnaie."

"No, ma'am. I have not."

"Where have you been, Miss Bowen? Living with the

pigs?" asked another woman who had gray hair pulled back in a bun so tight her eyes were almost slanted. They would have been, too, if she wasn't narrowing them so severely at Leah.

Leah sank further into herself, trying to come up with a suitable response. What would this lady think if she knew she really did live with pigs? She felt like a fly caught in a spider's web with an eight-legged beast heading directly toward her with one mission—to devour her.

That's what these women were doing—devouring her spirit. She needed to escape them. But she had no idea how to do that without being as rude as they were.

"Excuse me, ladies." Jake stepped next to Leah and looped her arm through his. "But I feel you have had the pleasure of my friend's company long enough. As much as I'm sure it will sadden you all to see her leave, I'm going to have to steal her away."

The women nodded. Their faces lit up with smiles. Jake's massive tall frame and extremely good looks would impress any woman. Even this group of snobby women. Several stared at Jake with dreamy eyes as if he were a prince of some kind. In a way he was. He was Leah's Prince Charming, rescuing her from the dragon ladies. Leah had never loved him so much as she did at that very moment.

They pressed their gloved hands against their lips, dipped their heads and blinked their eyes like schoolgirls with a crush. Not a single one of them could form a coherent sentence. They sounded like blathering idiots.

How did they like feeling the way they'd made her feel?

Leah raised her chin. "If you will excuse me, ladies."

Their heads bobbed jerkily as if someone were shaking them hard by the shoulders.

Jake led her away to a corner on the opposite side of the room.

Finally, Leah could breathe—well, kind of, with the infernal corset hemming her in and the tears of humiliation shimmering just behind her eyelashes.

They lowered themselves onto a white Chippendale bench seat. "How did you know I needed rescuing?"

He shrugged. "Just knew."

"Thank you, Jake." She sent him a shy smile. She'd never felt shy around Jake before.

"Told you I'd be here for you."

"Yes, you did. You're always there for me." Leah had to force her true feelings not to show when she fixed her eyes on him. She didn't want Jake to know she was in love with him.

Her gaze traveled around the room, and she leaned as close to him as possible without causing speculation about them, and for his ears only she said, "Are you doing okay in here?"

Jake skimmed the room. "Not too bad. There are several doors and it's not crowded. So far, so good. Should be fine."

"Oh, good. I'm so glad. When I came in here and saw all the space and doors, I had a feeling you would be." She smiled at him.

"You look really nice. I like the dress. It brings out the blue in your eyes."

A tear pooled in each eye.

"Did I say something wrong?" Concern drifted across his face.

"No. No." She held up her hand. "On the contrary."

"What are the tears for, then?" He brushed each one with his thumb from her cheek as they slid down.

She wanted to clutch his hand, press it into her heart and hold it there forever. But it wasn't hers to do with as she pleased. Her heart and soul heaved a heavy sigh before she answered him. "Since I arrived here, you're the first person to say something nice to me."

"What do you mean? People here been mean to you?" Jake's forehead furrowed.

She gave a long blink and nodded. "Those ladies that were so nice to you, well, they weren't to me. You should have seen the disgust on their faces when they eyed me up and down. Made me feel lower than dirt. Then they started talking politics. Things I knew nothing about nor care to, and some opera house in some place I've never even heard of before. I've never felt so stupid in my entire life. I wanted the floor to open and swallow me up."

The muscle in his jaw jumped. Leah could tell he was working to compose himself. "I wouldn't worry about what they think. You outshine every last one of them both in beauty and attire."

"Oh, you're just saying that to be nice. But thanks." She gave him a half smile.

"No. I'm not. I meant every word." Seriousness dotted each syllable he spoke.

Leah studied his beautiful gray eyes for the truth. She didn't see any falseness in them. Her heart warmed. She pressed her shoulders back, feeling taller and better than she had since she'd walked through the doors of this place. And she owed her renewed confidence in herself to Jake, who never once made her feel the way those ladies just had. Ever. In fact, she'd always seen the two of them as equals. "Thank you, Jake. I really needed to hear something nice. You look pretty fabulous yourself." Boy, did he ever.

* * *

Jake appreciated Leah's compliment. Her opinion was the only one there that mattered.

Leah played with her fingertips, rubbing and tugging at them. It crushed him to hear how cruel those ladies had been to her. He wanted to storm over there and give every one of them a good tongue-lashing. But he would not cause a scene and risk embarrassing Leah or Mrs. Bowen.

A quick glance at his outfit, and he couldn't understand why they'd been so nice to him. He was the most underdressed man in the place. He'd taken money out of his winter supply fund to buy a new pair of pants but the rest of his attire was his Sunday church clothes. If people didn't like the way he was dressed, well, that was their problem. He wasn't out to impress anyone. He was who he was and if no one liked it, then they didn't have to associate with him.

"Where's Elizabeth?"

"Don't know. I told her I needed to talk to you." He scanned the room but didn't see her.

"Does she correct your faux pas?" She tugged at her bottom lip and her head tilted at a slight angle.

"My what?"

"Faux pas. You know, social blunders?" She hiked a shoulder.

"Nope. Not once."

"You're fortunate." She glanced at him then down at her lap. "Fitzwilliam took me aside and rebuked me. He told me he couldn't believe I hadn't dressed properly this evening."

The muscle in Jake's jaw jumped as he bore down on his teeth.

"How was I supposed to know how to dress for an opera? I've never been to one before. Not even back in

New York. They were always held late in the evenings and we were in our bedrooms by then." She turned her face away from him.

"Leah." He tugged on her chin until she faced him. "Any man who cares about outward appearances instead of what's on the inside where it really counts isn't worth caring about. It's like all those people in *Pride and Prejudice.* All they cared about was outward appearances and how much wealth and power a person had. That ain't right."

"You've read *Pride and Prejudice?*"

Jake clamped his jaw shut. He couldn't believe he'd mentioned that book. No avoiding her question. "Yep."

"When?"

"Finished it the other night."

"What made you read it?"

"You."

"Me?"

"Yep."

"How come?"

Jake ran his hand across the back of his neck. "If you must know, it's because you kept talking about how you wanted a man like Mr. Darcy. I was curious what kind of man he was. Have to admit, I'm surprised you want someone like him. Even though he did turn out to be a nice fellow in the end."

"I keep hoping that's what will happen with Mr. Barrington. He's only trying to help me correct my social faux pas. I'm certain once I learn those things he'll be different, too."

"Leah." Jake locked his gaze on hers. Using his sternest tone he said, "Fitzwilliam isn't some hero in a fictional romance novel."

"I know that."

"Do you? Mr. Darcy isn't a real person, Leah. Life

isn't like a storybook, either. Fitzwilliam may or may not change. This may be the way he really is. You need to ask yourself if you're willing to take that chance."

She said nothing in reply. Only stared at him.

He'd frustrated her. But what kind of friend would he be if he didn't speak the truth to her? He had something else he needed to talk to her about, too. But now was not the time or the place.

"Oh, Jake. There you are." Elizabeth glided toward them, her dress swaying side to side like a ringing bell.

Jake rose. He turned to Leah and quickly said, "I have something important I need to tell you. Later, okay?"

Leah nodded.

Elizabeth curtsied at Leah and her smile appeared genuine. "Good evening, Leah. You look lovely this evening."

Jake sent Leah a see-I-told-you-so look.

"Thank you, Elizabeth. You do, too."

It was sweet of Elizabeth to compliment Leah. She would make someone a great wife. Not him, but someone. Elizabeth, too, was out of his league. Plus, Jake couldn't imagine having Fitzwilliam for a brother-in-law. He felt sorry for Elizabeth having a brother like him. And he would feel even sorrier for Leah if she ended up marrying the guy.

The thought of Leah marrying that phony fellow was terrifying. Jake couldn't let that happen. If nothing else, he had to at least talk her into finding someone else. He loved her too much to watch her marry a man like that. He started when he realized the thought that had just gone through his head. He loved her. More than that, he was *in* love with her.

"Time to be seated, everyone." Mr. Barker spoke loudly from the front of the room, stopping Jake's musings.

Fitzwilliam walked up and claimed Leah's arm, and

Elizabeth claimed his. Not wanting to lead her on, yet refusing to be rude, he allowed her to, and the four of them made their way to the chairs.

Jake sat in the chair directly across from the open doors and only feet away. Elizabeth sat next to him, then Fitzwilliam and then Leah.

Shortly after everyone was seated, a rotund man started singing. The man had a nice enough voice, but Jake couldn't understand a word he said. For the next hour, two other men and three other ladies joined him. The songs got longer and harder to endure. When the singing finally ended, to avoid getting trapped in the crowd, Jake got up immediately and went to stand next to the open doors. Elizabeth, Leah and Fitzwilliam joined him.

"Wasn't that a fine display of talent?" Fitzwilliam asked Leah.

"He sang beautifully, but I couldn't understand a word he said."

"You didn't? How very odd." Pomposity oozed from the man.

What did Leah see in this jerk?

"Nothing odd about it. I didn't understand a word, either," Jake said with no apology whatsoever.

"That doesn't surprise me—a country bumpkin such as yourself."

"Hey, don't talk about Jake that way," Leah blasted Fitzwilliam and disengaged her arm from his.

"Brother, please." Elizabeth bowed her head in embarrassment. "It was in Italian, after all."

Fitzwilliam turned his attention to his sister. The man was a pill, but he sure loved his sister. You could see it in his eyes.

"Very true, sister." He turned back to them. "My apologies to you both. I don't know where my manners are lately." He gazed down at Leah. "I fear jealousy is causing me to act in a manner most unbecoming."

"Jealousy?" She tilted her head.

"Yes. I must admit, I'm quite jealous of the relationship you have with Mr. Lure here. However, I'm sure I have no need to be alarmed on that account. For very soon, if I have my way, you and I shall be heading back to New York." His smile was fake at best. "In fact, what better time than the present to make my feelings on the matter known? Leah, my darling, please say you will be my wife."

Like a sucker punch to his middle, the wind whooshed out of Jake's lungs. *Marry?* His attention flew to Leah. Surely she wouldn't say yes. *No, Leah. Say no.*

She stared at the man with wide, blinking eyes and an open mouth.

Fitzwilliam fingered her mouth shut, shifted to the other foot, glanced around and then smiled. "Of course, you do not have to answer me straightaway, my dear. I shall give you this evening to consider my proposal. On the morrow you can give me your answer. I shall come by early in the morning if that is agreeable with you."

"Um. Oh. Um. Ye-yes. Th-that will be—be just fine."

A dagger ripped at Jake's heart, shredding it to pieces.

The day had come.

Leah would be leaving.

No! No! He refused to let that happen. He'd rather move to the city than live without her. How he would survive it he didn't know, but if that's what it took… His heart raced, and his palms turned damp just thinking about it. He swallowed hard, hoping the panic would go away.

Somehow.

Somehow he'd figure it out.

He had to.

Before she gave Fitzwilliam her answer, he had to talk

to Leah, to see how she felt about him, about them. In the next breath, he hoped and prayed she wouldn't reject him this time. For this time, with his heart on the table, her rejection would surely kill him.

Leah watched as Fitzwilliam gave Jake a smug grin, then he excused himself and headed to the group of prominent men he'd been visiting with most of the evening.

She shook her head, unable to get over how Fitzwilliam had asked her to marry him in front of everyone. More importantly, in front of Jake.

Jake.

She couldn't wait to find out what it was he wanted to talk to her about. But wait she must.

"It sure is warm in here."

Leah turned her attention to Elizabeth. Miss Barrington splayed her fan and waved it in front of her face. "Jake, would you be a dear and get me something to drink, please?"

He turned his attention to Leah. "Would you like something to drink, Leah?"

"Please."

He nodded, and Leah's gaze followed him as he headed toward the refreshment table.

"Isn't he the most agreeable man ever?"

Leah yanked her attention toward Elizabeth. "Isn't who the most agreeable man?"

"Jake." Elizabeth hooked arms with her. She glanced around the room and then she leaned closer to Leah. "He's been so attentive to me. So much so that I think he's in love with me."

Shocked to the very core of her being by Elizabeth's statement, Leah wondered if what she said was true. Was

Jake in love with Elizabeth? Leah's thoughts trailed back to how attentive he had been to the woman.

How he held Elizabeth longer than necessary whenever he helped her down.

How he saw to her comforts.

How the two of them laughed and joked.

How he'd gazed at her and had given her his undivided attention.

How willing he was to go every time Leah had invited him along. It had all been for Elizabeth, not for her.

Is that what he wanted to talk to her about? To tell her that he had fallen in love with Elizabeth and that he wanted to marry the woman?

What had she done? She'd driven the man she loved into another woman's arms.

Her mind scrambled to find a solution, but there was not one. If only God would have shown her a way to deal with the loss of her father. But He hadn't. And now she was about to lose the only man she'd ever loved. It was a no-win situation. If she married Fitzwilliam, Jake would be her brother-in-law. If she stayed, the nightmares and the loss of her father would continue to torment her. Earlier, she'd already made up her mind not to marry Fitzwilliam, and now that decision was cemented. There was no way she would marry Fitzwilliam and have to watch Elizabeth and Jake together all the time.

Jake married to another. That idea ate at her heart like a deadly cancer.

Lord, show me a way to make this work. I can't lose him. I can't. I know You have an answer. I'm asking You to reveal it to me. And soon. Before it's too late.

"Here you go, ladies." Jake's voice pulled her out of the heart-wrenching pit her thoughts had taken her to.

He handed them each a glass.

Elizabeth threaded her arms through his. Jake looked down at her. Never taking her eyes off of Jake, Elizabeth took a small sip. "Thank you, Jake. That was very sweet of you."

"My pleasure."

"Yes. Thank you, Jake." Leah forced a smile onto her lips. Even that was hard when her heart was breaking.

"Jake." His attention went back to Elizabeth. "I was wondering if you removed your advertisement yet. You said you were no longer in need of it."

Remove his ad? He hadn't told Leah he was going to do that.

"Yep. No need for it anymore." He looked at Leah, then back at Elizabeth.

He no longer needed it?

Elizabeth smiled at Leah and gave her a look that said, *See what I mean? He is in love with me. He's even stopped his ad as proof.*

Realization pummeled Leah's soul. Jake had said he needed to talk to her. Is that what he was going to tell her? That he'd removed his ad and that he no longer needed it because he was going to marry Elizabeth? Or that he'd finally decided to respond to one of the other women who'd answered his advertisement? Either way, it was too late for her and Jake. Or was it? Surely there had to be a way to work this whole thing out. She couldn't lose Jake. She just couldn't.

Chapter Sixteen

Leah skipped through the ranch yard and up into the trees singing, “Father. Father. Where are you?” She repeated it over and over as her eyes searched for him. Farther and farther into the forest she went. The foliage thickened as did the trees. Sweet syringa scents swirled around her. She stopped, raised her nose in the air and drew in deeply, then frowned as something awful went up her nose. She looked around, trying to figure out where the stench was coming from.

She watched as a tree fell in slow motion and landed with a crunch.

Leah walked over to the fallen tree and stepped on top of it. Her focus drifted to her feet.

Her eyes widened.

A man was trapped underneath the tree. She couldn’t see his face.

With one hop, she leaped off the massive trunk.

“Don’t be scared, princess.”

“Father?” Leah swung one direction and then another, searching frantically for her father.

“I love you, princess.”

“Where you are, Father? I can’t find you.”

"I'm right here."

"Where?"

"Here."

A single beam of light pierced through the darkness.

Leah shook her head. "No. No. I'm sorry, Father. I'm so sorry."

Leah's eyes bolted open, blinking, searching, trying to get her bearings through the morning twilight. When she realized she was in her bedroom and that the whole thing had been yet another nightmare, tears soaked her face as the fresh pain of losing her father assaulted her all over again.

Dear Lord, will these nightmares ever end? I can't take even one more of them. Please, won't You make them stop? She'd prayed the same prayer a million times over the years. Even though the nightmares hadn't ceased, she refused to stop praying. God was her only hope. And now she needed Him to deliver her even more than ever. Her future depended on it.

At first, she truly believed Fitzwilliam was God's answer for her and that once they were married and moved to New York the nightmares would end and she would be free from the place that had robbed her of her precious father. That might very well be true, but it wouldn't solve the problem of being in love with Jake or having him for a brother-in-law.

Jake? A brother-in-law? She tossed her coverlet off, stormed over to the washbasin and splashed cool water on her burning face.

Despite Fitzwilliam's certain disapproval, which she no longer cared about, when Leah completed her toiletries she dressed in a simple lavender dress—the one she always wore when church was held at their home.

Downstairs, she headed into the kitchen. Veronique had the day off, so Leah put a pot of coffee on the stove, cooked up a batch of Swedish pancakes and fried thick slices of ham. She'd just set them in the warmer when she heard the padding of slippers on the floor.

"Good morning, Leah." Mother entered the kitchen wearing her nightgown and robe. "I'm surprised to see you up and dressed so early this morning. I figured as late as it was when we got home last night, you'd sleep in this morning."

"Couldn't sleep. I thought I'd make breakfast so I could help get things set up for church today." Leah went to the window and pulled back the curtain. "At least it's another nice day today." The sky was covered with its usual large fluffy clouds sprinkled throughout the blue vastness. She let the curtain fall and headed to the stove. "You ready to eat?"

"No. Not yet. A cup of coffee sounds nice."

"I'll get it. You stay seated, Mother."

Mother nodded, placed her elbow on the table, rested her chin in her hand and sighed. "Why don't you sit down and have a cup with me?"

Leah nodded, poured them each a cup of the hot brew and sat down.

"Did you enjoy the opera?" Mother cupped her hands around the beverage.

Leah considered lying but realized she didn't have the energy to fake being happy. "Not really. I didn't understand a word they said. Some of the women's voices were so high they hurt my ears." Those high, shrill voices came from the very ladies who had snubbed her. "Did you enjoy it?" Leah blew into her coffee.

"It was all right. Not something I'd like to hear very often."

"Really?"

"Yes, really. It wasn't my type of music at all."

"Why'd you go then?"

"Because Charles asked me to."

"Does he host those kind of parties often?"

"No. He only did it because the man was his friend. Truth is, Charles doesn't care for them at all, and he couldn't understand a word they were saying, either."

That shocked Leah. Fitzwilliam had made her feel like there was something wrong with her and as if she were the only one who didn't understand. Well, she and Jake, that was.

"How are you and Fitzwilliam getting along? Do you think he's the one?"

"He asked me to marry him."

Mother set her cup on the table and leaned forward. "What did you say?" Was that concern on her face?

"I didn't. He said I could think on it and tell him today."

"Have you decided whether or not you're going to accept his proposal?"

"Whose proposal?" Abby stepped in the kitchen with her hair all rumpled, tying the string on her robe. She flopped into a kitchen chair. "Jake's?"

"Jake's?" Mother sat up straighter, eager eyes blinking in Abby's direction. "Why would you think Jake would propose to Leah?"

Abby straightened, and her gaze flew to Leah's and locked there, screaming, *I'm sorry.*

Leah sent her a brief warning glare to make an excuse and drop it.

Abby shrugged. "Just wishful thinking, I guess. I really like Jake, and if Lee-Lee married him, then she wouldn't leave."

"I understand that one," Mother said under her breath, but Leah heard her nonetheless.

If they only knew how that could never be. She sighed. Tired from all the tug and pull on her heart, Leah rose and gathered the food out of the warmer. Both Abby and Mother wanted her to marry Jake. She wouldn't mind it herself now. Except she was probably too late. As much as she wanted it to be so, marrying Jake wouldn't solve her nightmare problem, or seeing Mother with a man other than her father, or her hatred for the place that killed her father, or her desire to go back to where times were better.

Torn between her love for Jake and her desire to leave, Leah struggled to find a solution that would give her all of her heart's desires. Was that even possible? She wasn't sure. One thing she was sure of— She had to risk talking to Jake and telling him everything. If it wasn't too late, perhaps they could come up with a solution together. After all, he'd helped her so many times in the past.

Breakfast flew by with Abby regaling in her dramatic flair about the evening at Mr. Barker's and how fabulous it was. Leah wished she could say the same, but the whole thing had been torture. When they finished breakfast, each went to their bedrooms to get ready for church.

Leah loved when church was held out on the ranch. So did the rest of the town. Though they had an almost-new church building in town, everyone still wanted to gather at the Bowens' ranch at least once a month during the summer season, and Pastor James had readily agreed.

An hour and half later, the parishioners' wagons started rolling in, and Fitzwilliam and Elizabeth were among them. She didn't know what to tell the man because she hadn't had a chance to talk to Jake yet.

Fitzwilliam stepped down from the buggy and offered his sister a helping hand.

Leah drew in a deep breath and headed toward them, knowing she could not be rude.

"Good morning, my dear." Fitzwilliam kissed her hand. "You look—" His brown eyes took in her attire. He leaned close to her. "Is that what you're wearing to church?" Fitzwilliam straightened and looked around with a smile as phony as a three-headed animal.

Enough was enough. Leah refused to let him belittle her or criticize her anymore. She raised her chin. "Yes. This is what I'm wearing."

His countenance immediately changed to one of disapproval. "We'll discuss this later, my dear." Haughtiness tinged his voice.

"There's nothing to discuss."

"Brother, please." Elizabeth put her hand on his arm.

Leah turned to Elizabeth, whose big brown eyes were pleading with her brother once again.

"Good morning, Elizabeth." The warmth in Leah's voice was no act, even though the woman was a threat to her happiness.

"Good morning, Leah. I fear I must apologize for my brother."

Someone needed to. He sure didn't offer an apology for himself. "How are you this morning?" Leah asked. She really wanted to know. Elizabeth was a sweet lady.

"Very well, thank you." She looked around. "Is Jake coming?"

Guilt pricked Leah's conscious at the thought of hurting someone as sweet as Elizabeth. But then again, what if she and Elizabeth were wrong and Jake didn't love Elizabeth? Then what? The only way to find out was to talk to him. If Jake was indeed in love with Elizabeth and planned on marrying her, then as much as it would kill her, Leah would forget her plans about talking to him about everything. She would take that as God's answer to her prayer about the whole situation.

"Yes. He should be here pretty soon. Would you two like to go ahead and be seated?" She pointed to the side of the house where the chairs were set up in the shade.

"We're sitting outside?" Fitzwilliam's eyes widened in horror.

Leah wanted to yell, "Brother, please," but she didn't. "Yes. We are." She let out a long sigh, hoping he'd get the hint.

He emitted a disapproving breath. "Well, one time shan't matter, I suppose. But things will be different once we're married."

Leah mashed her teeth together. Now was not the time to say what was on her mind. Not before church. But the time was coming and it was coming quickly. Not quick enough, though.

"Shall we all be seated?" Pastor James said from the wooden podium.

Everyone flocked to their seats.

Leah sat in the last bench, purposely saving the end spot for Jake.

Jake. Where was he?

Jake had spent the past hour chasing down his goat. Meanie had escaped once again. He still hadn't found her, but he didn't want to be late for church, so he finally abandoned the search for his runaway goat, hoping and praying she hadn't gone to Mabel's again.

With a tuck to his horse's side, he galloped to the Bowens' and arrived just as everyone had gotten seated. Voices rose in worship to the Lord. He tied his horse to one of the hitching posts near the barn, pulled his Bible out of his saddlebag and strode to the side of the house.

Spotting an empty place on the end, and knowing Leah had saved it for him, brought a smile to his face. He slipped in beside her.

She looked up and her dimples made their appearance. Her smile was different. Warm. Inviting, even. Yet shy at the same time.

Leah turned her face toward the front and continued singing in a low, sweet tone. Jake wished she'd sing louder. She had a beautiful voice. One that kissed the soul of a man.

Minutes later, the worship ended, and Pastor James said, "Please be seated, folks." Everyone did. "If you have your Bibles, please open them to Matthew 6:33."

Pages rustled as Jake and several other folks searched for the scripture.

Pastor James glanced down at the makeshift podium. "Seek ye first the kingdom of God, and his righteousness; and all these things shall be added unto you." He raised his head and leaned his arm on the podium. "Is He first in your life and are you second? Or are you first and He's second?"

Pastor walked around to the front of the podium. "Let me tell you, folks. When we put God first in every area of life and read the Word daily and pray over every situation and decision, our lives will be blessed. I challenge you today to ask yourselves if there is something you're holding on to—an area in your life where you haven't put Him first. Perhaps it's money. Or your time. Or a relationship."

Jake glanced at Leah. Had he put God first in that area?

Pastor James continued, but Jake didn't hear what he was saying. He was busy repenting for putting himself first and God second. As hard as it was, Jake prayed for God's will and not his concerning Leah. He would accept

God's answer because he no longer wanted to be first in his life. From now on, he was second.

Leah leaned close to him and whispered, "So, did you really cancel the ad?"

Huh? Why was she asking him about that now? He nodded.

"Why?"

"'Cause my heart just wasn't in it anymore."

"How come?"

Tell her the truth. That still small voice spoke to Jake's spirit.

"'Cause I've fallen in love with someone." Now was not the time to tell her with whom. He'd tell her later.

"Please stand, folks," Pastor James said.

Church ended with a song, then everyone scattered to their wagons. Men handed baskets of food down to their womenfolk. Jake jumped in and helped move the tables and benches.

Fitzwilliam stood at the edge of the crowd, watching, the only man not helping.

Jake shook his head, then turned and hoisted another bench.

"I say, stop that. Get away from me."

Jake swung around with the bench still in his hands.

Meanie had the tail of Barrington's suit in her mouth, and she was yanking him to and fro as he fought to disengage her.

For once, Jake could just kiss that old goat. That wasn't very charitable, but he couldn't help enjoying the scene just a little.

Fitzwilliam managed to swat the goat on the nose, which seemed to have the intended reaction of her letting go. "Stupid animal." Fitzwilliam tsked as he examined his attire.

Meanie backed up and dropped her head.

Uh-oh.

Meanie lunged toward the man and rammed her head into Fitzwilliam's backside, sending him flying forward. He landed on his hands and knees, and his top hat bounced on the hard ground, rolling a few feet in front of him.

"Why you!" He jumped up just as the goat headed for him again.

Kitty stood in the background with her ears flapping and her nose jerking high in the air as if she were cheering Meanie on, as if saying "Hit him, hit him again."

The scene was hilarious. Jake wanted to laugh. But as much as he enjoyed seeing the man get what he deserved, Jake needed to stop his goat before she decided to do it again.

He set the bench down and strode toward Meanie, who was in hot pursuit of the gray trousers.

"Someone do something!" Fitzwilliam screamed like a little girl.

As Jake headed across the yard, his goat stopped and backed up.

Oh, no. Not again. "Meanie!" Jake picked up his pace, but he arrived too late.

Meanie rammed her head into Barrington again. This time he landed sprawled out on the ground.

Several men headed his way to help.

Meanie's focus darted to them, but only for a brief second. Mouth barred open, she chomped her teeth into Fitzwilliam's hat and shook it vehemently.

Jake caught her by the collar and tugged on the hat. "Bad goat. Bad Meanie. Give it back."

Meanie shook her head hard. Jake tugged even harder. So did the goat. But she wouldn't let go.

Rriipp.

Uh-oh. Jake glanced over at Fitzwilliam to see if he'd heard the noise.

Haydon, Michael and Jesse stood above Fitzwilliam, offering him a hand up.

"I can do it." He brushed them away, huffing as he stood.

They stepped back, holding up their hands in surrender.

A look of understanding passed between Jake and the three of them. Right then, Jake knew there was no way Leah would be marrying this man. Not if the four of them had anything to say about it, anyway.

In control of the now-shredded hat, Jake walked over and handed what was left of it to him. "Sorry about your hat."

Fitzwilliam snatched it from Jake's hands. Holding on to the brim, he mashed it onto his head. The whole brim tore off and the ring landed around his neck like a collar. Barrington closed his eyes, and his chest expanded. He brushed himself off, pressed his shoulders back and stormed away, mumbling something about being nothing but a bunch of hooligans.

Jake turned his attention back to Leah's brothers. He fought not to laugh, but when he saw Haydon with his head dipped, his hand over his face and nose and his peering eyes upward; Jess biting his quivering lip and looking everywhere but at him; and Michael with his flared nose, pursed mouth and chin twitching, Jake couldn't help it. Laughter rolled out of him, and the other three men joined him.

"Can you believe that guy?" Jesse shook his head, still chortling a bit.

"You'd think he'd at least try to impress us. But the man doesn't even try," Michael added.

"I don't much care for that pompous jerk. I can't figure out what Leah sees in him. Whatever it is…" Haydon rubbed his chin. "I know one thing. I'm not letting that man marry our sister."

"I agree. There has to be a way to stop her. But how?" Jess asked.

"I have an idea." The brothers turned their attention to Jake.

"Let's hear it."

Making sure no one could hear him, Jake shared his plan with them. "Do I have your permission?"

Haydon placed his large hand on Jake's shoulder and gave it a firm squeeze. "You sure do. Doesn't he, boys?"

The other two nodded their assent.

"Now, we'd better get back over there or they're going to eat without us."

Prayers were said over the food, so everyone fixed their plates. Jake, Elizabeth, Leah and Fitzwilliam sat at one of the smaller tables. Selina and Michael wheeled the prams over to their table.

"Mind iffen we join y'all?" Selina asked.

"No. We'd love to have you." Leah motioned for them to sit.

Jake noticed the scowl on Fitzwilliam's face when he had to move over to allow Selina and Michael to sit on the end of the bench across from each other.

What a jerk the man was.

"How you feeling, Selina?" Jake asked.

"Gettin' stronger than a bull every day."

"And ornerier, too." Michael jerked back in pain. "Ouch! Stop that." If his grin was an indicator, Michael didn't look one bit affronted by whatever just happened.

"Woulda never kicked ya iffen you'd behaved yourself." Selina wrinkled her nose at Michael and blew him a kiss.

"I say. Must you bicker at the table? You're acting like children and it is quite vexing."

Everyone's gaze slid to Fitzwilliam. Didn't he know they were teasing each other? It was all in fun. What an overstuffed shirt the man was.

"They aren't bickering, Mr. Barrington. They're having fun. You should try it sometime." The last five words were added under Leah's breath, but Jake heard them. He was certain a few others had, too, if their dipped heads and grins were any indication.

"Oh, don't go gettin' your trousers in a twist. We weren't bickerin', as you call it. Like Leah said, we was just teasin' each other." Selina eyed Fitzwilliam with disgust.

Fitzwilliam sneered at Selina. "You, madam, are—"

"Brother!" Elizabeth glared at Fitzwilliam.

He clamped his mouth shut. "My apologies to each of you. I can only blame my actions on that wretched goat for that beast has ruined my favorite hat."

Whom and what did he blame his actions on before Meanie?

The rest of the meal went fairly well. Everyone but Leah, who appeared down, talked in between taking bites of Selina's excellent Southern fried chicken, the fried trout, Swedish meatballs, potatoes sprinkled with parsley and melted butter, roast beef sandwiches and even a few foods from Jake's Norwegian ancestry such as lefse flatbread and potet klub—potato dumplings covered with butter. Jake wanted to try all the other dishes, but there were too many and his belly was full.

When everyone finished, Leah helped clean up the food, but the usual bounce in her step was missing. Jake couldn't wait to finish putting everything up and get Leah alone, hopefully before she talked to Fitzwilliam about his proposal.

Jake did double-time carrying the tables to the barn. With the last one in the storeroom, he closed the door and turned, nearly bumping into Elizabeth.

"Oh, sorry. Didn't see you there."

"My apologies. I never meant to startle you."

"No problem."

"Jake, may we talk?" Elizabeth fidgeted with the tips of her gloved fingers.

"Sure. We can go outside and—"

"No. May we talk in here, undisturbed, please?"

Her eyes looked down and then back up at him. The ends of her gloves were now twisted into points. He really didn't want to talk to her now, but he hated seeing any woman distressed. "Is something wrong?"

"No. Nothing is wrong. What I'm about to ask is extremely difficult for me."

"Oh, I see." He brushed the dust off a wooden storage container. "Won't you be seated?" He hoped this wouldn't take long. He couldn't wait to talk to Leah.

They sat down.

"What's on your mind?"

She chewed on her lip. Her chest expanded, then she looked him in the eye. "As I told you before, I lived in an isolated part of the country for years and adored it. I love country living. Especially here. Being a debutante is not for me. As you have daily witnessed, my brother cannot tolerate a lot of things. I, however, could care less about those things."

Where was she going with this?

A woman's shadow appeared on the ground outside the barn door. If he wasn't mistaken, it was Leah's.

"While what I'm about to say is highly improper, I cannot help myself."

His attention swayed back to Elizabeth, but using his peripheral vision, he kept watch on the shadow.

Elizabeth's eyelids lowered to her lap and she continued to massacre the tips of her gloves. "I no longer wish to live that kind of lifestyle. In fact, I detest it. What I'm trying to say is…" Her brown eyes met his. "I wish to remain here. With you. Would you consider marrying me?"

The shadow disappeared. Jake knew for sure it was Leah now. "Excuse me, Elizabeth. But I need to go." He pushed himself off the bench, but Elizabeth grabbed his arm.

"What about my proposal, Jake?" Hope filled her big brown eyes.

"I'm sorry, Elizabeth. You're a very nice lady, but I'm in love with someone else."

"Leah?"

"Yes. Leah."

Elizabeth nodded. "I already knew that. But, I was hoping—" She stood and her voice softened. "Leah's a blessed lady. Go after her, Jake."

Jake kissed Elizabeth's gloved hand, gave her one last look and darted out of the barn and into the trees.

Leah was right where he thought she'd be. The same place she always went when something troubled her. Her forehead rested against her arms that were pressed into the trunk of a cottonwood tree, hiding her face completely but not her sobs. Her body jerked with heart-wrenching cries. Jake's heart bled for her.

In an instant he was next to her, turning her around, pulling her into his arms and pressing her head close to his chest. "Leah, what's wrong?"

"Oh, Jake. I—I…" Sobs tore from her.

"Hey. Hey, what's the matter?" Panic brushed across his soul and settled there. Not wanting to let her out of the circle of his arms, he shifted her enough and leaned his head back until he could see her face. "Leah, please. Talk to me."

"I—I—I don't know how to—to tell you—" she said between gasps. "To tell you—"

"Leah, you know you can tell me anything, right? So whatever it is, just say it. It's all right."

She nodded and then waved her head back and forth. "No, I can't." She hiccupped. "Not now. Not this."

He set her away from him and tilted her chin up, and his gaze captured hers. "Listen to me. There's nothing you can't tell me. Now tell me what's bothering you."

She closed her eyes, then slowly opened them. "Elizabeth told me she thought you were in love with her. Then earlier today you said you'd stopped the advertisement because you had fallen in love with someone. I'm sorry, Jake. I know you're probably going to marry Elizabeth or one of the women who responded to your ad, and I have no right to tell you this, but I'm in love with you. You don't have to change your plans or anything, but—"

Jake pressed his fingertips over her lips and smiled. "I love you, too, Leah."

"What?" She blinked. "What did you say?" Her saturated eyes searched his.

"I said I love you, too."

"But—but what about Elizabeth?"

"I'm not in love with her. I'm in love with you."

She closed her eyes and opened them again. "Oh, Jake. I love you so much it hurts. But I don't know what to do. You see, I—"

"I do." Jake interrupted her. He placed one knee on the forest floor, ignoring the dampness soaking into his pant leg. "Leah, the first time I asked you to marry me was out of convenience. Now I'm asking because I love you. Will you marry me?" He looked up at her, waiting, hoping she wouldn't reject him again.

For one blessed moment he thought everything would be right again. But then her gaze fell from his.

"I—I want to, Jake, but I'm not sure I can."

Was she turning him down again? He stood and scraped his hand over the back of his neck. "I don't understand. You just told me you loved me. That you were *in love* with me. Is the reason you're not sure because I'm poor? Because you're determined to move to New York? Is it Fitzwilliam? What is it, Leah? Talk to me."

"Jake, this has nothing to do with Fitzwilliam. And it has nothing to do with you or you being poor. I don't care about money. You should know that."

No, he didn't. "You said you wanted to go back to New York to live the lifestyle you had before. So how can you say you don't care about the money?" Frustration mounted in him. He lowered himself beside her and studied her face.

"It's not about the money. Never has been. It's the memories. Honestly, Jake. I just don't see any way for us to make this work."

"You're not making any sense. What are you talking about?"

She chewed on her lip and looked around. Then she whooshed out a long breath of air. "I haven't told anyone what I'm about to tell you, so please don't interrupt me or anything or I'll lose my nerve." She didn't look at him or even in his direction. Instead, she spoke to the floor of the forest. "Ever since my father died, I've had horrible recurring nightmares where I'm searching frantically for my father. I'm in the forest surrounded by trees that come to life. Their limbs look like arms with long fingers that spread out and reach for me." She ducked her head down as if they were trying to get her now.

Jake wanted to comfort her but didn't know if he should. She had asked him not to interrupt. In his gut, he had a feeling if he did that he would be doing that very thing, so he didn't.

"I can feel evil all around me." Her body shuddered. Her eyes glassed over, not just with tears, but with the images of the dream.

His full attention locked on her, he struggled to keep his arms at his side.

"I beg them to leave me alone, but they don't. I scream for my father. I hear his voice, but it's gurgled as if he's choking. Then, I look down and see him. Blood is running out of his nose and mouth." Tears flowed through each painstaking word she spoke. "Just like they did the day he died."

He didn't know she'd seen her father buried under that tree the day he'd died. Ache for her drove further into his soul.

"The nightmares always end the same—with me saying I'm sorry." Her tear-drenched eyes finally met his. "I don't know what to do, Jake. I hate it here. This place stole my father from me." She laid her hand across his cheek. Her eyes overflowed with love and sadness. "I love you with all my heart, and it will kill me to leave you, but I don't see any way out of this mess except to go back to New York to where memories of my father are pleasant and peaceful, not horrifying. I can see now there is no other answer."

Yes, there was, and he would find it.

Leah's heart hurt more than it ever had before. She pressed her hand into her chest, willing the torturous pain to go away, yet knowing it never would. In leaving, she would be trading one heartbreak for another.

Jake pulled her hands into his. She latched on to them. To him. Needing the connection. Needing his strength. His love spread deep into her soul and wrapped its warmth around her heart. How desperately she needed the strength and love he offered her at this moment. She searched his face, memorizing every line, every crease, every detail.

"Leah."

Her eyes snapped up to his.

"I'm sorry for what you've been through. Wish I could take all your pain onto myself. Make it all go away. But, I can't. I won't ask you to stay here."

A huge chunk of her heart tore off, leaving a wide chasm. She pressed her hand tighter into her chest, willing with everything inside for the pain to leave. Yet how could it? The man she loved was lost to her forever. She doubled over, and the floods descended. Not only was she crying for the loss of her father, but also for the loss of the dearest, most cherished best friend she'd ever had.

Jake's arms encircled her like a protective shield as he pulled her tight against him. "Don't cry. If you'll still have me, I'll do whatever it takes to keep you. Whatever you need me to do, including moving to New York, if need be."

She yanked her head back and stared into his handsome face. The face she loved so dearly. "You—you would do that?" Her heart leaped with hope. "Move to New York with me?"

"I'd do anything for you." He swallowed, and a tremble emanated from him. Dampness moistened her back where his hands rested, and the veins in his arms throbbed faster. He pushed himself off the log.

Realization pummeled her brain. Jake was having a panic attack just thinking about going to New York.

Hope slipped from her heart. What had she been thinking? How selfish of her to even consider such a thing. She'd witnessed those attacks and how hard they were on him. He could never move to the city. Nor would she ask him to. She loved him too much to let him do that.

Her eyes trailed upward.

Jake stood in front of a large tree with his arms crossed. Behind that tree was an even larger, partially uprooted tree with a thick trunk leaning toward it and Jake.

Sunlight streaked through the trees, silhouetting him.

Quick as lightning bolts, flashes of memory struck into her brain.

Swatches of the day pieced together, spiking terror deep into every part of her being.

Her breath strangled to where not even a gasp could be gotten.

Leah leaped up and barreled into Jake, forcing his body as far away from the two trees as she could. He landed on his side on the cushioned forest floor with a thud. She ended up next to him.

"What'd you do that for?"

Panic gripped her so violently that sanity scattered. "I'm sorry. I'm sorry. I just… I couldn't let it kill you, too."

"Let what kill me?" Jake pushed himself off the ground, shaking the pine needles from his arms. Perplexed, he reached down and helped her up, then brushed the fern leaves and stems off the rest of him.

Looking up at the towering monsters above her, her body trembled so violently she thought her knees would buckle and her heart would stop beating. "That—that tree. I couldn't let it kill you."

Jake stared at her as if she'd lost her mind. Maybe she had. She didn't know. All she knew was something had snapped inside her. Something ugly. Something more frightening than anything she'd ever known before.

"You okay?" Concern covered every inch of his face.

"Yes." She nodded. "No." She shook her head so hard hairpins flew in all directions. "Oh, Jake," she cried as sharp talons shredded her heart and pierced her soul. She knuckled her hand into her chest, but nothing could ease this pain. "It's all my fault."

"What's all your fault?" He tried to pull her into his arms, but she stepped back, holding her arms in front of her like a shield. She didn't deserve his comfort—or anyone else's—for what she'd done.

"I now understand why my nightmares end with me telling Father I'm sorry." She stared at the ground, seeing nothing but her own guilt. Tears saturated her eyes.

"Leah, you're not making any sense again."

She tore her focus from the ground and dragged it over to his. Concern filled those soft eyes she so loved.

She couldn't hold his gaze, though—shame and guilt wouldn't let her. In fact, it was all she could do to choke out the next words. "When I saw you standing in front of those trees, it—it all came back to me. Every bit of it." She shuddered and pointed to the trees she had just shoved Jake away from. "See how that tree's almost uprooted?"

"Yeah?" He frowned. "What about it?"

"See how that other one is leaning toward it?" She pulled her hankie out and wiped her eyes then her nose.

"Yes. There's a lot of trees around here like that. What's that got to do with anything?"

"The day my father died…" She put her hand on the tree next to her to steady herself as reality peeled away leaving only the shadow of memories. "I remember the wind blowing really hard and the rain pelting down equally as hard. I was worried about my father being out in the woods in the storm, so I went to try and find him. By the time I spotted him, it had started lightning, too. It was cracking all around us. I hollered at him. He turned and looked at me and waved. Lightning struck the uprooted tree next to him. The tree toppled over—right on top of him. Don't you see?" Even though it hurt for him to know the ugly truth about her, she willed him to understand. "My father died because of me, Jake. It's all my fault." Uncontrollable sobs rent Leah's body. Her legs buckled, but her body never met the ground. Arms strong, yet gentle caught her.

Jake pulled her close, supporting her weight with his strength. "No, Leah, you didn't kill him. The tree did. It was an accident."

Unable to trust her legs to hold her up on their own strength, she clung to him, leaned her head back and gazed up at him. "No, it wasn't an accident. It's all my fault. If I had never gone looking for him, had never hollered at him, then he would have never stopped to wave at me, and he would be alive today."

Jake shook his head as he stared into her eyes. "Leah, no— You can't blame yourself. Did you know lightning was going to hit that tree at that exact moment?"

"No. But—"

Jake placed his fingertips over her lips. "There are no buts, Leah. There was no way you could have known lightning was going to strike right then and there. If you did, would you have hollered for him?"

"No." She shook her head.

"Well…" His sentence hung in the air for a moment. "Let me ask you this… If Haydon or Michael or Jess or Abby had gone out looking for him and the same thing happened to them, would you blame them for killing your father?"

"No. No. Never." Her response came out as fast as the lightning that had struck that tree.

Jake hiked one brow her way.

Her mind started to see the logic of what he was saying, was trying to grasp it even.

She would have never blamed her brothers or sister or anyone else if the exact same thing had happened. So why was she blaming herself?

The guilt fell away. Tears drizzled from her eyes, only this time they were tears of relief. "Oh, Jake. You're right. All these years I've carried this guilt inside me." She pressed her fisted hand into her chest where the constant pain had resided. "I never knew why until today. I never understood the nightmares, or why I had them when no one else seemed to. Oh, Jake. Thank you." she whispered into his heart beating against her ear. A heart that now belonged to her. "I love you, Jake."

"I love you, too." His whisper held a caress, one she held on to for more moments than it was there.

Then as if another lightning bolt of truth had struck her, she yanked back. "Sweet twinkling stars above."

"What?"

"Mother was right. I've been so blind and foolish."

"Now what are you talking about?" His brows puckered.

"You." Her eyes danced back and forth and the love she had for Jake reflected from hers into his. "Mother said that sometimes God places something right before our eyes but we don't see it because we're too busy looking somewhere else or for something else. I've always wanted a man like my father. A man who could make me feel protected. Secure. Loved. Who would comfort me and make me feel special. Jake, you're that man."

His lazy grin belied the glow on his face.

"I love you, Jake. But I can't ask you to move to New York with me. I can't do that to you."

His smile ended and his face dulled.

"So I'm going to stay here. I want to be with you."

In less than a heartbeat, he crushed her to him in the gentlest way. "My sweet, lovable princess. I love you."

"Hey, you called me princess." Her lips curled upward until she was certain they would take over her face.

"Yep. Sure did. You said being a princess was important to you. You'll always be my princess." Jake's mouth covered hers. His kiss went directly to her heart and soul, melting it with its passion, its warmth and its love. Long moments later, he raised his head and gazed tenderly at her. "I love you, Leah."

"I love you, too."

"So, does this mean you're gonna marry me?"

"Yep." Leah used his own word to answer him.

"Let's get one thing perfectly clear first."

"What's that?"

"This won't be a marriage of convenience, but of love."

"Good. I wouldn't have it any other way." She winked at him.

Jake kissed her again soundly. "Now, let's go tell your family the good news."

Leah quickly brushed her clothes and put her hair to rights. "What about Fitzwilliam and Elizabeth?"

"I have a feeling they won't be there."

"How come?"

"Because Elizabeth figured out that I'm in love with you."

"She did?"

"Yep. But if they are there, we'll share our news later."

"What about my brothers? I don't know how they'll feel about this."

"I do."

"You do?"

"Yep. Already talked to them about us and asked their permission to marry you."

"You did? Ah," she said. "That's so sweet. What did they say?" She tilted her head and a curl fell against her cheek.

"They thought it was about time I came to my senses and realized I was in love with you. They wished me luck and said they'd be praying for me. And for you to say yes." Jake settled the strand of hair behind her ear and ran his finger slowly over her cheek, across her lips and under her chin. He tilted her head up, his soft lips only a breath away.

"Kiss me again, Jake."

His eyelids drifted shut. His lips touched hers, softly, then playfully, then possessively. Her heart sighed and melted into his. The man sure knew how to kiss. She couldn't wait to become his wife.

Their lips eventually parted but with great reluctance.

Jake cupped her hand in his and they threaded their way through the wild ferns and trees.

When the noise of the festivities reached them, Leah stopped and strained to see if Fitzwilliam was anywhere around the ranch yard. She really wasn't looking forward to that confrontation. There was no sign of either him or Elizabeth or the carriage they'd rode in on. "They're gone," she told Jake with a huge sigh of relief.

"Good." Jake stopped her. "Leah, before we get married I want to ask your mother's permission."

"I think that would be nice. Thank you."

"One more thing. What if your mother marries Mr. Barker? Will your living here and witnessing it bother you?"

"I'm not sure. But one thing I am sure of… You'll be there for me if it does."

"Yep." Jake pulled her hand to his lips and kissed it. Love, warm and sweet, went from his lips straight into her heart. "One last thing— You sure you won't mind living in a small, three-room house?" Worry flitted across his face.

"Nope. I don't care about that. I care about you."

"But you said you wanted to go to balls and all that stuff."

"I thought I did. Truth is, after being around all those people at Phoebe's wedding, then at Mr. Barker's the other night, and then Fitzwilliam, I couldn't care less if I ever see another gown or attend another snooty gathering ever again. I no more belong with those people than a pig belongs in a mansion."

"A pig in a mansion, huh?" He grinned and so did she.

Her attention jumped from his to across the yard. "Oh, look. There's Mother. Let's go talk to her." She grabbed his hand and dragged him behind her. For someone who was so against the arrangement an hour ago, she sure had come around quickly. "Mother, can Jake and I speak with you for a moment?"

"Of course."

"I'll talk to you later, Mother." Michael glanced at Jake.

Jake nodded once.

Michael smiled and gave a quick nod of his own, then he turned and strolled over to Selina. Her brother leaned down and said something to his wife. Selina looked over at them, smiling from ear to ear.

Leah's heart warmed knowing they loved Jake and that they approved of her choice of husband. Well, God's choice, really. After hearing the pastor's message about putting God first and ourselves second, during that very service, she'd done just that and look what it had gotten her. The man of her dreams.

"Mrs. Bowen." Jake cleared his throat. "I would like to ask permission to marry your daughter."

"Oh, well, Abby's too young to marry. She's only seventeen." Twinkles glittered her mother's eyes.

"No. I meant…" Jake tugged at his shirt collar.

"Mother. Stop. She's teasing you, Jake."

"Yes, I am. Of course you have my permission to marry Leah. And God's, too."

"What do you mean 'God's, too'?"

"Well, ever since you and Jake ran the sack race, I had a feeling about you two and started praying way back then. And every time I did, it was as if I could sense God's approval."

"Thank you, Mother." Leah threw her arms around her. "Your prayers have been answered. And mine, too. Because of that, we have a wedding to plan."

"The sooner, the better." Jake winked, and getting his full meaning, Leah blushed.

The next morning, Leah bolted upright in bed. She pinched her eyes shut and a deep guttural groan leaked out of her. Her newfound love and revelation hadn't stopped the nightmares. "Why, God?" When no answer came, she hurried through her toiletries and flew toward the barn, hoping Jake was there alone, as was his norm in the morning twilight.

Leah stepped inside the dim interior of the barn. The instant she spotted Jake, she rushed over to him and threw her arms around his waist. Sobs tore from her.

"Hey, what's wrong?" Jake cupped her head snugly into his chest.

"I—I h-had anoth-another nightmare."

"Oh, honey." He pressed her head closer to his chest, his arm tightening around her.

She stayed that way for a moment before leaning her head back and gazing into his eyes. "I don't understand, Jake. Why did this happen? I thought because I'd finally understood why I had them that they would be gone. Or that love would make everything better. What do I do, Jake? I can't take the pain that each one brings. Do I have to leave you and everyone I love and go back to New York for this to be finally over?"

"Leah, love doesn't make bad go away. But it helps us to get through it. I don't know why you had another nightmare. Can't tell you what nobody can know. I can tell you that moving back to New York won't likely solve your problem, either."

"What makes you say that?" She tilted her head sideways.

Jake tucked a strand of hair behind her ear. "I live hundreds of miles from Atlantic City."

What did that have to do with her situation?

"Moving states away didn't solve my problem."

Leah frowned. "Huh? I don't understand."

"Leah, honey. My best memories are on my farm. My worst are in Atlantic City. Changing residences didn't solve what's happening on the inside—only God can do that."

"How? I've been praying about this for years."

"Don't know, princess. Only God knows what it will take. What I do know is 'Two are better than one, because they have a good reward for their labor. For if they fall, the one will lift up his fellow, but woe to him that is alone when he falleth, for he hath not another to help him up.'"

"Ecclesiastes four, nine and ten," she whispered.

"I can't fix everything, princess. Can't even stop the

nightmares. Wish I could, but I can't." The same finger that had replaced her curl now rested under her chin. "I can, however, promise to be here with you no matter what. To lift you up. To comfort you, and to protect you through those times."

Leah shifted out of his arms and put her back to him, struggling with what to do. She thought about Jake and how even though he lived miles away from where his problems had started—lived where memories of his family were sweet—panic attacks still plagued him. If Jake could survive what he had to endure, well, so could she. Only now neither of them would have to endure it alone.

Leah turned, and Jake was right there. Just where he said he'd be. Her eyes collided with his. She cupped his face. "My sweet Jake. I love you with all my heart. I promise to do the same and be there for you, too."

Jake drew her into the circle of his strong arms. "I love you, too. Together we can do this."

Their lips sealed the promise between them.

Epilogue

Twenty-one days had passed since Jake had proposed for the second time. During that time he'd courted Leah properly, bringing her gifts and taking her on picnics and evening strolls.

Those three weeks seemed like forever. Today they were finally getting married. Underneath the hot late-afternoon sun, Leah slowly made her way down the aisle, smiling at her friends and family sitting in the rows of benches lined in the yard of her family's ranch. Each step she took, her ivory silk taffeta bustle gown with layers of lace and an asymmetrical skirt with pale pink lace and bows brushed the top of her white button-up boots. It had taken her and Abby hours to sew on the delicate row of pink flowers draped diagonally across the boned corset bodice and neckline. Today she felt like a real princess.

Leah gazed at Jake, who looked more handsome than she'd ever seen him look before—something she thought would never be possible as he was already the most handsome man she'd ever seen.

Their eyes connected and held. Jake reached out his hand and she willingly laid hers in his.

"You ready?" Pastor James asked.

"Yep. Sure am," Jake answered in a rush.

The crowd laughed. When the laughter died, there in front of God and man, Leah said her vows and then Jake said his. He vowed to love, honor, cherish, protect and comfort her. All the things he had spent his life doing already. The very same things that reminded her of her beloved father.

"You may now kiss your bride, Jake."

"Yep. Think I will."

Everyone laughed again.

Jake tilted her chin and kissed her softly, lightly and yet not nearly long enough. When he raised his head, she tilted her head and sent him a questioning look.

He tucked her hair behind her ear. "Later, princess. Later."

She blushed.

After everyone had eaten and the gifts were opened, they said their goodbyes and headed to her buggy—their buggy—decorated with streamers of bowed ribbons and strings of rusty tin cans.

Her mother, brothers, sisters-in-law, sister, nieces and nephews gathered around them. Leah hugged and thanked each one, then Jake helped her into the carriage filled with her belongings.

She tucked herself under her husband's arm and snuggled into his chest on the way to his home. Their home. She sighed.

"What's that for?"

"I can't believe that you're mine. And that your beautiful home is mine now, too." She gazed up at her husband.

Jake pressed his shoulders back and pride marched

across his face. "Can't believe it, either. That you're mine, too."

"Yep." Leah laughed, then captured his lips in a long, breath-robbing kiss.

When the kiss ended, Jake breathlessly said, "Giddyup" and clicked the lines.

At her new home, they unloaded her belongings and while Jake went and put the horse and buggy up, Leah went to their bedroom, where her trunk rested at the end of the bed. She opened it and grabbed her diary.

Dear Mr. Darcy,
You won't be hearing from me anymore. Sorry to disappoint you by saying this, but I found someone even better than you—my very own prince who is everything I always wanted and more. A prince who is my beloved father's equal. So, Mr. Darcy, this is goodbye. Thank you for listening to me all this time.
Love,
Leah

Leah closed the book and clutched it against her chest.

"What you got there?" Jake came up behind her and slipped his arms around her.

Leah turned in his arms with one arm behind her back. She felt behind her and placed the book in her trunk and covered it with an item of clothing. "Nothing of consequence. Not anymore, anyway." With those words, she slipped her arms around her husband's neck and kissed him until her knees threatened to no longer hold her.

The next morning Leah woke up, wrapped in her husband's embrace. During the night, instead of a nightmare, she had dreamed about her prince of a husband. Hopefully it was the first of many good dreams. But even if it wasn't, she knew Jake's love would see her through the bad times, and that she had finally found the groom she had always wanted.

* * * * *

Dear Reader,

My wonderful church, Red Rocks Church in Golden, Colorado, did a series on I AM SECOND. That teaching, putting God first and me second, changed my life. In the past, I would get so busy with writing, deadlines and life itself that I would forget to read my Bible or spend time with the Lord. Since putting Him first, *Groom Wanted* was the quickest and easiest book I've ever written. Now I live by the motto HE IS FIRST, I AM SECOND. Some of you may already do that, but for those of us who don't, who let the busyness of life get in the way, this I AM SECOND motto is ginormous. Jake and Leah learned that lesson, too. They were so caught up in their own plans, placing ads and so on, that they hadn't put God first in their decisions. When they did, God worked on their behalf, as He has for so many others. In fact, if you'd like to hear some amazing testimonies about putting God first, visit *www.iamsecond.com.* It's my hope that this revelation helps you all as much as it has helped me.

God bless you and yours,
Debra Ullrick

Questions for Discussion

1. In your life, what is one time that you wanted something only to find that God had something better in mind?

2. Friendship is very important in the story. What friendship do you have that is most like Leah and Jake's—where you know the other person so well, you can tell when something's happened even from across the room?

3. When have you felt like a fish out of water? What happened? How did that make you feel?

4. The idea of prejudice—judging others by their social standing—is prevalent throughout the book. Where do you find prejudice in society today? Have you ever experienced prejudice? What happened?

5. Leah is tormented by nightmares she doesn't understand. What types of dreams have you had that you knew were about more than just the dream?

6. Leah had a close bond with her father and associated New York with the good memories of him. Whom did you bond with as a child? What memories do you have of closeness like Leah's memories of the stars?

7. Leah wanted to marry a man like her father. What kind of man do or did you hope to marry? Why?

8. When Jake realizes he loves Leah, he is still willing to let her go for her to be happy. If you've ever experienced loving someone that much, what happened?

9. Have you ever had a time in your life when someone close to you was going to marry someone you considered to be the wrong person? What did you do? How did it turn out?

10. Leah writes in her journal throughout the book. Why do you think it can be easier to write about what's really going on than living it?

11. Why is it so difficult to be yourself when you're surrounded by people who don't like you as you are? What do you do to help others know it is all right to be themselves?

12. Leah's mother wants to marry again. Leah is the only sibling struggling with this. Knowing the reason why Leah struggles, what advice would you give her to help her cope with her mother's remarrying?

13. Leah was willing to marry a complete stranger. Lots of women back then married for convenience and not love. How do you think you'd feel marrying a complete stranger you did not love?

14. Most weddings back then were a lot simpler than they are today. If you'd married in the late nineteenth century, how would you describe your wedding? Where would it be?

15. Life is a lot easier when you put God first. What areas do you need to start putting God first in?

COMING NEXT MONTH
from Love Inspired® Historical
AVAILABLE SEPTEMBER 4, 2012

HANDPICKED HUSBAND
Texas Grooms
Winnie Griggs

When ordered by her grandfather to marry, Regina Nash must convince the potential grooms—and her grandfather's handsome envoy—that she's *far* from a perfect bride!

THE GOVERNESS AND MR. GRANVILLE
The Parson's Daughters
Abby Gaines

Widower Dominic Granville needs a wife—and governess Serena Somerton is just the person to find him one! But could his matchmaker be his perfect match?

THE TEMPORARY BETROTHAL
Lily George

Groomed from birth for high society, Sophie Handley is devastated by her family's bankruptcy. Perhaps Lieutenant Charles Cantrill can show her the value of faith and love.

LADY OUTLAW
Stacy Henrie

Jennie Jones will do *anything* to clear her ranch's looming mortgage—even turn to a life of crime that could cost her everything...including ranchhand Caleb Johnson's heart.

Look for these and other Love Inspired books wherever books are sold, including most bookstores, supermarkets, discount stores and drugstores.

LIHCNM0812

When three bachelors arrive on Regina Nash's doorstep, her entire world is turned upside down.

Read on for a sneak peek of HANDPICKED HUSBAND by Winnie Griggs.

Available September 2012 from Love Inspired® Historical.

Grandfather was trying to play matchmaker!

Regina's thoughts raced, skittering in several directions at once.

How *could* he? This was a disaster. It was too manipulative even for a schemer like her grandfather.

Didn't he know that if she'd *wanted* a husband, she could have landed one a long time ago? Didn't he trust her to raise her nephew, Jack, properly on her own?

Reggie forced herself to relax her grip on her grandfather's letter, commanded her racing pulse to slow.

She continued reading. A paragraph snagged her attention. Grandfather was *bribing* them to court her! They would each get a nice little prize for their part in this farce.

How could Grandfather humiliate her this way?

She barely had time to absorb that when she got her next little jolt. Adam Barr was *not* one of her suitors after all. Instead, he'd come as her grandfather's agent.

Grandfather had tasked Adam with escorting her "beaus" to Texas, making sure everyone understood the rules of the game and then seeing that the rules were followed.

It was also his job to carry Jack back to Philadelphia if she balked at the judge's terms. Her grandfather would then pick out a suitable boarding school for the boy— robbing her of even the opportunity to share a home with him in Philadelphia.

SHLIHEXP0912

Reggie cast a quick glance Adam's way, and swallowed hard. She had no doubt he would carry out his orders right down to the letter.

No! That would *not* happen. Even if it meant she had to face a forced wedding, she wouldn't let Jack be taken from her.

Will Regina find a way to outsmart her grandfather or will she fall in love with one of the bachelors?

Don't miss HANDPICKED HUSBAND by Winnie Griggs.

Available September 2012 wherever Love Inspired® Historical books are sold!

SHLIHEXP0912